FALLEN MOUNTAINS

KIMI CUNNINGHAM GRANT

FALLEN MOUNTAINS

A NOVEL

AMBERJACK
PUBLISHING

Amberjack Publishing
An imprint of Chicago Review Press, Incorporated
814 North Franklin Street
Chicago, IL 60610

THIS book is a work of fiction. Any references to real places are used ficti-
tiously. Names, characters, fictitious places, and events are the products of the
author's imagination, and any resemblances to actual persons, living or dead,
places, or events is purely coincidental.

Library of Congress Cataloging-in-Publication Data

Names: Grant, Kimi Cunningham, author.
Title: Fallen mountains : a novel / Kimi Cunningham Grant.
Description: Idaho : Amberjack Publishing, [2019]
Identifiers: LCCN 2018037081 (print) | LCCN 2018038653 (ebook) |
ISBN 9781948705264 (ebook) | ISBN 9781948705189 (pbk. : alk. paper)
Subjects: | GSAFD: Suspense fiction.
Classification: LCC PS3607.R3629417 (ebook) | LCC PS3607.R3629417
F35 2019 (print) | DDC 813/.6--dc23
LC record available at https://lccn.loc.gov/2018037081

for Chris

And it's as if the past has claimed everything.

—Rainer Maria Rilke

AFTER

THE SUMMER'S HEAT ARRIVED IN FALLEN MOUNTAINS like a winged thing, swift and startling: the pansies drooped, the lettuce bolted, the trees shook off their buds. As Red walked back to the police station from the diner, crabapple blossoms, pink and white and wet, dropped from the trees that lined Main Street and stuck to his shoes. He fiddled with the locked door and stepped inside, wiping his feet on the mat, dabbing sweat from his neck with his handkerchief.

The letter announcing Red's retirement lay tucked in the top right drawer of his desk, sealed in an envelope he'd planned on submitting to his secretary, Leigh, at the end of the day on Wednesday. Today was Tuesday, and Leigh worked just two days a week. The truth was there wasn't a whole lot for a secretary to do at the police department of Fallen Mountains, Pennsylvania, which wasn't a department, really, just Red and Leigh, and the fact that the borough kept on approving the position at all was a small miracle. In the past year, the most egregious offense the two of them had handled had been when a bunch of kids broke into the high school at night and let a troop of farm animals run loose through the halls. Chickens, two pigs, one Nubian goat: mud on the walls, droppings scattered through classrooms. Red had seen to it that the culprits were put to work with the janitor one Saturday, scrubbing and mopping until the place glinted and sang with a piney-clean scent. He ended up feeling a little guilty about the punishment, though, those kids stuck inside working on a beautiful spring weekend, and he'd taken them some fried chicken from Wheeler's Diner for lunch.

There were, of course, minor transgressions that occurred in Fallen Mountains, small troubles that Red, over the years, had come to expect. The Baumgardners were always getting into it at their double-wide way out on 28, tearing into each other and carrying on until one of the neighbors would call Red to complain. (Mrs. Baumgardner was six feet tall and had a good fifty pounds on her husband, so he was typically the one who got the worst of it.) And there were the usual indelicacies: phone calls in the middle of the night, people overdoing it at the bar, folks trespassing and shooting deer out of season. Much of the time, Red also served as a game warden of sorts—he was the one people called when there was an animal mangled in the middle of the road, or a snake under their porch, or a skunk prowling around their garden. Red was proud, though, that Fallen Mountains was a place largely isolated from the greater sins of the world, a fact he was reminded of every night, watching the evening news from his living room recliner.

But Red was turning sixty in the fall, and he could no longer deny the fact that this was a younger man's line of work. Hauling drunks to the station late at night, dragging deer off the roads, squeezing under porches with a headlamp strapped to his forehead and praying he wouldn't come face-to-face with anything venomous—these were things he'd once done without difficulty, things he'd actually embraced with a manly vigor. But not anymore. He was tired, he was ready for a change of pace. As he geared up for his retirement, Red looked back on his time as sheriff with a sense of satisfaction.

Well, mostly. Twenty-two years of service and only one indiscretion, one real regret, a mishandling of sorts, and so long ago. In the grand scheme, it wasn't a legacy to be ashamed of, Red knew that. But recently, with Transom Shultz back in Fallen Mountains, with that unimaginable mess he'd fashioned out at the Hardy farm, Red found himself thinking quite a bit about that mistake—about what he'd let Transom get away with all those years ago, but even more about the boy who'd paid dearly for Red's silence. Possum, he was called then, and was still called, even though he was a grown man now.

As Red sat at his old metal desk, staring out the window into the steaming June afternoon, the cars sleepy and slow as they drifted past the station, he thought of his father. The man had spent his whole life working in a steel mill back in Pittsburgh; he'd quit school in the eleventh grade and been miserable for as long as Red had known him. But at night, for a tiny sliver of each day, his father would come alive, reading Faulkner aloud to Red and his brother: *Sanctuary, As I Lay Dying, The Sound and the Fury.* His father's favorite quote, the one he'd recited countless times to Red and his brother, was the famous one from *Requiem for a Nun*: "The past is never dead. It isn't even past." In an attempt to remind his sons that every action had a consequence, Red's father had their mother write it in her nice calligraphy and frame it, and that terrible truth had plagued Red and his brother all through adolescence. Every street race through McKee's Rocks, every skipped class, every rock thrown into the glass of old factory buildings, every girl he ever touched—Red thought of Faulkner.

Red pictured it now, that yellowed paper, his mother's fancy lettering, because he could feel it: the past, sweeping into the present like a giant ship. That one slipup from seventeen years earlier, it was back to shine its ugly face at him yet again. He was sure of it. Earlier that afternoon, as Red leafed through an article about trout fishing in warm weather and munched on a vending machine cookie, Transom Shultz's new girlfriend called to say she hadn't heard from him in four days. She was coming to the station first thing in the morning, she said, to file a missing persons report.

Red stood up from his desk, walked to the supply closet, and found a small black notebook that would fit in his front pocket. He eased back into his chair, grabbed a pen from the mug on his desk, and opened the pad to the first page. It seemed like the right thing to do, take notes, be prepared for that meeting with Transom's girlfriend. On the television shows, this was all computerized now, he knew—fancy tablets where you could maneuver information with a fingertip, fling it from one screen to another—but there was nothing wrong with a notebook. He spun the pen between his fingers and tried to think, sifting through the preceding months, piecing together some sort of timeline of events.

Transom had come back six months earlier, right after old Jack Hardy passed. Red remembered that because he'd run into Jack's grandson, Chase, with Transom at the hardware store a few days after the memorial service. Transom nodding his head and saying, *Sheriff*, and Red's heart shooting into his throat at the sight of him. Transom couldn't have been in town for very long by that point because otherwise Red would've heard about it. Within a few weeks of that, Transom had bought the Hardy farm off Chase: Red had learned about that in the *Fallen*

Mountains Gazette. As far as Red knew, Chase himself neither explained nor complained about the transaction, but the town had buzzed with the news. Why had Chase sold it? What would Jack Hardy say about the property changing hands?

Sometime in the spring, Transom had gotten the place timbered, all the trees in those magnificent old woods cut down and hauled from the property. For weeks, log truck after log truck rolled past the station, the brakes rattling the windows. Then came the oil company.

Red picked up the phone and dialed his friend at the *Gazette*, a reporter who fancied herself a bit of an environmentalist and who'd written a few stories about fracking in the newspaper. He asked her if she could find out when the oil company had started working out at the Hardy property. April, she told him. Five weeks ago.

Transom was the first to lease the mineral rights in Fallen Mountains, though there'd been drilling close by for over two years now. *Frackholes*, turning dirt and drilling deep into the ground for Marcellus shale. Excavators, dump trucks, rollers: all spring Red watched them knock through town and out 28 to the Hardy farm. He saw the workers at Wheeler's Diner and the gas station—men in pickups with out-of-state license plates, men he didn't know and didn't trust. He added another bullet point to his notes. He couldn't count that out, the possibility that something had gone awry with one of the workers.

But again Red thought of the Faulkner quote. The shale pit, that dreadful summer: Possum stuffed in the trunk of an old car, Transom standing at the edge of the woods. With just a touch of invention, couldn't Red link a multitude of sorrows back to that mistake, that terrible night? As the years had trundled past, hadn't he done that, drawn connections and questioned whether he was somehow responsible? He started writing one final thing in his notebook and then crossed it out, pressing his pen down so hard it tore the paper. Red wiped his forehead with his handkerchief and sighed. The words were gone but it didn't matter. Already his mind had started slinking in that direction; already he'd started to remember and doubt and unfurl the possibilities, and there would be no stopping it now, his dreadful imagination. Always when he remembered, he was ashamed. This time, though, was different. This time, Red realized, he was also afraid.

He grabbed an antacid from the bowl on his desk and chewed on it, the chalky berry substance sticking to his teeth. "You're getting ahead of yourself, old man," he whispered. He leaned forward at his desk, slid open the top right drawer, and held the sealed envelope of his letter in his palm. That letter would have to wait now, because he had to sort this thing out. He put the letter back in the drawer and shoved it closed. He could hardly believe such poor timing, such terrible luck. A few weeks before what Red had imagined would be his last day as the Fallen Mountains sheriff, Transom Shultz was missing. Again.

BEFORE

It was just before Christmas and all through the night, there'd been snow, a light, feathery dust that draped the pines and covered the black roof of the main barn. The snow came still, in a drowsy, slow fall, and Chase Hardy lay in his bed, watching the flakes flicker through the gray light. He heard a vehicle pull up but, peering out the window, didn't recognize the SUV parked out front. Next to him, Laney lay on her side, her arm draped across his chest, her blonde hair strewn across the pillow, lips parted. Pretty. Chase slipped from beneath the covers and dressed.

He trotted down the steps, buttoning his flannel shirt. He opened the front door before his guest even had a chance to knock, so that as it swung open, the visitor stood in a strange pose at the threshold, left arm held up and in position to tap. The two men took each other in for a moment, both equally surprised, until the one outside stepped forward and wrapped himself around Chase, gripping him in that same warm and prodigious embrace he had used for years.

"Transom," Chase said: an exhale, his breath pressed from him by his friend's thick arms.

"Brother," Transom said, and that word they'd always used to describe each other somehow felt both good and strange. He held Chase tight. "Been too long."

In the kitchen, Chase leaned against the counter and watched as Transom sat at the table, devouring a thick piece of pound cake someone had dropped off at the house a few days earlier. It had been a week now since his grandfather, Jack, had passed. A week since that terrible thud, the sound of flesh to floor, since he'd dashed up the creaking old steps of the farmhouse and held Jack in his final moments. Two days earlier, they'd buried him on the other end of the farm.

Jack, who could make Chase laugh on days when the chores loomed and the daylight was running out. Jack, who until the day his wife, Maggie, died would tell her she was the most beautiful thing that had ever happened to him. Jack, who'd taught Chase everything he knew about farming, the woods, life— sweet and gentle Jack. There was a reason why two hundred people had come to the viewing, the line snaking its way around the block of the funeral home, folks huddled in groups as a light snow quivered across the night. And there was a reason why Chase had made it clear that only he and Laney and the preacher were to be at the burial site. No need to have all those people clambering up the snowy hillside, saying everything all over again, looking at him with pity.

Laney had been taking care of everything for Chase, tending to all the tasks of mourning. Laney, who was, well, he wasn't sure what she was anymore, not a wife, not even a girlfriend, and at the moment he had no energy to try and put a label on their relationship, his mind spinning and hazed with grief. Chase regretted that, for her sake, because he did love her—he just wasn't quite sure he could characterize that love, at least not yet. In the meantime, Laney swooped in with grace and competence. She met with the funeral director on his behalf, set up the time for

Jack's viewing, had it listed in the local newspaper. She arranged for Jack to be buried at the little family plot on the farm, next to Maggie. Laney handled the guests, too, the friends and neighbors who kept showing up at the house, uninvited and without warning, shuttling coffee cakes and casseroles so that the refrigerator and countertops were covered in aluminum pans and Pyrex, the idea being that food and company could fill the void left by the dead. Although of course that was ridiculous. Chase knew that every person dropping by was rallying around him out of love for Jack and support for him, but deep down, he wished they would leave him alone.

When they'd buried Jack, Chase and Laney stood with the preacher, the winter sky gray and sour, the wind cruel and biting as they huddled on the hill where four generations of Hardy family members had been laid to rest. Afterwards, he'd told Laney he'd prefer to be alone, but when he'd gone back to the farmhouse, the intense silence had been unbearable: no sputtering coffeepot, no humming woodstove, no radio buzzing with the old Gospel tunes Jack loved. Even walking the woods, which almost always could put him at ease, hadn't helped. The night before, even though he felt selfish about it, even though he knew she would read into it, he'd asked Laney to stay.

Transom took a drink of coffee and made a face. "I see you still haven't learned how to brew a decent cup of coffee, Boss," he said, wincing as he swallowed. A yellow crumb stuck to the side of his mouth. "I don't know how you can drink this. Seriously."

"I see your appetite hasn't waned."

Transom grinned: wide beautiful teeth that his parents had spent a fortune on back when they were in middle school. "True enough." He folded his hands and looked around the kitchen. "It's good to be back," he said. "It's good to be home. Place looks the same."

"How long has it been this time? Four, five years?"

"Something like that." Transom looked Chase in the eye. "Listen, Brother, I was sorry to hear about Jack. Real sorry. He was a good man." He paused. "Best man I ever known."

Chase shifted his weight and looked down. "I appreciate that. I do." He flicked his wrist to dump the last sip of cold coffee in the sink and turned to look out the window.

"Is he buried here on the farm?" Transom asked, rubbing his thumb along the rim of his coffee mug.

Chase nodded. "Up top that hill with the rest of them. Maggie, my parents." He put his mug on the counter.

Transom shook his head. "I should've come sooner, I know that. It was selfish of me. Stupid. I had all sorts of excuses. I was busy. It had been too long. Truth is, I've never been good at good-byes. And you know, as long as I stayed away, I could sort of convince myself nothing had changed." He paused. "If it'd be all right with you, I'd like to go up there. Pay my respects."

Chase shuffled his feet. It was the last place he wanted to go, back to the hill where his entire family was buried. "Sure."

Transom sliced another thick piece of pound cake and took a bite. "Anything in season?" He grinned. "I thought maybe we could go out and take the gun for a walk."

"Rifle's over. Small game's in," Chase said. Grouse, squirrel, pheasants. "Might be able to flush out a rabbit or two." With small game, you spread out, maybe fifteen feet apart, and walked the field, pushing whatever was hiding in the grass and brush from its hiding spot so it took off running.

Transom stood up. "You've got a shotgun for me, right? I know you've got an arsenal in Jack's room." He grinned, shoving the last bite of pound cake in his mouth. "And some clothes. I've got a pair of boots in the car, but I'll need pants, and a heavy jacket if you've got one." He walked to the door. "Be right back."

This was how it was with Transom, how it had always been in the twenty years he'd been Chase's best friend. He had a way of sweeping people toward him, pulling those around him into whatever he was doing, good or bad. The strange part was that people never seemed to mind. When you were around Transom, you felt important, somehow; you felt interesting, funny. You liked yourself a little more.

Chase left the kitchen and walked into the adjacent room, Jack's office. He felt around the top of the gun cabinet until his fingers grasped a key, then he unlocked the gun case. He felt a stab of grief as he glanced at Jack's old gun, a gift Maggie had inherited from her grandfather and given Jack as a one-year anniversary present, back when he'd hunted ducks. On its barrel was gold plating with a picture of a man and his German shorthair, the dog pointing, the man kneeling, gun raised toward the ducks that were flying overhead. Jack was not the type to put much stock in stuff—store up your treasures in heaven, he liked to say, quoting the book of Matthew—but if there was one worldly possession that Jack had treasured, it was that gun. Chase grabbed the gun next to it.

Transom came back into the kitchen from his SUV. "Chilly out there," he said, rubbing his large hands together rapidly, holding them to his mouth and blowing.

Chase handed him the sixteen gauge and reached into his pockets for a fistful of red shells.

"What about you?"

Chase shook his head. "Just gonna walk today."

"Don't tell me you're still not hunting."

"Still not hunting." He tossed Transom a fluorescent orange hat. "You gotta wear this," he said.

Transom rolled his eyes and pulled the hat over his head. "It's private property," he said, climbing into a pair of insulated coveralls. "You got someone else hunting here? Someone who might shoot us?" He struggled to zip the front. Transom had always been thick-chested, much more so than Chase, and he hadn't gotten any smaller over the years.

"Just wear it," Chase muttered. "And by the way," he added with a grin, remembering how his friend had always hated the job, "you're just in time to help me milk the cows."

———

Upstairs, Laney woke to the sound of men's voices, two of them: laughter, the ease of familiarity, simmering up from below, through the kitchen ceiling, through the floorboards and into Chase's bedroom. *Jack.* That was her first thought—Jack and Chase, up early, done already with the milking and now in the kitchen making breakfast—and she felt happy. She was in Chase's bed, where she'd dreamed about being for a very long time, in a house she loved. But then she blinked and as she stretched out of her sleep, she remembered: No. All that food, all those mourners in black and gray, shuffling through the Hardy farmhouse and Chase, Chase with his tired blue eyes and his grief hanging on him like fog. Jack was gone.

So the voices in the kitchen—she recognized Chase, but who was he talking to? Another neighbor popping in to pay respects, another old-timer friend of Jack's? These farmers, they were early risers; they could show up at such an hour and feel sure someone would be awake. She sat up in bed and peered out the window. Snow. The sky white-gray, everything dusted, the rooftop of the barn, the fields beyond it, the world an opus of white. Beside her truck, a black SUV.

A shot of loud laughter swelled through the floor and she knew. She'd recognize that laugh anywhere, the roar from deep in his gut, the way it would float higher and higher into an octave that was surprising for a man of his size. She could picture the way his face would break into a hundred beautiful lines with the laugh; she could feel it, too, his face pressed against hers, a memory. She knew the way his eyes would glisten and his teeth would shine, and she hated how her heart darted upward at the thought of him because, just last night, Chase had invited her to stay for the first time ever. Whatever new thing might be unfolding with Chase—she wanted it. At least she thought she did. But hearing that laugh made the sweet clarity of that desire shift and blur. Transom. Transom had come home.

AFTER

RED TOOK OUT HIS HANDKERCHIEF AND DABBED HIS forehead: another stifling June day. Across from him sat Transom Shultz's girlfriend, Teresa, slumped in a soft, whining chair in a room with glass walls at the back of the Fallen Mountains Police Department. There was no place at the station to interview, interrogate, or even have a private conversation, so while the room was by no means ideal, it was the best spot for such a meeting. Once a month, the school board gathered in this room, eating donuts and drinking coffee and arguing over salaries and textbooks and whiteboards, and their minutes from a previous meeting lay stacked in the middle of the table.

In the main room, Leigh sat at her typewriter and punched letters onto speeding tickets, looking up at them from time to time, curious. This was big news in Fallen Mountains, someone missing, and a beautiful, weepy girlfriend here at the station to drum up help. In the window behind Red's desk, an air-conditioning unit moaned and sputtered. The past few days had been oppressive, a heat heavy and suffocating. *Close*, people called it, and that was just how it felt, like someone was hovering nearby, and you wanted to shrug them off because you needed some space. June wasn't supposed to be so hot.

"Last time I saw him was Memorial Day weekend," Teresa said to Red. "The Friday before." She wiped her eyes with her bare, skinny arm and quivered. "So it's been five days now." She and Transom had fought that Friday night. Originally, they planned to go to her place, but instead she drove home alone. When she called his mobile phone the next day, and the day after that, he didn't pick up. "I figured he was just mad," she added, "ignoring my calls. Which he did that sometimes, you know. Played games. But then when I still didn't hear from him, I started to worry."

Red jotted things down in his pocket notebook, and his right hand, which his doctor had informed him had arthritis that he could manage by alternating ibuprofen and Aleve, protested as he squeezed the pen. He wrote the number five at the top of the page and looked at Teresa, waiting for her to go on.

"I know what you're probably thinking, you and everyone else," she said, rubbing her knuckles together. "He up and left again. But I'm telling you, that ain't what happened this time. I'm sure of it, and I need your help." She was startlingly pretty, this woman, with her shiny brown hair, her oversized brown eyes and wide, perfect mouth, her delicate face and frame. "He told me about it: his travels, he would call them. Sometimes he just got an itch to drop everything and leave, and that's what he did. It sounds bad when I say it, but it wasn't like that. He just never had a reason to settle, to stay put. This time, that wasn't the case." She sniffled and shook. "We were in love."

Red tapped his pen on the table. He didn't like the way this conversation was headed, with Teresa so sure something had happened to Transom. He clicked the pen. "People do it, you know. Leave. It's hard to accept, but some people—they just can't stay put." He was reaching for it; he was leading her. He knew it and he felt a little guilty about it, but his desire to put an end to things before they completely unraveled was overpowering. He couldn't help himself. "I guess what I'm saying is that, with Transom's history, it could be hard to prove that's not what happened this time."

Teresa reached her left arm across the table and held out her hand. "How's this for proof?"

Red stared at her bright red nails and a tattoo of a rose that wound its way up her wrist.

"It's over a carat," Teresa said. "He worked with a jeweler out in Pittsburgh and designed it himself. He asked me to marry him just last week. I'm telling you: he wasn't going anywhere."

Red looked at the ring, sparkling and enormous on Teresa's tiny fingers. He took a sip of coffee and tried to swallow the anxiety that was lodging itself in his throat. "Where you from, Teresa?" he asked. She wasn't local, he knew that.

"Empire."

Empire was twenty-five miles north, up Route 666, the Devil's Highway, people called it, a winding, skinny road that rolled through thick pines and ended in a town even smaller than Fallen Mountains. For years Red had heard about a meth ring on its outskirts, but recently there were other troubles: people stretched thin for too long and fraught, selling off the mineral rights, hundred-acre farms, small plots, too, and trucks and drill rigs and strangers rolling through in their pickups, starting fights with the locals, knocking up girls, too. Empire. How had a pretty thing like Teresa come from a place like Empire?

"And how long have you and Transom been together?"

"Since February. We met at a bar up in Empire."

"So not even four months."

"I guess when you know, you know."

He couldn't argue with that. He'd known he wanted to marry Sue the day he met her.

"He was under a lot of pressure," Teresa said. "Mostly with that property, the Hardy farm. Chase, the oil people. Once you sell the rights, you don't got no say in how things go: when they come, where they set up, what they do. Which, that's just how it works." She wiped her eyes with her arm. "He changed his mind, you know. He tried to get out of it, the contract, after he seen what it done to Chase. 'Course, the oil people wouldn't have that."

Red plucked a tissue from the box on the metal cabinet behind him and handed it to her. He made a note. Had Transom gotten into a disagreement with someone from the oil company? A foreman? A worker? He envisioned a struggle in the woods of the Hardy farm, two men warring in the heat, things getting out of hand. An accident, maybe. This was exactly why Red had been pushing so hard for that ordinance to keep the oil companies out of Fallen Mountains. There was nothing but trouble with those outfits, nothing but disturbance of various sorts: the land, the roads, the streams, the people, most of all. Trouble.

"He was just so tore up about it," Teresa said. "The farm, Chase. Said he loved both. People don't know this about Transom—he comes across as not caring about anybody, always doing what he wants—but inside, he does care. He's soft like that." She paused, rifling through her purse. She pulled out a piece of gum, slid the gum in her mouth, and refolded the silver wrapper back to its original shape. "I grew up in a trailer park in Empire, and we didn't own the trailer or the land it was on, so I never really understood how a person could love a place. I told him, business is business. You gotta keep your emotions out of it. But he couldn't."

"Tell me again about the weekend he disappeared," Red said. "What happened?"

Teresa wiped her eyes again. "We went to the shooting match. We got into a fight, and I drove home."

Red interrupted. "A fight about what?"

She sighed. She didn't want to say.

"Miss," Red said, leaning closer. "I'm not trying to pry, you understand that. Just need to piece things together, best we can here."

Teresa nodded. "About them pills he was on." Painkillers. She didn't know where he'd been getting them, but he'd been on them since they met. "He kept taking more and more, and, you know, he'd drive and stuff. He'd drink. Sometimes he'd get disoriented, forget where he was going, what he was doing. He'd get a look, eyes glassy, like he wasn't really there. I told him he needed to get off them or else—" Teresa stopped there, and tears welled in her brown eyes. She tried to fight them, but as soon as she blinked, they spilled, ambling down her cheeks.

"Or else what?"

She began sobbing, doubling over and tucking her head. "Or else it was over between us," she said, her face buried in her knees.

Red glanced up and saw Leigh standing, tiptoed, craning her neck, hands raised to her sides as if to ask, do you want me to do something?

He shook his head at her and placed a hand on Teresa's bony shoulder. "Did you say anything else? Did he say anything? Like maybe something about leaving." He paused, hoping, leaning forward. One mention of it would be all he needed, really, and he could close the books. Transom had a fight with his fiancée, he threatened to leave, and did, just like he had before. Red could have Leigh type up a quick report. He could hand in his resignation letter the very next day and be done with it. "I need you to try to remember. This is important."

"I called him all sorts of names, said things you say when you're mad. I told him I never wanted to see him again. But, Sheriff, that was just talk. We said those things to each other, both of us did, that was the way things was between us, but we always made up in a day or two. I kept calling him all weekend, he wouldn't return my calls. Finally, Monday, I called the farm-house, and that's when Chase told me he hadn't seen him, either."

At this point Teresa's crying turned into a wrenching wail that overtook her. She bent over onto the boardroom table and wept, and Red wasn't sure what to do—reach out and pat her on the back, ease out of the room? He had the plummeting sense that he was in over his head, that Transom really hadn't just run off again, also that the thing with Possum he'd buried all those years ago lay just beneath the surface, ready to burst through. He raised a hand and motioned for Leigh to come in—Leigh the comforter, with her sweet voice and cherub face, Leigh who was surely better able to handle such a thing. She hopped up and walked quickly to the room, high heels clattering across the checkered linoleum. Red slipped out of the room and then out of the building, too, into the abominable heat, and he thought of the letter in his desk drawer and wished and wished and wished he'd decided to hand it in last month.

BEFORE

 AT THE HARDY FARM, CHASE AND TRANSOM HEADED toward the western fields. The December ground, frozen for weeks now in northern Pennsylvania, was hard and dusted with snow, and their boots crunched with each step.

"Beautiful here," Transom said as he stopped walking and turned to look over the farm behind them, the rows of short dry stalks of corn, the mountains gray and white in the distance. "You're gonna stay, right?"

Chase kicked at a stalk and shrugged. "Not sure if I can." He was quiet for a moment, trying to figure out how to explain things. Just the day before, he'd sat across a wide, tidy desk in town, where an attorney leaned back in his dark leather office chair, shaking his head.

"It's not good, Chase," the attorney had told him. "I won't lie to you. Your grandfather, God love him, he left things a real mess here." Jack had been in default on the mortgage for eight months. Last year, he hadn't paid the property taxes. There were equipment loans, too. In all, tens of thousands of dollars. "You got any cash?" the attorney had asked Chase. "A savings account? Sometimes these things can be negotiated a bit."

Chase had some money stashed, but he'd never had a job besides working at the farm, so he had nowhere near enough to pay his way out of the kind of hole the attorney was talking about. He'd shaken his head and stared out at the street in front of the office, watching the wind pelt freezing rain against the wavy old glass, the heat of their bodies fogging it up.

The attorney had then asked if Chase had considered leasing the mineral rights. "You got Marcellus shale there, whole town does. Might be a way for you to keep the place, farm parts of it if you wanted to." He'd paused and adjusted a stack of paper on his desk. "I know Jack didn't support that, initially. But things have changed now. Perhaps he'd understand your predicament."

Fracking. Not that long ago, two men had come to the house, making small talk, asking about the Holsteins. They'd shown Jack a contract, explained the benefits of leasing the mineral rights. Jack had sent them on their way. He'd been opposed to it from the start, long before the oil companies had started knocking on the doors of local farms—the very idea of people coming in and stomping around the property, drilling deep and taking what they needed and potentially hurting the land he loved—and Chase wouldn't dream of doing something he knew Jack was against.

"Fracking's not an option," he'd told the attorney.

The attorney had handed Chase a small stack of papers tucked in a folder. "Well, take some time to think things over," he'd said. "I'll do my best to keep the sharks at bay for now. But try to get back to me in a week." He'd walked Chase to the foyer, gestured a good-bye that was almost a bow, and backed into his office.

Now, as Chase plodded through the snow with Transom, he thought about that conversation; in his mind he marked a day off the week he'd been given. Six days left. Six days to figure out some way to save the farm that had been in his family for two centuries, the farm his grandfather had loved and tended, the farm he loved, too. There was no way out of the mire Jack had left, and Chase suddenly grew angry at his grandfather for leaving him with such impossible odds.

"When Maggie got sick, there were a lot of medical bills to pay," Chase said, taking a deep breath, forcing out the anger in a great white puff, "and we had to make some sacrifices. Well, I guess that's what must've happened. Jack let the other bills pile up, taxes, too. I didn't know any of this, not until yesterday. You know Jack: he wouldn't want to 'burden' me with his problems." He shrugged. "Anyway, to answer your question, I don't know that I *can* stay."

Transom shook his head. He reached into his pocket and pulled out a small brown bottle of pills. He popped one in his mouth, tilted his head back, and swallowed. "I'm sorry."

The two walked in silence for a few minutes. They climbed over an old barbed-wire fence and stepped into an overgrown field, where the switchgrass was tall and the autumn olives rose up in thick clusters.

"This is probably a good place to load," Chase said. He didn't feel like talking about his sadness over Jack's death, and he certainly didn't feel like ruminating on how disappointed Jack would feel about losing the farm. He didn't feel like talking at all, actually.

Transom loaded his gun with three shells and flipped on the safety.

They walked through the field, their breaths heavy and white. Ten yards ahead, a rabbit darted out from a shrub, zigzagging through the snow, shuffling in and out of sight. Transom was slow, pulling his gun to his shoulder awkwardly and firing far too late. Snow flew up where the BBs pelted the ground. The rabbit was gone, disappeared in the brush ahead and out of range.

Transom looked at Chase. He flipped his safety back on. "Out of practice," he said with a laugh. He spat to the side. "I'll get the next one."

Chase nodded, and they continued walking through the field. "What you been up to, all this time?"

Transom was breathing heavily, struggling in the snow. "Working, here and there. Business." He smiled. "Getting old."

Back in high school, Transom had been in phenomenal shape. He'd run from the Hardy farm to town and back, an eight-mile loop. The star of the high school baseball team, he pumped iron in the dingy high school weight room every day after school. In the ninth grade he and Chase had installed a metal pull-up bar in the barn, and the two of them would have contests to see who could hold himself up longer, arms bent, chin atop the bar. Also who could do the most pull-ups. For years Transom had won both contests. Chase had begun to lose interest, never winning, but then in their junior year, things changed. It wasn't just that Chase got stronger, though that was part of it. It was that Transom, somehow, seemed to get weaker. In fact, by the time they graduated, Transom refused to even try: "Gotta save my arm for the game," he would say, shaking his head.

Ahead of them, another rabbit shot out, frightened and crazed, darting left, then right. This time, Transom was ready: he pulled the gun up fast, nudged it deep into his shoulder, aimed, and fired, all in one swift, confident movement. They walked ahead and Transom picked up the rabbit, a heap of fur and blood in the snow. He held it out at arm's length and grinned. The rabbit's neck hung limply, body folded.

"Let's go home and grill it up," Transom said. "You got a knife?"

He knelt in the snow and Chase pulled from his pocket the knife Jack had given him for his eleventh birthday. The pang of that memory—the gift wrapped in the comics page, Jack tousling his hair and telling him that a man needed a good knife—assaulted Chase, and he could feel it again, the smack of grief, another blow. He held out the knife.

Transom gripped the rabbit by its legs and twisted the skin, pulling it off one leg, then the other.

Chase stood a few yards back, looking away.

"Hey. What if I bought the place?"

Chase turned and studied his friend's face, unsure if this was another one of Transom's jokes. "What?"

"The farm. I could buy it. You'd still live here, farm it like you always have. It'd still be the Hardy farm. Only difference would be the name on the deed." He used the knife to remove the head and feet of the rabbit, tossed them aside. Steam rose from the warm body.

"Why?" The smell of the animal began to lift, and Chase stepped back.

"What do you mean, *why*? We're family, aren't we?" Transom said, cutting down the rabbit's middle and pulling out the insides. He took his thumb and rubbed it in the rabbit's cavity, then smeared a streak of blood under each of his eyes. He held up a hand and motioned for Chase to step closer.

"Naw, man. None of that for me."

"Suit yourself." He wiped the blood from his hands in the snow, two red streaks, and stood. "Here with you and Jack and Maggie, this was more home than anywhere else ever was. You know that. Besides, I've been missing this place. And I've sort of been itching to settle in somewhere for a bit, stay put."

Chase could feel his throat tightening, the kindness of the offer crushing him in his grief-heavy state. He turned away and kicked at a clump of snow. "I really don't know what to say."

Transom brushed snow from his pants and gave Chase a shove. "Hey, don't go getting soft on me. It's not a handout or anything. It's an investment. A business transaction."

Chase nodded. Transom and his multitude of contradictions: pensive and generous one moment, hard and detached the next.

"You don't have to answer right away," Transom said. "But promise me you'll think it over."

"All right."

They lumbered down the hill, half walking, half sliding through the snow, a layer of ice beneath the fresh stuff, their legs and feet gathering snow, heavy. From far away, the farmhouse, white in a world of white, looked warm and comforting, though not as comforting as it once had, Chase realized. He took another look. Candles. A long time ago, Maggie used to place candles in all the windows, the day after Thanksgiving. He would walk up from the barn after the evening milking, and every window would glow and send off a warmth that made him want to go inside.

By the time they got back to the house, Laney had left. Chase wondered what was going through her mind. Was she annoyed that he'd left with Transom without a word or note? Was she hopeful? He would never want to hurt Laney. In fact, the past few weeks—their closeness in the wake of Jack's passing and then their night together—had made him start to wonder if maybe there was something more between them than friendship, if there could be a different type of future for the two of them. But he was also fairly certain he didn't want to dive into anything, at least not now, with so many big decisions looming.

Transom announced he needed a nap and slumped into the couch, and Chase slid into his coat and slipped back outside. He hopped onto his four-wheeler and headed up the farm road to the far end of the property, the vehicle teetering back and forth in the ruts and snow. When he arrived, he quieted the engine and climbed off. He walked briskly through the woods, endless woods, it seemed, this part of the land connecting to a half million acres of the Allegheny National Forest. He made his way to Church Hollow, the place he loved most of the whole farm. Originally, this particular hollow had just been called The Hollow, but during his teenage years, Chase, not wanting to join Maggie at Grace Bible Fellowship, had begun telling her that The Hollow was his church. That place where he could think clearly, feel as close to his Maker as he ever did.

When Chase would make those refusals to attend church, which he did try to space out so that it was never two consecutive weeks, Jack would look at Maggie from across the kitchen table and communicate, without a single word, that she must back off, give him his space. At some point or other during his adolescence, The Hollow had become Church Hollow.

The name was appropriate. Tall boulders jutted up at the top and on the sides of the hill, so that if you stood at the bottom of the hollow and looked up, you could see the likeness to an old cathedral. Chase climbed onto his favorite rock and settled himself on top. Soon, the cold of the stone crept through his jeans and chilled him, and he liked it—that deep, unsettling feeling of cold. He pulled his hat down over his ears and looked out at the trees. American Elm, *ulmus Americana*. Black Ash, *fraxinus nigra*. Northern Red Oak, *quercus rubra*. He'd memorized the names as a kid.

Chase rubbed his thumb along a rough, green patch of lichen and peeled a small piece of it off. He looked up at the gray winter sky, the thin clouds shifting quickly, almost imperceptibly, above. He exhaled, watching the white air dissipate, and as he thought about Transom's offer, as he tried to make sense of things and come to a good decision, his grief took hold of him again. Not just because the farm itself was so closely linked with his grandfather, but because Jack was the person he'd always gone to for advice. Jack had a way of guiding you without flat-out telling you what to do or say. He never made you feel judged, either. But now, as Chase was facing the most difficult decision of his life, Jack wasn't around. More than anything, Chase wished he could have a few minutes—rumbling in the truck over a farm lane or sitting on the front porch after a long day of work or eating one of Jack's slow cooker stews—to seek his grandfather's guidance.

The wind picked up and Chase leaned back on the cold rock. The treetops, tall and sparse this time of year, swayed and moaned. A squirrel scuttled up a nearby white pine, clucking, eyeing him warily. It whisked its fluffy tail back and forth. Maybe it wouldn't be so bad, selling Transom the farm. On paper, it wouldn't be the Hardy farm anymore, but people would mostly still think of it as such, and after all, Transom was prac-tically family. Though they weren't related, Transom had lived there full-time for two years, and he'd spent dozens of afternoons and weekends there, all through their childhood. Chase thought of him as a brother, and he knew Transom felt the same.

The year they turned sixteen, both of them suffered terrible losses—Chase's parents were killed in a car accident, and Transom's parents split. The boys had always been friends, two kids whose circumstances had tossed them together before they were old enough to know or care otherwise. Chase and his parents lived a quarter mile down the road and because his mom worked in town, he'd spent much of his time at the farm since infancy, and for extra income, Maggie watched Transom four days a week. Chase and Transom had learned to crawl and walk together; they'd taken the training wheels off their bikes the same day and taught each other to ride. They'd spent countless afternoons shooting pigeons off the rafters in the barn, catching bullfrogs in the summer dark. In their suffering, however, the boys grew closer than ever. A few months after Chase's parents died, Transom showed up at the front door of the farmhouse one Saturday, with two huge duffel bags slung over his shoulder, his cleats and baseball bat at his feet. He just stood there, forlorn and speechless, and Maggie pulled him inside and told him to take his things to the guest room. It was the week after his mother had attempted suicide—Transom didn't need to explain himself; they understood why he was there. Maggie called Transom's father, JT, and told him Transom was welcome to stay as long as he needed to, and he'd simply never left. For months, JT had called. For months, he'd come to the farm in his Lincoln, trying to get Transom to talk to him, leaving envelopes of cash. A year later, when JT announced he was selling his factory and leaving Fallen Mountains, he hadn't even protested when

Transom said he wasn't moving somewhere else to finish his senior year of high school.

It could be a good thing, Transom staying now, and Chase
liked the idea of it. He stooped, snapping the end of a thin pine
branch off and holding it to his nose. He loved that smell, so
gracious and clean. He reached his fists toward the sky, stretching off the cold, breathing in the forest. The squirrel climbed
higher up the tree. Chase scooted down the rock and headed
home. As he made his way back toward the house, he made up
his mind, and like Jack had taught him, he would stick to his
decision. No second-guessing himself. He would sell the farm
to Transom.

AFTER

As soon as he finished his interview with Teresa, Red climbed into the driver's seat of the Fallen Mountains police car, a white GMC Jimmy that, a long time ago, had been the nicest vehicle in town, if you didn't count JT Shultz's small fleet of Lincolns. In fact, JT Shultz had been the one to purchase the Jimmy, donating it to the town, "for the purpose of law and order" at one of his big company events out at the factory. Back then, Red had loved driving around in the thing, exploring the winding back roads of the Allegheny National Forest, learning all the names of those roads, the names of the farms, too. Stopping by school to pick up his son, Junior, the look of pride on Junior's face at the sight of him standing outside the schoolyard, leaning against the Jimmy in his tan sheriff uniform.

Now, though, with JT Shultz long gone and no one in any position to purchase a new vehicle, the Jimmy required a ritual to start: pump the gas pedal three times, turn the ignition, hold it, wait. Most of the time, if he did it just right, the Jimmy would grumble to life. The air-conditioning had been broken since the summer before. Red wasn't going to pay to have it fixed, nor had he been able to convince anyone else to. ("I don't got air-conditioning in my truck," the township supervisor had said with a shrug, "and you don't hear me complaining about it.") Last month, when Red had been cleaning the Jimmy, he'd removed the floor mat on the passenger side, and he'd peered in and seen pavement through a hole that had finally rusted all the way through. He couldn't imagine it would pass inspection come October, but hopefully, that would be someone else's problem, not his.

It was hot, even at suppertime; the Jimmy was a rectangle of stifling warmth. As long as he was driving over forty, enough air would whip through the open windows that he could keep it tolerable, but through town, it was bad. He drove out 28 and pulled into the lane of the Hardy farm, wider now and rutted worse than he could ever remember, all the traffic coming through with the oil company. The Jimmy teetered back and forth, bottoming out twice. Red wondered whether the road would bust through the hole on the passenger-side floor—maybe that would get the township supervisor's attention.

He parked beside Chase's truck, climbed out, and crossed the yard to the house. He knocked on the door, and when no one answered, he peered through the white lace curtains of the front windows. The living room. Dark hardwood floors. A woodstove. A couch and two chairs. A large braided rug in the center of the room. Everything the same as it had always been, the way Maggie Hardy had set it up decades ago, when she'd married Jack and moved in. On the porch a wasp began to circle him, and he looked up to see that there was a nest in the corner of the window: the small, tan cylinders tucked together like a fist. He swatted at the wasp that was after him and stepped back quickly.

He wandered down to the barn but, seeing the Holsteins push and nudge each other and then eye him warily, he turned around and headed back to the Jimmy. He didn't like cows, never had.

The stench, of course, was unbearable, but there was more to it than that. Red was a Pittsburgh boy, born and raised in McKee's Rocks, along the south bank of the Ohio River. The Rocks, everyone called it. When his class had visited a Westmoreland County dairy farm for a field trip in the second grade, all he could think about was how the bones in his foot would collapse beneath the weight of one of the animals. He thought, too, of how his small body could sink into the knee-deep mud and disappear. All the other kids in his class had loved that field trip, everybody getting a turn at squeezing a cow's udder, milk spraying into a metal pail—they'd talked about that for weeks—but Red had hated every minute of it. Looking at the barn now, he felt the same way.

He paused and turned, looking over the farm: one large field of perfect rows of corn, not even knee-high this early in the year, three fields of hay, some soybeans. Beyond the barn, in the field Jack had let grow wild the summer Maggie was sick, he saw it—a massive metal-sided building, red tanks, a bright yellow backhoe clawing at the hillside, enormous fans on the beds of three trailers. Movement, human specks floating across the too-flat, cindered gray site. This was the first he was seeing it, and it was bigger than he'd imagined—acres and acres. More sites were coming, he knew. The Witherspoons had just sold. The Franklins, too. Following Transom's lead.

He wandered toward Transom's black Lincoln, fished his camera from his pocket, and snapped a photograph. He slid on a pair of blue rubber gloves he'd grabbed from the storage closet, tight and pulling at the hair on his knuckles—Leigh used them when she cleaned the bathroom—and he tried the front passenger door. Not locked. Inside, a vanilla-scented air freshener in the middle console. An old Styrofoam cup. Clean, very clean inside. He took another picture. He clicked open the glove compartment. A bottle of prescription pills tumbled forward onto the ledge. Red took a photo and then turned the brown bottle in his palm and read the label. Transom's. Vicodin, from a doctor in Philadelphia. He snapped another photo. He carefully slid the bottle into a Ziploc gallon bag and then turned his attention back to the glove compartment. Wallet, cell phone. He picked up the phone: dead, not surprisingly. It'd been sitting in the vehicle for six days. Red dropped it into the bag, along with the wallet. Nothing in the back seat, nothing in the side pockets. Plenty in the trunk: a baseball and glove, a cooler with a six-pack of Rolling Rock, a sleeping bag, two down pillows, expensive. Also an accordion file stuffed full. He peered inside and grabbed a sheet of paper. A cell phone bill. And a thick stapled stack, from a few files back: a contract from an oil company. Strange, Red thought. Most people didn't keep their paperwork in the trunk. He tucked the file under his arm and carried it over to the Jimmy.

He paused to look at the garden in the front yard. Tomato plants, zucchini: no blossoms yet, but he recognized the leaves. Cosmos, not yet in bloom. His wife Sue's favorite flower. She would've stopped to pull her fingers from the stem up and over the delicate buds. He kneeled and touched one.

"Hey!"

Red stood quickly, his knees protesting, the left one especially, and he thought of old hinges, whining from overuse and rust. He turned, nearly losing his balance.

Chase Hardy stood behind him, a huge tan bag slung over his shoulder. He wore a baseball cap, worn jeans, a blue t-shirt, and knee-high rubber boots. "Sheriff? Sorry, didn't mean to startle you. You all right?" He stepped closer, placed a strong hand on Red's shoulder. "You gave me a scare," Chase said. "I didn't hear you pull up, wasn't expecting to see anyone here. Thought maybe you were from the oil company, someone snooping around."

"Sorry," Red said. "I knocked, nobody came to the door. I figured you weren't here."

"I was in the root cellar out back." He bent and placed the bag on the ground and leaned it against his leg. He gestured to the garden. "Maggie always liked them, too. Cosmos. I plant them every year, get a packet of seeds at Tractor Supply." He looked at the sky and shrugged. "Sort of to remember her by. Plus sometimes I think, whatever heaven's like, if she can see the farm, it'd make her happy to look down at her old garden and see them."

Red hadn't planted a garden for two years now, not since Sue passed, a ruthless bout of pancreatic cancer, the only mercy of which had been its swiftness. Some things, he'd realized, were just too hard, and the garden was such a thing.

"You here for business or pleasure, Sheriff?" Chase asked.

Red pulled his handkerchief from his pocket and dabbed his forehead. "Business, I'm afraid. Transom's girlfriend came into the station yesterday. Fiancée, I should say. Reported him missing." He tried to read Chase's response to the news. Surprise? Anxiety? Concern? Those unnaturally serene eyes of his, the gentle face: Red looked but could find nothing there. "Did you know? I mean that she's worried about him."

Chase kicked at a stone. "She called the house asking for him."

"And?"

"I told her he wasn't here. But sometimes I didn't see him for days. I figured he was up at her place. Honestly, Sheriff, I didn't keep track of him." He took off his hat, ran his fingers through his hair. "You know how he is."

Red thought of Teresa's doe eyes, her pretty face. "Did she come here often? Teresa."

"Yeah, sometimes she would stay for a week or so. Put near drove me crazy. Sometimes Transom went up to her place in Empire."

"Didn't either of them have jobs? I mean, to be able to up and leave for a week at a time—that's unusual."

Chase's eyes darkened. "Transom ran his own business. I guess you probably already know that." He put his baseball hat back on his head. "Listen, I've got cows to milk. You're welcome to come along. You can give me a hand. I'm willing to talk, but you know, when them cows need milked, they need milked."

Red didn't have much choice: he followed Chase to the barn, the accordion file still tucked beneath his arm. A brood of cats watched with anticipation as Chase approached. They dashed toward him, swirling about his feet, purring and mewing. He kicked at them gently, plowing his way through. One scrawny yellow cat hunched down, whisking his tail back and forth, hissing at Red.

Chase maneuvered through the cats to a large metal garbage can. He lifted the lid and scooped cat food into a low white bucket. Then he flicked open a pocket knife, cut open the bag, and dumped cat food into the garbage can. The cats immediately turned their attention to the food, shoving their little heads toward the bowl, pushing each other with a graceful violence.

"This way," Chase said, walking deeper into the barn. Red felt relieved to be in the shade: at least it was cooler there, although the stench was nauseating. The cows were walking toward them, their hooves clacking on the cement. A few of them moaned, as though protesting the presence of a newcomer. "We don't have as many cows as we used to," Chase said. "Back when I was a kid, we had one hundred eighty or so. You probably remember. Now I've got seventy-six. It's all I can manage. And tell you the truth, it's hardly worth it, with milk prices so low."

Red nodded, walking briskly to keep up with Chase, whose height gave him a long stride. "You were saying you and Teresa didn't get along," Red said.

Chase stopped, looked at him, and cocked his head to the side. "I never said that."

"Well then, what is it? You said she drove you crazy. That's surprising to me, Chase, you being such a reasonable man. Never met a soul you didn't get along with, truth be told. So level with me here: Is she stable? I mean mentally." A flicker of hope: maybe Teresa was at the heart of all this. Maybe there was more to that argument than she'd told Red about—maybe Transom had left town again, after all. Red pictured her wailing, the way she'd flung her body onto the table at the police station. Maybe she was crazy.

Chase snorted. He moved a wide shovel out of the way and placed it against the metal gate inside the barn. "She's stable. She's just, I don't know. She'd just take over the place," he said at last.

"What do you mean?"

Chase sighed. "I don't know. Perfume in the bathroom, candles everywhere. She'd move my stuff sometimes, get rid of it without asking. Just annoying stuff like that. Listen," Chase said, turning to Red. "He's done this before, just up and left. You know, you remember. Truth is, he's done a lot of damage here that I've got to figure out." He pointed to the field where an excavator was parked. "Frackers up there doing who knows what, more equipment every day. There's a trailer up there. I think they sleep here, the workers. Where else would they be sleeping, right?" There was no hotel in Fallen Mountains. He sighed. "Besides, he might show up here, one point or another."

He motioned for Red to follow him into an all-cement room with twelve milking stations. The parlor, Red knew it was called, which had always seemed like a misnomer. A dozen cows shuffled their way in, one at each station, six cows on each side of the room. Chase walked down a set of stairs into a pit of sorts.

"You don't think it's strange that he just left his car here, all his belongings, and just—" Red waved his hands around for emphasis—"disappeared?"

Chase shrugged. "He done it before."

"But he'd need his things, if he were gonna try to go anywhere. His vehicle, too. Wouldn't he?" The wallet in the glove compartment, the phone. The news was sinking in as Red heard himself say it aloud. "Have you considered that something might've happened to him? That he might be hurt? Dead?"

Chase was in the pit, wiping each cow's udders with a thick orange substance, then hooking up tubing and metal cups to the cows. He worked efficiently, effortlessly, someone whose body had memorized the movements long ago, finishing one cow and then moving onto the next. The room smelled intensely of bleach, and it burned Red's nostrils. "I guess not," Chase said, bending over.

"And what if you considered it now?"

Chase paused. He looked up from his position below. "I been through this too many times, him leaving and me here, wondering was he all right, to think about it in those terms. I never understood why he done it, left us like that. There's a lot I don't understand about Transom. We grew up together, but still, we always been real different, him and me. You got a brother, Sheriff? Maybe you can understand."

Red thought of his older brother, Tim. Back in The Rocks, they used to stand on their porch, when their mother wasn't looking, a game: punch me as hard as you can. One of them would always end up bawling, and once, Red knocked Tim's front tooth loose, an awful, bloody mess that made his mother scream. He thought of how Tim had asked Tammy Jamison to the prom, when he'd known Red had a crush on her. As payback he'd slipped an egg in Tim's back pocket so he'd sat on it when he went to pick Tammy Jamison up, the rented tux stained and, by the end of the night, reeking. Tim tearing through The Rocks in their father's '69 Chevelle, Red in the passenger seat, knuckles white, picturing the Faulkner quote on the wall, sure they would crash and face eternal consequences. Tim howling with delight. Brothers: Red understood. He shuffled his feet. "Can you think of anyone who would want to harm Transom, someone he might have angered?"

Chase shrugged. "There's a lot of people that didn't like him," he said. "That's how it's always been, ever since his family come to Fallen Mountains. Heck, you know this better than I do." He nudged one of the Holsteins forward.

Red slid his notebook from the back pocket of his jeans. "What about Possum?" He tried to sound casual, but he could hear a quiver in his own voice, the memory of that night scuttling back to him again: Possum battered and filthy in that trunk, Transom stealing into the trees.

"Possum?" Chase cocked his head to his side and wrinkled his nose, confused. "What would Possum know about anything?"

Red snapped the notebook closed. "I don't know. Just trying to consider every possibility here."

Chase finished hooking up the last cow and climbed the steps to Red. He flipped some switches, and the room erupted into noise: motorized humming, suction. "Was there anything else, Sheriff? You want to poke around the house a bit?"

"Next time," Red said, the thought spinning to him: he should get a warrant. He extended a hand and Chase removed a rubber glove, sticky with the orange substance, and took it. "I may be back," he said. "You understand."

"Sure."

"Unless he turns up."

"Right."

Red turned and headed back to the Jimmy. The sun had heated up the vehicle to the point where it was overpowering, and Red reached over and took great swigs from his water bottle, the contents now warmer than the temperature of his mouth and not refreshing at all. What had Transom been up to, cell phone and wallet in the glove compartment and that file in the trunk? Red drove out the long Hardy farm lane, the gravel crunching beneath the tires, the warm air starting to circulate. He looked up at the hill where Chase had pointed. Who was up there, ferrying every sort of truck a person could name, drilling deep into the ground that a family had worked and loved and considered sacred for two centuries? And what, exactly, had unfolded over the past six months?

BEFORE

 LANEY HAD GONE TO MARYLAND TO SPEND CHRISTMAS and New Year's with her mother, but now she was back in Fallen Mountains, and she stood in her coat closet, dialing the numbers on her gun safe. Left 46. Right 58. Left 93. She took out her .38 special, checked to ensure the safety was on, and placed the pistol in her holster. She slid into her winter jacket and orange vest, then pulled her thick fluorescent orange hat down over her ears. It was January—rifle season was over, but some die-hards would still be out there, flintlock and late archery, and if she were to come across anyone during her evening walk in the woods, she wanted to be seen.

It was Jack Hardy who'd taught Laney to shoot a gun, how to carry a pistol, how to be sure of herself with a weapon—although she'd taken it upon herself to learn a lot more about guns than Jack ever knew. A friend, Joanna Dean, had been assaulted after leaving a bar, and while that hadn't even happened in Fallen Mountains, but in Empire, the event had shaken her. The man who attacked Joanna—he'd been watching her. The police searched his home and found photographs, a piece of jewelry she'd thought she'd lost. It had been going on for months, and Joanna never suspected a thing. Laney was a woman who'd always taken pride in her ability to live alone and be happy alone, but after what happened to Joanna, everything changed. She was looking over her shoulder constantly, thinking she saw movement in the shadows outside her windows. Haunted by the idea that someone might be watching her, she would close the blinds any time she was home. She could no longer enjoy the long walks she liked to take in the nearby woods. She tried to be home by dark. The mace she kept in her purse or pocket did little to soothe her, and after a few months of living in what seemed like constant fear, she took matters into her own hands. She enrolled in a self-defense class at a martial arts center thirty miles away. She bought a German shepherd, Kip, who joined her on her walks and who grew to love her fiercely. When Jack offered to let her try out his handgun one afternoon when she was visiting, she jumped at the opportunity. At the time, she'd never even shot a weapon before.

She would never forget that first time: a pistol in her hand, held out at arm's length, lining up the bead with the D on a Mountain Dew can ten yards away. The exhilaration—the power she felt—when she pulled the trigger, slowly and carefully, as Jack told her, and then watched the soda can leap up from the stump it had been sitting on. She knew immediately that she wanted one of her own. Within a few weeks of that lesson, she had researched and decided on a .38 special snub nose, a small gun with good kick and decent accuracy at short range. True, it only held five rounds, but it felt like the right fit for her needs. She went to the sporting goods store and paid cash for it. A week later, she took her paperwork and twenty dollars into the county courthouse and got a license to carry a concealed weapon. It was that simple.

She whistled for Kip, who was waiting patiently by the kitchen table, watching her every move, thick tail twitching with excitement. Somehow, the moment she got it in her mind to head to the woods for a hike, Kip would begin pacing anxiously, following her around the house, whimpering with anticipation. They walked out the back door. She removed the pistol from the holster and placed it carefully in the glove compartment, then motioned for Kip to hop into the front seat.

Laney most often went to an unnamed access point to the Allegheny National Forest that was less than two miles from her house, about a four-minute drive. There was a nice loop there that took her to a stream and then circled back to the parking lot, and she liked it because of the mountain laurel that grew thick along the trail, as though someone had carved a path through it. In the summer, you walked through a tunnel of white flowers. Nobody ever went there to hike, either, although she'd shown her cousin Possum the place, and sometimes he went there looking for mush-rooms. And once, many years ago, she'd taken Transom.

Kip stood beside her on the bench seat of the truck, lifting one paw and then the other in excitement, whining quietly. A long string of drool made its way to her lap. She kept her eyes on the road but reached over and patted his chest.

Spending Christmas and New Year's with her mother had been a welcome distraction from the squall of events that had unfolded through December. She'd been put to work making royal icing for a church baked goods sale; she'd trimmed the tree; she'd basted ham and turkey. But she'd also had time and space to think, to grieve. Losing Jack Hardy had flung a double sadness at Laney. She hated to see Chase suffer—he was her best friend and she knew how heavily Jack's death, and all the issues with the farm, weighed on him—but while she was holding it together well in front of him, Laney was mourning, too. Had

Chase not been sinking in his own grief, he would've been aware of this fact, would've recognized that Jack's death was a terrible loss to her as well. But through it all, he'd been oblivious. Laney understood the way grief could blind you like that, swallow you up like a bad snow and make you entirely unaware of anyone else's feelings, and she tried not to hold it against him.

The truth was she had loved Jack and Maggie, and the farm, too, for as long as she could remember. Those early years when her mother was too depressed to take care of her—when Laney was getting herself up, fed, and dressed for second grade while her mother lay in bed, staring out the window onto Locust Street—it was Jack and Maggie who'd reached out and brought her into their world.

And what a world it had been, back then, when the farm hummed and spun with activity: the hired hands dashing from one task to the next, Jack smoking his pipe as he puttered by on his old Farmall, Maggie harvesting and baking, and everyone, farmhands included, gathering at the kitchen table at noon for lunch. Laney had never seen such a place, with so much happening and yet with so much order. Maggie made sure of that—she kept everyone on task and on time, she liked to say. What Laney didn't see at the time, but marveled at later, was how seamlessly Maggie Hardy had welcomed her into that life, as though Laney were no inconvenience at all, as though there'd never been a time when she hadn't been there. It was, Laney told Maggie years later, a magnificent rescue.

Maggie had laughed at that. "Rescue," she'd said, shaking her head. "I'm the one who needed rescued. All these men and boys. I needed a companion, a little girl." She'd pulled Laney in close, pressed Laney's cheek against hers. "You're family, dear, you always have been." That was the thing about Maggie and Jack—that was why everyone who knew them loved them—they never let you feel indebted, like you were leaning on them, even when you were.

Through the holidays, Laney had also had time to contemplate what was evolving between Chase and her. Or what might be evolving. As a girl, she'd viewed Chase with a sense of wonder. Well, she'd seen both of them like that—Transom, too, but in a different way. With Transom, there was an inexplicable draw, a pull he had on her that simultaneously made her swoon and shrink. With Chase, it was more a matter of blissful compatibility. They looked at the world the same way; they understood each other. The two of them together, it made sense, and when Jack died, she saw it: all those hours she'd spent at the farm taking care of the arrangements, taking care of Chase—it hadn't felt like a burden. In fact, it had been just the opposite: she'd felt like that was what she was made for. When Chase asked her to stay, when she'd followed him upstairs to his room that night, the day after they'd buried Jack, it had felt right: it had felt like coming home.

But now, with Transom back in town and with things looking like he had every intention to stay a while—in just three weeks he'd bought the Hardy farm and settled in out there—Laney worried that things might never unfold with Chase. Because sooner or later, there would be trouble. Sooner or later, Transom would show up at her place.

—

Since the first time he left, Transom had been doing the same thing. He'd go to the Hardy farm first, but eventually, he'd come to Laney's. She'd shown him where the key was long ago, tucked in a fold of cloth she'd sewn into the pad on the porch swing at the front, but he never used it. Instead, he'd park in the alley and come to the back door. He'd knock quietly, and when she'd lift the yellow curtain on the door to peer out, he'd be there, smiling through the glass pane.

She would let him in. There would be no hellos, no questions, no catching up and filling in the details of the long stretches of space and time that had lapsed since they'd last been together. They had an understanding, the two of them, that this was about body and desire and need, about people who on some level cared for each other but who, in the end, cared more about themselves. There was, she'd thought sometimes, a type of love in such an arrangement, maybe.

When Laney lay in Chase's bed the morning Transom came back, listening to the voices floating up through the floor, her first thought after realizing it was Transom had been to wonder when he would come to her. And right after that, she'd felt ashamed of herself for going there, for the little flurry of longing that had traveled her body at the thought of him standing at her doorstep, looking for her. She wasn't that type of woman. She was still in Chase's bed, she'd scolded herself.

Laney pulled her truck into the small parking lot of the national forest, her favorite spot for her evening walk. She reached over to the glove compartment and took out her handgun. Kip began pawing her thigh softly, whimpering to be let loose. She climbed out, Kip scrambling past her, and pulled on her thick gloves. The night's cold was starting to set in. She checked her watch: about forty minutes until dark. Laney holstered the gun and set off into the snowy woods.

AFTER

RED KEPT TRYING TO CONSIDER THE VARIOUS THINGS that could explain Transom Shultz's mysterious disappearance—run-in with the frackers, car accident on some remote back road, some primordial itch to cut loose and get out of Fallen Mountains—but despite his great efforts not to think about it, he kept coming back to Possum. Possum Miller, with his oversized eyes and his white t-shirt and red puffy vest, every day of the year, even in this oppressive June heat. A year after what happened at the shale pit, Possum had taken a bronze figurine of an eagle and pummeled his drunk stepfather to the point where the man's eye permanently strayed left and he never could quite utter a complete sentence anymore. Had Possum had another breakdown? Had he snapped again?

Back then, Leigh hadn't been hired yet, so it was just Red, and he was forty-three and happy. Back then, JT Shultz had a hold on Fallen Mountains like a crooked king. He was mayor at the time, no one else wanting the responsibility for the pathetic stipend the town offered, but more importantly, he owned the electronics factory, where at least one member of every family in town worked, including Red's wife, Sue. JT didn't pay well, but he offered benefits. Twice a year, in the spring and fall, he hosted a town picnic with a spread of food so magnificent people would talk about it for weeks. Games, too. He'd set himself up in the dunker, and people would pay a dollar per pitch to see if they could make him drop into the water. Nobody in Fallen Mountains liked working for Shultz, and nobody liked *him*— overbearing, barrel-chested, handsome, mean—but the thing was, nobody was in any kind of position to turn down a job, period, let alone one with health insurance.

Red and Sue had bought a place on Crocus Street, a two-bedroom cape cod that was in dire need of paint, but its foundation was solid, its windows in good shape. That was Red's sixth year as sheriff. He'd only been in Fallen Mountains for seven, and people still thought of him as an outsider, the city slicker from Pittsburgh who'd married Sue Philips. He only became sheriff because the previous one dropped dead of a heart attack, mid-term. He had an associate's degree in criminal justice, so in some ways he was more qualified than any prior Fallen Mountains sheriff, although not knowing the lay of the land or the quirky politics of the town certainly made things difficult at first. Now, Red had more than twenty years under his belt and a much better understanding of life in Fallen Mountains. Junior was done with college and out on his own; his ears were all fixed and his surgeries, paid for with the health insurance from Sue's job at the factory, were a small chapter of family history. JT Shultz and his stupid picnics were out of the picture, too. Red was in a position to handle things differently.

The day Possum lay into his stepfather was Junior's sixth birthday; he remembered that. They were outside blowing bubbles and Junior had on a blue and red Spider-Man outfit, the usual cotton balls stuffed in his left ear to catch the drainage. It was months after the big surgery, and things were looking good for him. He hadn't woken up screaming and writhing in pain for weeks, and Red and Sue were finally, finally getting to a place where they could sleep at night.

Red's in-laws were at the party; his parents had driven in from Pittsburgh, too. They were all in the backyard and Sue had just served the cake, also blue and red, Spider-Man. Inside, the phone rang, its jingle singing through the screens and into the yard, rang and rang and rang and Red knew the rule: people had his home number and he always had to pick up, no matter what. This was before the days of pagers and cell phones, before 911, too, which didn't come to Fallen Mountains until 2002.

He went inside and picked the kitchen phone off the receiver. "Redifers," he said.

"This is Possum Miller." The voice calm and feathery. "I'm calling to report a crime."

Red's heart plummeted in his chest. He gripped the kitchen countertop and thought *no*, because this was June, a new summer. The cicadas from the previous year were long gone and it was ten months after that incident out at the shale pit: he'd thought he'd managed to avoid dealing with it. He'd thought it was done.

"Possum," Red said. "Where are you?"

"My mom's trailer."

"I'll be right over."

Red shoved the last of the birthday cake in his mouth, grabbed the rifle from the gun case, caught Sue's eye, and leaned his head toward the car. He mouthed an apology, and her face fell, but she nodded. He didn't say good-bye to Junior because he was having such a good time there with all four of his grandparents doting on him, ripping around the yard in his Spider-

Man outfit, playing with his new remote-control truck. Interrupting him would only put a damper on things. Red slipped out, hopped in the still-new Jimmy, and drove four blocks to the trailer park.

Inside the small gray trailer where Possum lived with his mother, Lissette, and stepfather, Vance Taylor, Possum sat on the floor with two bodies close by, a bronze figurine of an eagle in his hands, and blood, so much blood, all over the yellow linoleum floor and cabinets and bodies.

"I thought you would come before this," Possum said quietly when Red first arrived and walked across the threshold. He looked at Red: those wide, dreadful brown eyes. "You said you would come."

Red swallowed hard. He knew what Possum was talking about, the thing from the summer before, Possum skinny and bruised and soiled and Transom standing at the edge of the woods, watching, before slipping into the trees, and Red wanted to say something—apologize, explain, because there *was* an explanation—but no words would come out, the stench, the sight, overwhelming him. He knelt to check pulses on the bodies, the blood soaking up through the knees of his jeans. Both alive, for now.

Possum glared at Vance's limp body on the floor. "Bastard had it coming."

"Sure," Red said, his throat tightening at the sight of the blood, the pasta salad and burger and birthday cake threatening to soar from his abdomen. The smell. Possum looking out the window: a goldfinch at the feeder, bright yellow with summer, head cocked. Red stood and picked up the corded phone in the kitchen and called the closest hospital, a number he'd memorized his first week on the job. Fifteen miles south. He gave his name, a few details, the address, then he squatted across the room from Possum, and told himself twenty minutes, max. Twenty minutes he had to keep things exactly as they were, Possum still and serene, and then help would arrive. He imagined an ambulance and a police car trundling north up 28, past the Orvetto dairy farm, past Shultz's factory, the baseball field, Red's own house and the birthday party in the yard. "Sure, son," he said to Possum, willing his voice to stay calm. Agree with him, don't say anything to set him off. Keep him right where he is and in twenty minutes you can step out of the room and get some air and decide what's next.

"He had it coming," Possum whispered. The finch darted away, a flash of yellow at the window. Over and over, that was all he said. He had it coming.

—

Which is what Red kept contemplating now, as he thought about Transom Shultz. Vance, beaten to a pulp by a fist-sized figurine, and Possum, sixteen years old and scrawny and his big eyes, looking at Red and saying, in a voice so tranquil Red would dream about it for years, that the man had it coming. After what Transom had done, he would've had it coming, too. Red knew that. But obtaining a warrant to search Possum's trailer and that enormous metal shed of his that held who-knew-what, or even bringing in Possum for questioning was, well, sort of out of the question. As far as Red knew, there were only three other people on earth who knew about what had happened out at the shale pit, and Red was in no hurry to start exposing any of it, especially right before he was about to retire.

More troubling than the idea of digging up that misstep and airing it for the town, though, was a different possibility, and as Red drove along 28, the hot air whipping through the Jimmy, the thought began to stitch its way into him. What if Possum had indeed exacted his revenge on Transom? What if Red was next? Images began tumbling into place, like cards being shuffled and stacked up: years and years of unnerving encounters. Possum holding his gaze at the diner, refusing to look away. Possum trailing him in the grocery store, lingering by the eggs.

For now, Red told himself, he needed to stay calm, stay focused. There was no need to start stirring up trouble, no need to go jumping the gun. He would keep an eye on Possum, see what he could scrounge up without making things messy, without making any dangerous assumptions.

So on his second day on the case, six days since anyone had seen Transom Shultz, Red headed to the Allegheny National Forest, a spot two miles north of town, a little pull-off where he'd seen Possum Miller's red pickup parked off and on all spring. From what he'd heard around town, Possum hunted for mushrooms there, which was very likely what he was doing, and which of course wasn't a crime. Besides, people were free to park in a public lot if they wanted to, after all, and people did in fact park there all the time, workers carpooling to the mill up in Empire, teenagers fooling around on fall nights.

Red had a feeling that if Transom hadn't disappeared on his own accord—if he wasn't gallivanting around Tahiti or Costa Rica or wherever it was he might've decided to go—if he was indeed *dead*, he was somewhere in those woods. But that Allegheny land spanned over 500,000 acres, more land than any search team could ever dream of covering. The truth was, Red had trouble conceptualizing how much ground that was, how many hills and gullies and trees and streams would comprise such a tract. The body could be anywhere. But don't go getting ahead of yourself, Red: that's what he kept saying. Maybe there was no body. Lord, he hoped so.

Red pulled the Jimmy into the empty parking lot, a gravel area on the side of the road with nothing but a sad brown sign with painted white letters to indicate you were in the right place. A skinny, overgrown trail veered off into the woods to the right of the lot. He slipped into the plastic fluorescent orange vest he'd picked up for two bucks at the gas station. It wasn't hunting season, but he figured better to be safe than sorry. Before he'd left, he'd told Leigh where he was heading. She was typing up traffic violations and she'd dipped her head and peered at him over her bifocals. "You want me to ride along?" It was a long-standing joke, that Leigh, fifty-three years old and barely a hundred pounds, Leigh in her skirt and high heels and hot-rolled blonde hair, would accompany Red on his patrols.

"Next time," he'd said with a smile.

"Be careful, Sweets." Leigh called everybody *Sweets*.

That morning, Red had started leafing through the accordion file he'd found in Transom's trunk, and by studying the checkbook he'd found there and then making three phone calls, he had pieced together already that Transom had a knack for identifying good tracts of land, buying them on the cheap, and then making loads of money off them. In the past, he'd had luck partnering with a particular real estate developer who'd divvy up the land into decent-sized lots that attracted a very specific clientele. This had worked well for him in the middle of the state, in Harrisburg and State College. More recently, though, he'd shifted his attention: he'd been focusing on the western half of Pennsylvania, buying up land and selling the mineral rights to the oil companies drilling for Marcellus shale. The Hardy farm was the third property Transom had worked. Red couldn't help but wonder— had it been Transom's plan all along to return right after Jack Hardy passed, to buy the land off Chase, when his old friend was in a pinch? And then, a more troubling thought, a thought that unfolded a new chain of troubling possibilities: Had Chase Hardy figured out all of that? Had he tried to do something about it? "Not a chance," Red said aloud. Chase Hardy was as phlegmatic as they came; he was harmless and solid.

Red climbed out of the Jimmy. He caught a whiff of the tall green trash receptacle sitting next to the sign, where yellow jackets churned and hummed. He grabbed his backpack. At the trash, he paused and slipped on a pair of rubber gloves, struggling to pry open the bear-proof metal container. Fast-food bags heaped in the middle. An old t-shirt hung over the side. Whose job was it to empty these? State employees? Volunteers? How long had it been since someone had tended to it? Surely this much garbage hadn't accumulated in a week or so. He grabbed a stick and poked through the bags and rotten food, holding his handkerchief over his face, gagging at the stench. After a few minutes Red closed the lid, and it reverberated loudly, metal to metal. No dead body in there.

He wiped his forehead with his handkerchief and sighed. At the edge of the woods, he stood, squinting in the bright sunlight, pondering what to do. The map he pulled from the wooden box in the parking lot wasn't very reassuring; it merely showed a winding, dotted line that headed south. White marks, small circles spray-painted about eye-level, indicated the route.

He took a swig of water from the plastic bottle he'd bought with the orange vest and began walking. Although he was sweating profusely in the midday heat, he felt an urgent need to move. He paused, checking the Ruger .380 he'd slid into his pocket. The Borough of Fallen Mountains had issued him a rifle, a 30-30, but nobody wanted to lug a rifle around on patrol, and he couldn't very well go around with it strapped over his shoulder all the time. So years ago, he'd had Sue give him a handgun for an anniversary gift. He'd picked it out, of course, and bought it himself, but she'd wrapped it, in shiny silver paper. He'd bought her an herb garden that year.

"What kind of person buys himself a handgun for an anniversary gift?" Sue had said. "You understand that's weird, right?"

"It fits right in my pocket," Red had replied. "See? You can't even tell it's there. And to answer your question: the kind of person who wants to protect the people he loves, that's who." He'd smiled then, leaning in and kissing her.

The trail led Red into a copse of dense, tall mountain laurel that arced above him, creating a sort of tunnel that he had to forge through, ducking at times. White flowers like teacups held to the branches, fragrant and delicate, their dropped petals dotting the dirt path. Close by, a stream bubbled along, but in the mountain laurel tunnel, he couldn't be sure of where the sound was coming from: maybe it wound all around him, maybe it lay just ahead.

When Red stopped to take a drink, he thought he heard the sharp sound of a stick cracking, breaking under the pressure of weight. He turned around slowly, searching the woods behind him, but he could only see a few yards. The mountain laurel, dense in the peak of summer, arched over the path.

"Hello?" he called, resting his hand on the Ruger. His heart thundered in his chest. "Is someone there?" Silence. "Who's there?" Possum, he thought again, the name rumbling through his mind. Possum gathering mushrooms or doing whatever it was he did in those woods, seeing an opportunity and moving on it.

It could be an animal, Red told himself. A bear, a deer, maybe even something smaller. Would his .380 be enough to stop a bear? Should he fire it into the air?

Maybe there'd been no sound at all. He questioned himself sometimes, doubting even his own senses—he hadn't slept well for two years now, since Sue had passed. He couldn't get used to it, the dip on the other side of the bed where she used to sleep, the quiet. So the noise: Had he imagined it? He waited for a moment, then kept walking, until he heard it again: a stick snapping. He spun around quickly this time, raising his piece. This time, he thought the noise may have come from his left. "Who's there?" he yelled. Red pictured Possum sitting on the floor of his mother's trailer, Vance at his feet, blood pooling at his head and Possum with the bronze eagle in his hand, staring at the refrigerator. The finch quivering at the window.

Red wished he could see a little better, wished it wasn't so dark and tunneling right there. No sound, no movement. But then—he was sure of it—the sound of retreat, something thrashing through the mountain laurel: twigs breaking, footsteps. Red stood on the trail, surrounded on all sides by the tan, curling branches and large, thick leaves of the mountain laurel. The white flowers. He rotated, looking all around, and then realized with a great deal of anxiety that he could quickly become disoriented if he didn't keep track of the way he'd come in. At that point he realized he had no choice but to head back; he must acknowledge his limitations and be willing to call it a day. Sweat slid down his forehead and into his eyes, and he dabbed his face with his handkerchief. His shirt was soaked, and his pulse raced. With his Ruger out of its pocket and clenched in his hand, wrist aching, he walked back to the parking lot, back in the direction of whatever—whoever—had followed him.

BEFORE

POSSUM HAD EARNED HIS NICKNAME IN THE THIRD grade, when the class was learning about the local fauna and one of his classmates, Katie Johns, had made the observation that Tommy Miller looked like an opossum. When Katie made her remark, the entire class turned to look at Tommy's face. Even Possum could see why Katie had drawn the connection: he did resemble that scrawny, wide-eyed creature known for playing dead. He was plagued by a terrible cowlick that made his light brown hair stick up in the back, and despite his enormous appetite, he had always been skinny. His eyes were disproportionately large for his thin face, and, despite his efforts to stop, he had the unfortunate habit of staring, mouth half open, in a look of constant bewilderment. Eventually he decided to let the name stick, mostly because after a while, nobody thought of him as anything else. In their small town of nine hundred, even the adults picked up on it, even the teachers at school.

Nobody seemed to care that maybe he might prefer his real name, Thomas, any version of it, really, anything but Possum. The truth was nobody cared much about Possum at all, as long as he minded his own business, which he was more than happy to do. After nearly two decades, the town had mostly forgiven him for what he'd done to Vance—some people had never held it against him to begin with—and to them he was just a quiet, awkward misfit who hunted mushrooms and collected junk.

What nobody besides his cousin Laney knew, however, was that Possum ran a lucrative business selling that junk on the Internet. When he gave his mother, Lissette, a new Dodge Neon for Christmas one year, a gift he had proudly paid cash for, she'd frowned and said, "Promise me this is from them antiques of yours, not something else." He'd assured her it was.

Possum lived in a trailer next to his mother's at the edge of town, just across the Ninth Street Bridge, behind which there was a shed where he stored all of his wares. The shed was twice the size of the trailer, and Possum kept it meticulously organized so that he knew exactly where every item was. He traveled the state and even ventured into Maryland or New York attending auctions, yard sales, and flea markets gathering items for his business. He knew his antiques well, knew which kinds of nesting hens were more desirable than others, knew the best angle for photographing Depression glass. And perhaps most importantly, he knew how to sell these things with vivid but not dishonest descriptions. That's what often gave him an edge, he believed. He'd always been a good writer, at least that's what his English teachers had told him in high school, before he'd dropped out. Recently, he'd purchased China Rose Spode china, service for twelve, for a hundred bucks at a garage sale, and turned around to sell it for nine times that price online. That type of situation wasn't typical, by any means, but he could live off that profit for weeks.

After what happened with his stepfather, Vance, Possum never went back to high school, although he did earn his GED from jail. It was in jail that he began getting into antiques. He read book after book, memorizing names and dates and numbers. His mother took them out from the library under her name and brought him one or two each week when she visited. As soon as Possum got out, he borrowed some money from his mother and used it to pick up a handful of items at an auction: a Walter Bosse Metzler Ortloff figurine, a garnet pendant, and a brass hotel bell. He sold them, and with the profit, paid back his mother and purchased a couple more things. Within a few months of his release, he had established a viable business.

He also foraged for mushrooms, in the spring and summer. The very first book he read in jail was one someone had left behind in the pathetic stack of random titles the guards called the library, a thin book titled *Pennsylvania's Edible Mushrooms*. He read it carefully, cover to cover, and then he read it again, memorizing the names—king bolete, chicken of the woods, horn of plenty, morel—and then the descriptions and where to find them. When he was released, he ordered the exact same book for himself and started looking for those mushrooms, wandering the trails of the national forest nearby, following the book's instructions on how to prepare them, too.

He told Chase Hardy about his new endeavor, and Chase invited Possum to roam the property looking for morels. He'd found his best spots on that Hardy land, and like all morel hunters, he'd never told a soul about his good luck—it was a secretive business, mushroom hunting. Not far from the farmhouse, there was a tulip poplar with a patch of them at the base, but the greater treasure was way off, deep in the woods, close to the national forest line. There, two dying elm trees with the bark sloughing off created the perfect environment for morels, and every spring for years now, Possum had gone there with his Adirondack pack basket and gathered dozens.

———

He thought of that sacred spot in the woods now, on the stoop of his trailer, as he finished his cigarette and stomped off snow. With Transom Shultz back in Fallen Mountains, running the Hardy farm, what was Possum supposed to do about his morels? Ask for permission? Drive right past the farmhouse and hope he wasn't noticed? Sneak in some other way? He had a few months to figure it out, but the mere thought of it—Transom ruining yet another thing for him—was enough to make his blood boil.

The thing was, it wasn't that hard for Possum to blame everything that had ever gone wrong in his life on Transom Shultz. If it hadn't been for Transom, maybe Possum would've been a better student. Maybe he would've gone on to college and moved away. Maybe he wouldn't have snapped that day after school, his junior year, when he came home and found his mother on the floor, knocked out cold by one of his stepfather's heavy fists, and Vance standing over her, so drunk he didn't even recognize Possum in the doorway. If it weren't for Transom, maybe he would've ended up living a regular life. Maybe he would've been normal.

In recent years, Possum had been training himself not to think about Transom Shultz, and he'd convinced himself he'd let it go, all that anger and hate that used to burn at him, deep in his gut like a coal blistering its way out. It was in the past, he told himself. They were just kids, stupid kids. He'd moved on. He'd carved out a decent enough life for himself in Fallen

Mountains. He was good at his work; he enjoyed it. He had a chunk of change in the bank. He'd even recently started talking with a woman, a Russian named Alla, in an online forum.

But now, with Transom Shultz back in town, Possum felt as though he'd been flung right back to his school days. Transom shoving him into the janitor's closet, crushing him with his incredible strength and hissing, hot against his face: "You call out, you tell anyone, I swear: I'll mess you up so bad you'll wish you were dead." Then the heat, the smell of bleach and pine-scented cleaner in the closet. The mice, too. And all his classmates shuffling past, unaware that he was trapped, their shadows flickering across the small crack at the bottom of the door. Then, of course, there was the other thing, that summer when the cicadas had teemed and eaten their way through the treetops, Transom hovering above the trunk, dumping kerosene, Transom saying, *I don't want you to be afraid*, the trunk easing closed.

In the kitchen of his trailer, Possum grabbed a butterscotch crumpet and plopped down at his computer. As he logged in, his hands continued to shake. He needed a distraction, something to shift his attention from the fear. That'd been his technique in the past: find something else to think about, focus on it until his body could recover and the shaking would subside.

For three weeks now, Possum had been talking to Alla, a fellow antiques dealer whom he met in an online forum designated for discussing wares. He'd picked up a hand-painted Ukrainian egg at a flea market and was trying to estimate its age and value; he posted four pictures and a description, and Alla responded to his post. Alla lived in Moscow and specialized in folk crafts, and the two sort of hit it off, at least as far as Possum was concerned.

Sometimes Possum found himself staring at the photograph Alla had posted in her profile, her blonde hair shimmering in the sunlight and lifting with a gust of wind, her head tilting just to the side. He felt a little strange doing this—he hated creeps who stalked people on the Internet—but he couldn't help himself. She was beautiful, just breathtaking. Of course, Possum was savvy enough to know that Alla could be a fat man in his forties who snapped a picture of a random woman on the street, but something told him she was real, that the person in the photograph was the same one he'd been talking to online. Possum wasn't someone who allowed himself the luxury of imagining he would get married one day, have a family, be happy. It never felt like something that was in the cards for him, and he'd come to terms with that. So this thing with Alla was new to him, and scary—he couldn't stop thinking about her.

On this day, though, even chatting with Alla didn't help. His hands still juddered; he sweated profusely; his heart pounded. After a few minutes, he told her he needed to go and signed off. In a brown bottle in the medicine cabinet were anxiety pills, and he could take one, he knew, but instead, he stepped back outside, into the bitter January morning, and lit another cigarette. Knowing Transom Shultz was back in Fallen Mountains, feeling that fear that had consumed him for all those years, and then sensing how quickly that same old rage engulfed him again, Possum realized he'd been deceiving himself, all that time. He wasn't over anything at all. He hadn't let it go, and he never would.

AFTER

RED LAY IN HIS BED, FIGHTING FOR SLEEP, THE JUNE air still and heavy, the heat ruthless. The crickets bellowed outside his open window, and their noise, which he usually didn't mind, put him on edge. He realized just how deafening they were—just how much they limited his ability to hear anything else. Like someone prowling about the house on Crocus Street. Or a vehicle pulling up outside.

He couldn't shake off the experience in the Allegheny National Forest from that afternoon, playing it over and over in his mind. What had it been, there in the woods? Had it been an animal, or had someone been following him? Red remembered the words from that night at the trailer, long ago. *He had it coming. Bastard had it coming.* Like a bad song they kept playing on the radio, no escaping it. Maybe he, Red, had it coming, too? His mind darted through all the questions, all the possibilities.

But then came the doubt. It very well could have been an animal out there in the woods. Worse—maybe he'd imagined the noise, the thrashing through the mountain laurel. Maybe he'd made the whole thing up. Was he getting paranoid in his old age? Was this how dementia started?

Beside him, in the filtered white light from the streetlamp two houses down, the sheets and comforter lay flat, and as he looked, the same old sadness swept over him. Perhaps the cruelest part of grief was that it kept on winding back, over and over, so you didn't lose the person once, but again and again. Two years in and he'd still wake up sometimes and forget Sue was gone. He'd reach for her, the small of her back, her shoulder, and when his hand grabbed at air and fell to the bed, he'd remember.

Red wasn't sure what he thought about the capacities of people who'd crossed that threshold into the life beyond—did they float among us, soul-presences that we could sense but not see? Did they watch from above, defying the laws of nature, leaping about the clouds? He didn't know, but there were times when he'd talk to her, there in the bed, when all the houses around him were dark and still and nobody would hear the voice of the lonely sheriff swimming through the thin glass of his home on Crocus Street. Late, late at night. Pretend Sue, Ghost Sue.

"I messed up," he said now, his voice a whisper. "Way back, when Junior was small. I hid something that shouldn't have been hid." He looked at the ceiling, stained in the corner from a leak in the roof the fall before. "I know this is a disappointment, you being the most ethical person I ever met. You wouldn't have put yourself in such a predicament. The thing is, now I don't know what to do."

He'd met Sue at the wedding of a mutual friend, a wedding he hadn't wanted to go to because, like all weddings, this one would no doubt depress him. He'd earned his associate's degree, but he was working as a clerk in an auto parts store back in The Rocks, living in a run-down duplex two blocks away from his parents. At nights he'd sit with the window open and watch the headlights glide over the bridges, the river glittering below, everything alive and moving, and he was stuck. Most of his friends were married by then, most of them had at least one kid, some of them three, and he was that guy, the bachelor that the husbands sometimes envied and the wives pitied and tried to fix up with their friends, single women who were single for a reason he could always put his finger on right away. Red had pretty much given up on the idea that he'd meet someone wonderful and have a family. And then he'd gone to that wedding and been seated next to Sue at the reception on the lawn. Sue, eleven years his junior and from a town he'd never heard of, Sue who would toss her head back in laughter, Sue with auburn hair gleaming in the October light. She'd asked him to dance and he'd asked for her number and a year later they were married and living in Fallen Mountains in the house on Crocus Street.

Now, in his bed, he imagined Ghost Sue scooting across the sheets and pulling him close. Everybody makes mistakes, she would say. You'll find your way, you always do. And you look at me, John Redifer. Look me in the eye. (This is what Sue used to say when she really wanted his attention: Look at me, John Redifer, when every other time she'd call him Red, like everybody else.) You're a good man, Ghost Sue would say. You're a good man.

For so many years, he'd convinced himself that was true. But was it? Or maybe, all along, it had been Sue's goodness that he'd felt. It had radiated off her, a warmth, and he'd been able to absorb some of it himself. Maybe it was just that he was a great pretender, and because he'd been able to convince everyone around him that he was a good man, including Sue, he'd started to believe it himself.

—

That terrible summer, seventeen years earlier, had been hot, like this one—hot in a way that the air always felt heavy and your clothes never felt dry, and yet it never rained, and even in June the grass had already fried to hopeless brown tufts. There were more rattlesnakes that year than usual, the creatures descending from their isolated spots in higher elevations to lower areas, creeks and springs, desperate for water. But what Red remembered most of all were the cicadas, seventeen-year locusts, emerging in multitudes from the ground, their brown shells everywhere, litter crunching beneath your feet. Then their sound, a paranormal thickness, deafening to the point that you'd have to lean in closer to hear a person talk.

Junior was five that year, and sick. He'd had trouble with ear infections since he was a few months old but the year he turned five, the doctor said he needed surgery, and when that didn't work, he needed another. It was on the schedule for September, the big procedure. Recurrent acute otitis media. Adenoid hypertrophy. The surgeons had gone over the diagnoses and shown him and Sue a plastic model of an ear, the pink folds and blue canals—eustachian tubes, middle ear, inner ear—but none of that meant anything to them, only that Junior would emerge from the other end of it all with ears that worked right, his balance restored, the raging pain that would shake his body, gone. He and Sue hoped.

The night the incident at the shale pit happened, Red and Junior sat on the porch on Crocus Street studying a cicada Junior had caught in a jar.

"Scary, huh?" Red said.

Junior, obsessed with insects, shook his head. "Not scary," he replied. "Different. Look at their wings." He unscrewed the lid and took one out, holding it in his palm and watching as it crawled up his arm.

It was Possum's cousin, Laney Moore, who called the house phone that evening to say Possum hadn't shown up to work at the Dairy Freez, that he wasn't home, either. "Sheriff," Laney had insisted on the phone, when Red tried to assure her that there was no need for concern, "something's wrong. He wouldn't just skip work like that. I know him, and that's not the type of thing he'd do."

When he hung up, Red sat with Junior, the boy's tiny hands folded inside of his, and prayed, as he did each night, *Dear Lord, please help Junior to sleep safe and sound. Please help his ears not to hurt tonight. Amen.* He told Junior to be a good boy and go to bed for his mother, kissed them both good-bye, and grabbed the 30-30 from its case at the back of the hall.

He fired up the Jimmy and decided to head to the shale pit out along 28—if kids were involved, that was always a good place to start looking. They drove quads there and partied, their tire tracks and IC Light cans and cigarette butts and Twinkie wrappers as evidence. Afterward, Red saw that if he hadn't gone there first, he may not have gotten there in time; he may not have arrived before things went south, really south.

Red pulled the Jimmy into the parking lot. Night was folding in, the sky with just the slightest hint of blue left in it, the sun gone, and darker there in the pit, with heaps of shale piled high like small mountains. He grabbed the rifle and slid a bullet in the chamber, skimmed his thumb over the safety mechanism. The cicadas were tapering off with the waning daylight, and the crickets were taking over.

Red clicked on his flashlight. "Hello?"

The insects too loud.

"Someone there? Hello?" he called again.

It was impossible to hold that light and the rifle at the same time. He slung the 30-30 over his shoulder. As he rounded the bend, he saw the shape of a person, standing on one of the mounds of shale, his silhouette dark and looming against the sky. Red flashed his light, just before the person turned to dart off into the woods, and he saw the body, the face, and he was sure of it, *sure*—that big figure in the dark, it was the Shultz boy, the pitcher for the baseball team whose name was in the sports page of the *Fallen Mountains Gazette* all the time. Transom.

"Hey!" Red called into the darkness. "What you doing out here?"

And then pounding, bang bang bang, muffled voice, he could barely hear it with the crickets, filling the dark with their song. Red flashed the light around, into the woods again, flickering left and right across the trees. An old car was parked about fifteen yards away, tucked between two heaps of shale. Was someone in there? He pulled the rifle off his shoulder and held it, his left hand on the barrel, right hand on the stock. Flashlight in his mouth now. He walked closer, the noise growing louder, faster, more desperate. The trunk. He set the rifle on the ground and struggled with the handle, old and rusty, not wanting to move. He struggled to pull it open, both hands, light still in his mouth, jaw sore from the stretching. Finally it gave, wailing as he opened it, and there, in the trunk of the old car, hands and wrists and mouth tied with pieces of a t-shirt, his own, it turned out, a shirtless boy, skinny, back blue and purple with bruising, squinting in the light, the stench of urine and kerosene rising as Red leaned in.

"Possum?" he said, recognizing him as Lissette Miller's son, the boy with the wild hair and big eyes. Red reached in, removing the cloth from the boy's mouth. Possum began to shake hard, whole body convulsing. "Possum, you all right, son? What happened?" He looked up, shining the light over the trees again, the shadows large across the lot, the insects loud and night closing in, no sign of anyone in the woods.

—

Seventeen years had passed, but how many times had Red lived through that evening, catching cicadas with his son, the phone call from Laney, then driving out to the shale pit, seeing Transom slip into the woods, finding Possum in the trunk. All of it, a bad dream that kept on trembling back. Try as he could, Red couldn't seem to free himself of it. The past: never dead. Maybe if there'd been a different chapter after that, maybe if he'd told Possum's mother and encouraged her to press charges and they'd gone to the state police, maybe if he'd done the right thing, the events of that night wouldn't haunt him the way they did. But there was no undoing any of it now, no taking it back.

Red sat up in his bed and flipped on the light, squinting in the sudden brightness. Behind the light, on the nightstand, was the green accordion file from Transom's trunk, and he reached for it. He pulled his reading glasses from their sleeve and slid them on. He'd been systematic about looking through the file, pocket by pocket. In one, stubs from a logging company. Apparently Transom contracted the same outfit to cut the timber, regardless of where a property was located. Earlier, Red had sat at the police station with a microwave dinner and a calculator, peering through his glasses, leafing through the papers, tapping in the numbers. Close to a hundred grand Transom had brought in, from logging alone, over the past year. Six properties, scattered across the western end of the state. In another pocket, three contracts from oil companies, mineral rights in perpetuity, all for Marcellus shale, all within an hour of Fallen Mountains. The last one, signed in February of this year, four months earlier, was for 8817 Old Oak Lane, the Hardy property. How long had Transom owned the place before he'd sold off the mineral rights? Red had walked across the street from the police station to the courthouse and looked it up in the records. Five weeks. Not very long. The loggers had come even sooner. Again, the thought: Had it been Transom's plan all along, buy that property, cut the good timber, sign with an oil company? Had he known about Jack's strong stance on the issue?

Red had one pocket left, at the back of the file. He reached in and grabbed an envelope. Sea to Sea Travel Agency, Pittsburgh. Relief flooded over him—here he would find a receipt, an itinerary. Transom had gone off again and there was evidence to prove it. Red would hand in that retirement letter tomorrow, first thing, and he'd tell Leigh right off that he'd intended to hand it in before, but then the whole Transom Shultz thing had come up, and he hadn't felt right about leaving until it was wrapped up. He'd call Junior and make plans to drive out to see his new apartment in Shadyside and go to a Pirates game. He'd go bass fishing; it was too hot for trout.

What he found instead in the final pocket was not a receipt, but plane tickets, two of them. Red scanned the names: Transom Shultz and Teresa Bradley. Pittsburgh to Atlanta, Atlanta to Jamaica. Red dumped the rest of the contents from the Sea to

Sea Travel Agency envelope on the bed. Reservations for a week at a swanky beach resort in Negril. A pamphlet on scuba diving, a pamphlet about a booze cruise at sunset. And a personalized, typed plan, not just their names and a date and time but also additional details—private ceremony on the beach, pink orchids, torches, table for two.

He remembered pretty Teresa sitting across the table from him at the police station, her hand extended, the ring gaudy and brilliant in the fluorescent light. Red's heart sank. He looked at the empty spot in the bed beside him. A wedding. Transom had been planning his wedding.

BEFORE

BY THE MIDDLE OF JANUARY, LANEY HAD COME TO terms with the fact that she needed to prepare herself for when Transom showed up at her place, because one way or another, she'd need to explain that things were different now. Even if her relationship with Chase bore no official title, she hoped that, in time, it would. With Transom, there was chemistry and comfort, a heat lightning that flashed and loomed, but there was only the moment, nothing beyond it. With Chase, she could see a future that stretched on and out: a life together, a family. And that's what she needed to hold to; that's what she had to keep reminding herself of. Because when Transom showed up at the back door, his beautiful face peering through the glass in expectation, she needed to be ready to send him on his way.

She devised a plan. She could not let him in the house, she knew that, so no matter how cold it was, no matter how bitter the wind sweeping off the mountains was, she would open the door and step out onto the back porch. "Things have changed," she would tell him. "So this can't happen anymore. This is in the past." She imagined the events, rehearsed the lines. When her mind veered toward Transom, toward the feel and smell of him, that terrible pull he could exert on her, she'd force it back to Chase.

The problem was, Transom didn't come to the door. Instead, Laney was in the meat section of the grocery store, looking for a ribeye. It was brutally cold and it was one of those days when the absence of Jack and Maggie hung on her like a backache. Chase hadn't invited her to stay again, and when she'd seen him, he'd been distant, standing far away from her, avoiding eye contact. Laney figured a steak, maybe, a fattening slab of protein, might make her feel better. She was reading the labels, looking for a cut that would allow her to have a good portion and the dog some, too, when she felt someone come up behind her, the body so close she could feel it graze her own.

"I was hoping we'd cross paths eventually."

That voice, the feel of the speaker so close, after so many years of silence and distance, caught her off guard and sent a shudder through her because this—this she had not prepared for. This, she had not rehearsed. She whirled to face him, those sea green eyes that penetrated, the face, familiar and lovely with its symmetry and grace. "What are you doing here?"

"Same as you," he replied, breaking into a smile. "Looking for a piece of meat." He laughed and nudged her, that smile with a hundred lines, those brilliant teeth. Although years had passed since she'd last seen him, Transom didn't look much different, just older, a little more worn. Still handsome, plus he seemed thicker, somehow. Stronger.

"You look good," Transom said, tilting his head. He reached out and brushed a stray hair from her forehead.

She became self-conscious then, in her ripped jeans and dirty jacket. She hated that she'd come straight from her walk with Kip, that her face was flushed from cold and wind, that her fluorescent orange beanie was pulled above her ears and way up on top of her head, like some kind of odd Christmas elf. She contemplated yanking it off and shoving it into the shopping basket, but then she worried that such a move might reveal an even uglier disaster: her disheveled, frizzed hair, which she hadn't washed for two days.

Why was she so embarrassed about all of that? Why was her heart racing, thumping in her chest? Why, after all these years, did she still feel so enthralled, and so ashamed for being enthralled, in Transom's presence?

"You want company for dinner?" he asked, his eyes twinkling.

"I can't," she said, pushing past him to grab a strip steak, the closest package she could reach without touching him. She needed to get out of there, away from him.

He reached out and grazed his knuckles against hers. "Come on. It's just dinner."

She shivered, her red shopping basket hanging from her arm and resting against her hip, and she turned to look at him. She tried to read him, wondering if Chase had told him anything. Well—maybe there was nothing to tell. Maybe he'd just been lonely, and she'd been there, a friend, a body. After all, it wasn't like he'd made some sort of commitment; it wasn't like he'd said anything at all. Her mind began to spin.

"It's good to see you," Transom said.

Everything with Chase, those conclusions she'd come to over the holidays about the two of them belonging together—all of it muddled and bent. "Dinner," she said. "Just dinner."

And that's all it was that night. Dinner, steak and beer and frozen French fries in the oven. Transom told stories from high school: pep rallies and four-wheeling at the farm and wild parties out at the lake. Billy Ferguson drunk and forgetting to put his

truck in gear, the pickup sliding into the water, the bubbles floating up and everyone too hammered to do a thing about it.
Remembering, Laney laughed so hard she cried. Corning the
principal's house on Halloween, all three of them dressed as zom-
bies, Chase and Transom and Laney, too—pelting the front door
with field corn from the farm. Eleventh grade, that had been.

"Remember that night?" Transom asked, looking at her.
"That was the first time, you and me. I dropped off Chase first."

Her mother hadn't been home, and he'd pulled around back.
When she'd reached into the back seat to grab her purse, he'd
kissed her neck.

"I remember." She could feel Transom's strong pull then, his
eyes on her, and she stood and started clearing the plates from
the table. "Listen, I don't mean to be rude, but I have things I
need to do."

"Right. I should get going."

She dumped soap into the sink, filled it with hot water, and
sunk her hands into the suds. "Well, thanks for this. It was nice.
It was good to catch up."

Transom stood and carried his plate to the sink. "Laney."

She couldn't look at him, not when he stood that close, not
when he said her name like that. She shook her head and kept
her eyes on the pot she was scrubbing, her arms deep in the
water. "I can't."

Transom stepped back. "Okay." He slid into his coat. "Thanks
for dinner," he said. "I can let myself out."

From the sink, she watched as he paused at his Lincoln,
looked back at her through the window, and raised a hand good-
bye. And when he'd gone, when she'd watched his taillights disappear down Locust Street and turn left onto 28, she didn't feel

guilty about having spent time with him. Instead, she slumped on the couch and felt a wash of relief but also a stitch of grief, a sense that she'd missed out on something. If this was the right thing to do, send him on his way, why was there such a sense of loss, she wondered.

—

Laney still hadn't heard from Chase when, two days later, Transom returned, stood at the back door, and knocked quietly. She was balancing her checkbook at the kitchen table, tapping numbers into her calculator, and all at once her plans to step outside, to meet him on the porch, scuttled away from her. She opened the door and he stepped inside and pulled her close and then the two of them were entwined and breathless and hungry and stumbling through the living room. Even in the moment, she knew there would be no freeing herself from that thing she'd been so drawn to over the years: like the June bugs that jolted to the bug catcher humming on her back porch each summer, she just couldn't keep herself from lurching toward the light.

But right after, she felt the weight of her choice, heavy and ugly and whirling. Laney rose from bed, dashed to the bathroom and vomited, her fingers wrapped around the white porcelain rim, her body wrenching. Kneeling on the old tile floor, she closed her eyes, gathering herself. The room spun, white and yellow, and the floor was so cold, the old house with its thin windows and drafty halls. She thought of all those times the three of them had roamed the Hardy farm together, the times, too, that they'd insisted she stay behind, because it was Boys Only, Brothers Only. As a child, she'd resented that, being left behind, but she'd admired their closeness, too: she'd envied it. Transom and Chase, inseparable, two friends who'd navigated the multitude of adolescent trials without a hiccup, and now she'd somehow managed to position herself between the two of them.

"You all right?" Transom called from the bedroom.

She pulled herself up, cupped water from the faucet and splashed her face, then sobbed into a hand towel. She brushed her teeth and stumbled back into the bedroom.

"There's something I need to tell you," she said, her voice hoarse.

Transom rolled onto his side and propped himself up. "What is it?"

"We can't do this anymore," Laney said, shaking her head. "We just can't."

"I've heard that before." He rubbed his eyes and shrugged his shoulders, smiling, sinking back into the pillows. "And yet, here we are."

"No, it's different this time. Things have changed."

"What's changed?"

"Chase."

"What about Chase?"

"I'm with him."

Transom sat up. "What?"

"Well, I mean, we might be getting together. I want to." She took a deep breath. "It's complicated."

Transom frowned. "Am I supposed to understand what that means, 'it's complicated'? Because I don't."

Laney sat down on the edge of the bed. "Nothing's official. Nothing's been said."

"But you guys have hooked up."

She bit her lip. "Once."

"Recently?"

She nodded.

"Why didn't you say something?" Transom shook his head, rose from the bed, and pulled on his jeans. "Why didn't you tell me? I never would've—" he paused then, sliding into his shirt and slumping over, the burden of her announcement heavy on him. He sighed. "Does he know about the other times, you and me?"

She shook her head. "I never told him. Did you?"

"No." Transom struggled with the buttons on his shirt. "He's my best friend, Laney. I don't pretend to be the most upstanding guy, you know that. But even I have lines I don't cross."

She sat on the bed and began crying again, hiding her face in the pillow. "I know. It's just—you know how he is. So hard to read sometimes, so distant. And then you and I had dinner. You came over."

"I came over because I didn't know."

"I should've told you. It was a mistake. I'm sorry."

"Maybe we should just tell him. Come clean. I'll tell him I didn't know."

"You can't do that." Laney grabbed his hand. "You can't throw me under the bus. Transom, please."

Transom seemed to consider this.

"Listen, try to understand. You come and go, you always have." Did he wince when she said that, or did she just imagine a flash of emotion on his face? "This is my life now. We're here, me and Chase. We're never going anywhere, neither one of us. And I want things to work out with him. I really do." She thought of all the years Chase had spent serenely in Transom's shadow—Transom the better-looking one, the stronger one, the more popular one. Chase, quiet and unassuming, never complaining about his position. But something told her that if there were any hope of the two of them being together, he couldn't find out about Transom and her. Not the numerous times before, and certainly not this time. In a moment of sudden clarity, she realized what she really wanted: Chase, the farm, a life together. "He can never know," she said.

"We had a good thing going, you and me."

Was that sadness she detected in his voice? Had she hurt him? She couldn't be sure. "I'm sorry."

He headed down the steps.

"Promise me you won't say anything to Chase. Please."

He turned to look at her over his shoulder. "I can let myself out, Laney," he said, and walked out the front door.

AFTER

RED DROVE SLOWLY PAST THE TRANQUIL HARDY FARM-house, the Holsteins dawdling in the pasture. In the rearview mirror, the dust rocketed up, everything bone-dry and the cicadas roaring, filling the air like a bad fog. A memory scampered back to him: he and Junior crawling around the yard after the ugly, black creatures with enormous folded wings and diabolical red eyes, stuffing them into an old mayonnaise container. Out at Sue's parents' place, they pitched the little critters at the hens and watched as the chickens dashed to peck them from the ground. Junior loved every minute of it.

Red turned the Jimmy up the gravel road to the plateau where the oil company was in the thick of construction: a huge swath of cleared land, a spot carved into the hillside and rolled flat. Cylindrical metal containers everywhere, a maze of piping. To his left, a forklift and, he counted, nine pickup trucks. To his right, a tan, windowless construction trailer, and another beyond that. Red quieted the engine and looked around. Before he even got out, a man in a hard hat, fluorescent yellow vest, and sun-glasses approached. Thick in the middle with a wide, menacing mustache, the man walked up to the Jimmy and tapped on the window. Red cranked it open.

"Who are you?" the man asked.

"Redifer, John Redifer."

"What do you want?"

"The man who owns this property, Transom Shultz, has gone missing. Is there someone I can talk to? Someone in charge?"

"Sit tight." The man pulled a radio out of his back pocket, and when he reached back, his shirt lifting, Red could see a handgun holstered at his hip. The man motioned to Red to step out of the Jimmy. "Boss is in the trailer," he said. "Come on."

As the man turned away to spit, Red cautiously slipped his Ruger into the pocket of his khakis. He had a bad feeling about this place and, remembering Teresa's comments about Transom's attempts to get out of his contract, he decided he wanted the weapon on him, just to be safe. Cautiously, he followed the man to the work trailer a hundred yards away.

Inside the trailer were three more men, two of whom were dressed like the one Red had met outside, and one of whom wore a light blue polo shirt and sat behind a desk.

"Afternoon," Red said, nodding to the three of them.

"What is it we can help you with?" the man in the polo asked, leaning back in his swivel chair. In his hand, he squeezed a purple grip strengthener, over and over.

"Well, as I mentioned to your associate," Red said, "the landowner has gone missing, and I'm here to see if you fellows have heard from him."

"You a cop?"

"I'm the Fallen Mountains sheriff."

"You got a warrant?"

Red began rethinking his plan, wishing he'd stopped by Judge Hess's to get a warrant. He should've told Junior where he was, or at least Leigh. With Sue gone, there was no one at home to miss him, no one to say, *He should be home by now*. Maybe Chase had seen him drive up the hill? "I ain't asking to poke around," Red said. "Just wanted to know if anyone has seen him."

"He used to come up here all the time," the man with the thick mustache said. "But we ain't seen him for a week or so."

"I need you to check on whether Sailor's done loading those pallets, Bill," the man in the blue polo shirt said. "Go on now." His voice twanged; he wasn't local. *Frackholes*, shuttling in from all over. Oklahoma, Texas. They drove their pickups and put up their rigs and stirred up trouble and left; that's what they did. You couldn't even drive through the national forest—the national forest!—without crossing paths with them anymore. The last time Red had driven through one part to go fishing, they'd had two men standing along the road in orange vests, directing traffic, radioing ahead. You had to stop at a kiosk and tell them who you were, give them your driver's license. They'd write it in a log before they let you through.

The mustached man, Bill, backed out of the trailer.

"So you been seeing him?" Red asked.

"Mr. Shultz leased us the mineral rights," the man in the polo explained, leaning forward in his seat, his knuckles white as he continued compressing the grip strengthener. "And there were times when he came up here, poking around. Caught him on video snooping in the dark. Three, four in the morning. I had to double up on security, got a crew working the night shift now." The man stretched his thick fingers. "Once, he showed up, barged right in here without checking in, and started hollering about the contract. My boss happened to be here that day, in from Texas. Which I took a lot of heat for that, looking like I don't know how to run the place."

"What was Transom mad about?"

The man shrugged. "Didn't like the way things were going up here, I guess." He shook his head in disgust. "You people just don't seem to get it. You sign a contract, you're paid. You don't get to come in here and say how things go anymore." He turned to the man beside him and began to laugh. "I think I'm gonna tell corporate I have an idea. They can hire me to start teaching classes on what a contract is." He laughed harder and turned to Red. "You guys have schools out here in the sticks?"

Inside, Red was seething, this guy talking down to him, making fun of his town and his people, but he forced himself to remain calm. "I just want to know the last time you saw Transom Shultz, and what happened."

"Don't get your panties in a wad, old man. I see what you're getting at, and I assure you, he ain't here. Haven't seen him for over a week. We've got men here, equipment, machines." He looked closely at Red, his gray eyes piercing. "You're a man of the law. You understand the need for rules and regulations. Order. We can't have people up here who aren't with the company. It's not safe."

"Right."

"Which is why I have to ask you to be on your way now."

Red grimaced at the self-assured smirk on the man's ugly face. There was nothing he could do at that moment in the confines of this dark, simmering trailer, him against the two men, at least one more outside, and with all those pickups, more around, somewhere. His arthritic right wrist, his whining knees. He stared. "All right," he said at last, the words lisping through his clenched teeth.

"Let me get your name and number," the man in the polo said. "You got a card or something?"

Red wondered whether or not he should give it, his paranoia humming, but he reached into his wallet and pulled out one of the green and white business cards Leigh had made for him. It was the first one he'd ever used.

The man slipped it into a drawer without looking at it. "If something comes up," he said, squeezing the grip strengthener, "we'll give you a ring."

Red nodded and muttered a thank-you, and as he stepped back out into the blinding June afternoon, the heat slamming his face, his eyes struggling to adjust to the intense light, the man in the polo called after him, in that singsong drawl of his, "Be careful out there. You hear?"

BEFORE

 IT WAS FEBRUARY ALREADY, AND CHASE FOUND HIMSELF exhausted each night, a heavy winter tiredness that tugged at his limbs. This was supposed to be a slower time of year for him at the farm, but day after day he was dragged into another one of Transom's projects. These tasks were on top of the usual chores, feeding and milking the cows, twice a day, mucking the barn, all of which Transom never helped with. Too busy, he said every time Chase asked.

Transom possessed a kind of wild energy—he always had—that could be infectious. He began by gutting a bathroom in the house, one that, once it was pointed out, Chase realized was indeed hideous. The toilet wailed and sputtered with every flush. The tile was an unbearable peach-but-almost-pink shade, and the sink was shaped like a seashell. Chase knew nothing about remodeling, but Transom knew a great deal. They drove to a home improvement store thirty miles away and came back with everything they needed, piled in Chase's truck: paint, a new vanity, dark bronze fixtures, vinyl flooring, a toilet, a fan and light. Within six days, the two of them had transformed the room. Transom taught Chase how to plumb the sink and wire the light and fan, and he liked it, learning these new and useful things from his old friend.

After Transom finished the bathroom, he insisted they move on to Jack's "office," a room that was more of a junk storage area than anything else. In there, they unearthed all sorts of things. Ticket stubs to a 1977 Pirates game. A receipt for the Farm-All that Jack had sold ten years earlier. Calendars, photo albums, instruction manuals, birthday cards, stacked neatly in an old shoe box, decades' worth, some of them from Chase and Transom. And traps, lots of traps, newer ones and ones that hadn't been used for decades. Transom sat on the floor amidst the mess, transfixed. He held them up to get a sense of how they worked, ran his fingers along the metal, pressed the sharp, deadly edges into his palms.

"Careful," Chase warned. The mere sight of the ugly contraptions made the hair on his body stand up. There'd been a time, long ago, when he'd run lines with Jack, but he'd sworn off trapping when he'd sworn off hunting, all of it at once.

In the dim light of Jack's office, Transom began sorting the traps, placing them into separate piles. Chase asked what the method was to the organizing. Transom shrugged his shoulders. "Rusty, not rusty."

"What you gonna do with them?"

"Some of them we can get rid of, right?" He motioned to a heap behind him: a stack of seed trays, an aquarium, the blade to the old rototiller. "Thought I'd take a load of stuff to the transfer station, get some money for the scrap metal." Transom ran his fingers along one of the traps. "The other ones, I'm gonna use. Try my hand at trapping." He looked up and held Chase's eyes. "I mean, as long as you think you'd be all right with it."

Chase looked away, out the window, where a light snow had just begun to fall, the flakes slow and deliberate, mesmerizing. He knew why Transom was feeling him out, trying to get a read on him. They were both remembering the day, eighteen years ago, that had resulted in Chase giving up hunting and trapping for good. He didn't want to go there; he didn't want to think about it. "You got to be organized about it, you know. You have to know how many you set, and where."

"Yeah, I know," Transom said. He placed another rusty trap into the heap.

The traps, Chase knew, were like so many other things with Transom: he would argue and insist and nag until he got his way. And half of the time it was all bull anyway. It was easier just not to get into it. Mostly, Chase found himself grateful for his friend's presence, for his ability to absorb those around him in his undertakings. If Transom hadn't been there, Chase felt sure his grief would've yanked him into a dark, winding funnel. Instead, Chase remained busy, in a useful way, with all the projects and outings. Things had been good between them, simple. Having Transom around had also given him a welcome distraction from whatever was transpiring between him and Laney. With so much up in the air, with so many emotions swirling through his head, he wasn't ready to make any commitments. He just couldn't.

Chase still missed Jack all the time. He continued to be caught in that chapter where he would be able to think about something else for a while, and then he would be plunged back into the grief, a bad baptism that kept on happening. It didn't take much to trigger a memory. The nuthatch, his grandfather's favorite bird, that came and settled on a branch just outside the kitchen window, tilting its head curiously instead of darting away when Chase shifted his weight. The sweet, pungent smell of chewing tobacco, a whiff he caught in line behind an older fellow at the grocery store.

He found himself missing Maggie, too, more than ever. When Maggie passed away, Chase didn't have the luxury of grieving her. The farm was in shambles; Jack was in shambles. Chase held everything together, plodding ahead with the everyday demands while Jack took all the time he needed to start functioning again. Now that Jack was gone, it was almost as though Chase was grieving the both of them. He wondered if the heaviness that seemed to have permanently settled deep in his chest would ever go away. Would he sleep through the night, soundly, restoratively, again? It seemed that years had passed since he had slept well, even though it had only been six weeks.

Chase continued staring out the window of Jack's office. In some places, the snow was sticking to the ground.

Transom held up a large, heavy object. "What's this one for?" he asked, frowning, squinting his eyes. Folded in half and turned on its side, it looked like the wide, toothy grin of an ape. Chase knew that, when opened, the trap looked like a crown.

"Bear?" Transom said.

Chase nodded.

"Man." Transom ran his index finger over the perilous rim of teeth.

"Jack got that at an auction," Chase said. "It was in the bottom of a box of hinges. He never used it. Look at all the rust. Thing probably don't even work."

"I could get it to work."

"Transom, they ain't even legal." He reached out. "Give me that."

Transom flashed him a smile, that same smile Chase had seen so many times, the one that suggested Chase was attempting to ruin all the fun. "No one would ever know. No one would care."

"Like I said, just leave it be. Besides, why would you want to kill a black bear? You ever even seen one?" Chase knew Transom didn't have the attention span to go through with all of this, but still, the sight of the traps, the thought of animals suffering, made his stomach churn.

"For a rug, that's why. Right in front of the fireplace. Nothing says, 'I'm a man,' more than a bearskin rug. I can assure you of that." He grinned. "Just picture it. The rug, a female companion. The good life."

Chase was about to say something to the effect of 'not on my property,' but he caught himself. The month before, the two of them had sat in the attorney's office, each signing through a two-inch stack of papers—the farm, technically, was Transom's now. The realization stung as Chase had to rethink his approach. He reached out again. "Here, give it."

"You've become a regular pansy, you know that." Transom kicked all the traps into one giant heap and pitched the bear trap on the pile. He continued sorting through Jack's stuff, leafing through a stack of old receipts, shuffling gear. Chase watched him for a moment, keenly aware that he was being ignored. Irritated, he mumbled something about needing a few things from town, grabbed his wallet and jacket, and walked out of the house.

———

Later, when he returned to the farm from his trip to town, Chase put the groceries in the refrigerator and went to find Transom. He was still in Jack's office, but the room had been cleared out: the traps, along with the aquarium, seed trays, and rototiller blade, were gone.

Transom was rummaging through Jack's chest of hunting clothes in the office. He held up a heavy Gore-Tex camouflage jacket and placed it beside him. Two pairs of long johns were strewn over the arm of Jack's chair. Jack's favorite Jones hat, the one he would replace every three years because it would grow thin and ragged and Maggie wouldn't tolerate it, sat on Transom's head.

"Hey, I've been meaning to tell you," Transom said. "I planned us a camping trip on the Clarion." They could hike and then camp along the river, he continued, drink beer by the fire. It would be good to get away, get out in the wild. Like old times.

"It's winter," Chase said.

Transom shrugged. "It's supposed to warm up next week, be in the mid-forties. So what do you say? You in?"

"Yeah, I'm in," Chase said, with reluctance. He knew that if he didn't agree to go, Transom would nag him until he got the answer he wanted, anyway, so there was no point in arguing. "I picked up some burgers," he said. "I stopped by Laney's. She's coming over tomorrow."

Transom stared at him for a minute, then removed Jack's cap and laid it in one of his stacks. His gaze dropped to his lap.

"You all right?" Chase said.

Transom reached in the corner and grabbed the beer he'd been drinking and tilted his head back. "Just needed a drink," he said. "How's she look? Still got them legs?" He licked his lips and grinned.

Chase leaned over and picked up an old No Trespassing sign from the floor. "Don't," he said, and he was surprised by the protectiveness in his voice. What was it he felt then, that tingling on his flesh? Jealousy? An urge to keep Laney safe? And if so, from what? Transom?

He'd known Laney since kindergarten, since she'd plopped into the seat beside him on the bus, the first day of school. All through high school, all through their twenties, they'd remained friends because of Jack and Maggie. In recent years Laney had been the friend that Transom should've been, had he stuck around. But the thing that had happened right after Jack passed—he and Laney growing closer than ever, the two of them hooking up, the contentment he'd felt in her arms, the naturalness with which it had all occurred—threatened to make everything messy, and messy was something he couldn't handle. He left occasional messages on her phone when he knew she was at work and couldn't answer, but for the most part he was keeping his distance, hoping things might somehow just not be awkward, with a little time and space. When he stopped by her house earlier, he realized he'd been wrong: if anything, avoiding her had made things worse. He was almost certain he'd hurt her feelings.

He flung the sign at Transom, who deflected it.

"What?"

"I'm serious," Chase said. "Don't."

Transom stood up suddenly. The No Trespassing sign dropped to the floor. In one swift movement, the kind of quick movement that a man of his age and stature should not have been able to manage, he tackled Chase to the ground, on top of the pile of hunting clothes. "Why?"

Chase struggled to shove Transom, who was much heavier—but, he was happy to realize, not as much stronger as he had been when they were younger—off him. He lay on his back, barely able to catch his breath. "Get off me," he said, pushing to free himself. "What's wrong with you?"

Transom laughed his deep, guttural laugh. "Answer the question. Tell me about the two of you." He rolled to the side.

Chase sat up and gave him a shove. "There's nothing to tell."

"You're lying. I'm your best friend, and I can tell when you're lying." He still lay on the ground. "Good Lord," he said, turning away. He reached into his pocket and grabbed a pill, then took a swig of beer. "You're in love with her."

"I'm not in love with her," Chase said firmly. As he said it out loud, though, he realized Transom was right: it did sound—feel—like a lie. Panic swelled in his throat: Was he in love with Laney? Was he that far removed from his own emotions that he hadn't been willing to face even that?

"Have you—" Transom stopped himself here, pausing, re-choosing his words. "Does she sleep over?"

"Like I said, there's nothing to tell, except that she'll be here tomorrow."

"I'm happy for you, man," Transom said with sincerity, squeezing Chase's shoulder, and then added, "Wish you would've said something sooner."

———

The next day, as Laney drove her truck out the road that led to the Hardy farm in the waning blue-gray light, she couldn't help but wonder whether agreeing to have dinner with Chase and Transom was one of the worst decisions of her life. Ever since she'd seen Chase the day before, her mind had been swirling through various scenarios, all of which ended horribly. Transom spilling the news to Chase right before she got there, so that she arrived and had to witness the disappointment and disgust on his face. Transom making an offhand comment at the dinner table.

When Chase stopped by and invited her over, her first instinct had been to come up with an excuse. If things weren't going to pan out, if he had no interest in her, he could at least have the decency to say so. But then yesterday, he'd been different: less reserved, even a little affectionate. Maybe there was something there, after all?

At the farmhouse, Chase greeted her at the back door, taking her pan of brownies and slinging an arm over her shoulder. Behind him, Transom stood in the kitchen, arms across his chest, his cheeks red from the warmth of the house, and, she suspected, the beer he was holding. She tried to read his face—what was going through his mind? Shame? Jealousy? Regret? Maybe nothing at all.

Transom stepped forward. "Laney," he said, "it's been a while."

Nineteen days, it had been. She was hopeful, though: he seemed prepared to play along.

But as Transom leaned in to embrace her, she could smell alcohol on his breath, in his skin. He held her too long; it was too conspicuous, too intimate, his cheek against hers.

She wanted to shrug him off, push him away, but Chase stood just a few feet away, seasoning the steaks. She had to be careful. "Drunk already?" she said, forcing a smile. She gently freed herself and offered to help with dinner. Transom stepped aside and threw his head back, finishing his beer. She hoped he was done drinking for the evening—how many beers would it take before he'd get careless, the words tumbling out, the secret spilling like water?

Chase stood at the counter, slicing mushrooms, his flannel sleeves rolled to his elbows. He smiled. "Beer in the fridge. Help yourself," he said. He grabbed the cutting board with the burgers and headed outside to the grill. "Be right back."

With Chase gone, Laney turned to glare at Transom. "I thought we agreed to put the past behind us."

"That expression: put the past behind." Transom smiled and shook his head. "It's never made any sense to me. Besides, we didn't really agree to anything. You asked, but I didn't agree." He grabbed two beers from the fridge, cracked them open, and handed her one. He shook his head. "I don't know how you do it, act like nothing happened."

"Transom, please."

Chase came back into the house, the cutting board red from the meat. "Cold out there," he said, sliding it in the sink and washing his hands. "They said it might snow later." He set the timer on the stove and picked up his beer. He raised it to Laney and Transom. "To old friends," he said, smiling.

"Yes, yes," Transom said. "To history." He stared at Laney.

Her face burned. She clinked her bottle to theirs and took a swig.

Chase grinned. "This is great, the three of us together. Like old times."

Chase seemed so happy, so unsuspecting, and that made Laney feel even worse. She watched as he continued humming about the kitchen, steaming the broccoli and then dumping the water off the boiled potatoes. He seemed energized tonight, happier than he'd been for a long time.

"You're worse than Maggie," Transom said, "buzzing around here, fretting over vegetables." He eased himself into one of the kitchen chairs.

"I'll do the potatoes," Laney offered. She got out the beaters from the cupboard where Maggie had always kept them, flung a slice of butter into the pot, and added milk.

The timer went off.

As Chase stepped back outside to check the burgers, Laney turned off the beaters. "If you ever cared about anybody but yourself, I'm begging you—let it go. If not for me, then for Chase. Keep your mouth shut."

Transom crossed his arms. "You've got a lot of nerve, talking to me about whether I care about anyone but myself." His eyes traveled her body.

"That's not fair." She traced the rim of the bowl of potatoes with her fingertip. "I do care about him, and Transom, I want to believe that you do, too."

He stared at her and finished off another beer. Chase came back inside, and Laney immediately began mashing the potatoes again, the beaters loud against the ceramic bowl. Chase turned off the broccoli on the back burner. "You look nice," he said to her.

"Thanks," she said. She looked at her sweater and jeans, the sixth outfit she'd tried on before coming. With each one, she'd stared at herself in the mirror, turning side to side, telling herself it was Chase she was hoping to impress.

Transom pulled a brown bottle of pills from his pocket and popped one in his mouth.

The rest of the evening passed with considerable smoothness, given the awkward nature of the situation. Thankfully Transom laid off, and the three of them ended up telling stories and laughing, deep into the night. But in the background of that laughter lay the fact that Laney had betrayed Chase, and it haunted her. She hated herself for hooking up with Transom; she hated that she hadn't had the self-control. Most of all, she hated her own confusion, the way her heart still seemed to pitch in two different directions.

She hoped this wasn't a snapshot of how life would look from now on: a precarious almost-happiness tempered at all times by the cloud of Transom looming nearby, threatening to burst and rain havoc. Because he might do that—burst, spill her secret. Transom had always been unpredictable. She couldn't live like that, holding herself back from each moment in fear that a word, a glance, a gesture, might set him off. Maybe Transom would leave again. Maybe things would simply improve with time. If they didn't, something would need to be done.

AFTER

RED SQUINTED AS THE DOOR OF THE FALLEN Mountains police department swung open and the heat from outside soared into the room, cool air sailing out, the whole morning's worth of work for the old sputtering air conditioner undone, in a matter of seconds. The man stood just across the threshold, looking around the place, still wearing his sunglasses. Unabomber glasses, Red had always called them, thinking about the Montana man whose sketch had filled the nightly news for weeks back in the nineties, until Junior had explained once, "They're called aviator glasses, Dad."

"I'm looking for Sheriff Redifer," the man said, taking off his glasses and tucking them into the pocket of his collared black shirt.

Red stood and stepped forward, extending a hand. "That's me." He wished Leigh were here. She had a knack for lightening up a tense room.

"Mick Dashel," the man said, taking Red's hand and squeezing it firmly, Red fighting the urge to wince, arthritis acting up with the humidity. "P. I."

The day before, after finding the plane tickets and wedding plans in the middle of the night, Red had come into the station and flipped through the names in his Rolodex. He'd stopped in the S's and pulled out an old business card that JT Shultz, just before he'd closed his factory and left Fallen Mountains, had handed him. "You ever need anything," JT had told him, "you give me a call." What Red had wanted to do, back then, was set a match to it. *I ever need anything*, he'd thought, *you're the last person I'll call*. Instead, he'd kept it, tucked it into that Rolodex Sue had bought him shortly after he got the job, mostly forgotten. Junior had helped him set up an address book in his cell phone, so the Rolodex had spent the last few years in the bottom drawer of his desk at the station.

After finding the tickets and wedding plans, though, Red knew he needed to fish out that number and call JT Shultz. Even if the man was a lying, manipulative jerk, he was still a father, and Transom was still his son. If something, God forbid, ever happened to Junior, Red hoped someone would do the same thing, call him.

On the phone he was shuttled through two different receptionists and placed on hold for eight minutes, having had to explain, twice, that he needed to speak to JT directly, that it was about his son, that no, he could not leave a message. When JT finally picked up, Red had just slid a Werther's candy into his mouth. Heart racing, he slipped the candy onto a napkin at his desk. "Mr. Shultz?"

"Yes."

"Mr. Shultz, this is John Redifer, from Fallen Mountains. I was sheriff, back when you were here. Still am, actually."

A pause. Had JT forgotten?

"Sheriff Redifer, of course. What can I do for you?" The voice on the other line suspicious now.

Red took a deep breath. "I'm afraid I have some upsetting news, Mr. Shultz. Your son was reported missing a few days ago, and, well, we sort of figured maybe he'd just left town again, him never being one to say good-bye and all, but still, you know, we would follow up on something like this because that's, well, that's what we would do. Anyhow, I been looking into things, and last night, I come across two plane tickets in a file of his, one for him and one for his fiancée, Teresa. That's who reported him missing. Dated for next weekend, it turns out. Also a packet with arrangements for a special event, down in Jamaica. A wedding, it seems."

No response. Red was rambling, he knew that, his nerves all twisted up over having to explain such a thing to a father. Maybe Red had spat out too much information, too fast. Maybe he hadn't been clear? "So what I mean to say here, Mr. Shultz, is that it's starting to look like Transom didn't just up and leave this time."

"Yes, I see that," JT snapped.

Again, a long pause. Red tried to picture what was happening on the other end of the line. Was JT motioning to a troop of assistants? Was he typing things into a computer? Dialing Transom from a different phone? Did he know something, did he hold some piece of information that Red lacked? Was Transom with him? "Mr. Shultz, you there?"

A deep sigh. "I'm here. Listen, I have a guy: I'll send him out there."

Strange, Red thought. He knew JT and Transom had a falling-out, years ago—he remembered Jack and Maggie telling him how Transom showed up at their doorstep one weekend—but he couldn't help feeling like something was suspicious about this. If *he'd* received a call informing him that Junior had disappeared, he wouldn't dream of sending someone in his stead; he'd go himself. Was there something JT knew and wasn't telling him? "Mr. Shultz, that won't be necessary," he said.

"A private investigator, very experienced. He can take care of things, here on out."

"Sir, I assure you we are putting every resource on this case." Red felt his skin prickle at the lie. Not so much a lie as a stretch. Every resource. Him.

"He'll be there tomorrow, first thing."

"All right."

"And Sheriff?" Another pause, long enough for Red to detect a flicker of ache behind that sober, dangerous voice. "Appreciate the call."

—

So, as promised, here he was, that private investigator JT Shultz had said he would send. Mick Dashel with his aviator glasses and black polo shirt and khakis, crease down the legs, shiny black shoes. His hair was clipped short and spiked, some kind of gel holding it in place and giving it an unnatural luster, strong jaw-line that he clenched as he stood there, hands folded across his groin. Every cliché Red had ever envisioned in a private investigator. Also a backpack. He was young, maybe thirty or so. Broad-shouldered and fit, and Red felt self-conscious then, with his knees that droned when he bent for too long, his stiff right hand, his thick midsection. When had all that happened, those small betrayals by his own body? He was only fifty-nine. Not that long ago, he'd lobbed a football with Junior in the back-yard; he'd dug a walkway and laid the stone.

As Red filled him in on the details of the case, Mick nodded with mild interest, moving around the room, taking stock of his surroundings. "Mr. Shultz mentioned something about a file you have?" Mick Dashel said, when Red was done.

Red turned to his desk. "Yes, here. This will need to stay at the station, though. You understand."

"Of course. Mind if I take a look?"

Red handed over the green accordion file and eased back in his desk chair.

"May I?" Mick Dashel asked, pointing to a chair across the room.

"Make yourself at home. Coffeepot over there, water in the mini-fridge. Soda, candy." He motioned to the small kitchenette at the back, across from the room where the school board met, the vending machine where Leigh would slip coins every Tuesday and Thursday, the coil unwinding and releasing some treat that would drop to the bottom. Until two years earlier, Red had rarely bought a thing from that vending machine, but with Sue gone, no one to pack him lunch, sometimes he'd wander back there, fishing quarters from his pockets, hungry.

Mick Dashel took a chair and began leafing through the papers in the file. He pulled a calculator from his black backpack and quickly keyed numbers. He frowned and jotted notes in some kind of tablet with a fancy electronic pen. Any other Monday, Red would lock the doors and head out with the radar, tuck the Jimmy in one of his spots. Behind the Graysons' white barn on 28. Along the tall hedge of Douglas Fir on Weaver Avenue, bottom of a hill, people always going too fast there, and it was close to the elementary school. More recently he'd been venturing farther out of town, nabbing frackers that hummed past in their fancy pickups, out-of-state plates. "Didn't know you was a cop in that heap of junk," one had said to him, the week before. Two hundred fifty-eight bucks for that guy. He'd nabbed him for speeding and driving too fast for conditions, the conditions being that it was when the school buses were out delivering kids.

Today, though, no tickets. He couldn't just leave Mick Dashel at the police station. Red took out his little notebook and flipped through the few pages of things he'd written down. So it looked like Teresa had been right, after all. He remembered her sitting across from him, eyes wide, breasts pressed to the boardroom table. *That ain't what happened this time. We were in love.* Had things gone according to Transom's plan, the two of them would be packing up for that fancy beach resort right now.

Mick Dashel rose from the chair. "You been out to the Hardy place?"

"Sure, checked Transom's vehicle. That's where I found the file."

"You got a warrant?"

"Yeah." Anticipating this request, he'd gone to Judge Hess's yesterday, right after he'd hung up with JT Shultz.

"The Hardy man, the one who sold the farm, what's his name?"

"Chase."

"Right. He's probably our guy."

Red tried to picture it, Chase as a guilty man. Chase Hardy, feeder of barn cats, one of the only men in Fallen Mountains who didn't hunt. Chase, who stepped in to break up playground scuffles, who had a herd of little kids that looked up to him and followed him around the playground. A gentle giant, Sue had called him. "What makes you think that?" Red asked.

Mick Dashel gathered his things, placing them carefully into his backpack. He slid the papers back into the accordion file and handed it to Red. "Looks like he sold that farm under pressure to an old friend, someone he trusted. And I'd go out on a limb here and say Transom violated that trust, logging it as hard as he did, selling to the oil companies. Chase also stands to inherit the farm should something happen to Transom. Did you see that in the file? Which means Chase Hardy had motive." He slung his backpack over his shoulder. "Can you take me out to that farm?"

Red grabbed the warrant from his desk and tucked it in his pocket. He hated the idea of showing up again at Chase Hardy's place in the Jimmy with Mr. Aviator Glasses and a warrant. "Air-conditioning's broke in my car," he said. "Let's take yours."

BEFORE

POSSUM HAD A THOUSAND REGRETS ABOUT HIS LIFE, but if there was a single day he could go back and redo, it would be the one when he found the letters. Dozens of them, tucked beneath his mother's bed in a fancy metal box, varying in length but all handwritten in black ink, some with newspaper clippings, three with poems. It was 1998. He was fifteen and home alone as usual, watching Pearl Jam and Stone Temple Pilots on MTV and roaming the trailer, bored. His mother was at work, supposedly, and she was never home before eight, so Possum carefully pulled off the lid and began sifting through the contents of the box. All of them signed JTS, all of them signed *Love*.

JT Shultz, Possum thought to himself, perplexed. After looking through the first four letters, Possum realized they were dated. He began searching first for the dates because this was a mystery, a story to be pieced together, one letter at a time, like the Hardy Boys books he used to read, like the Christopher Pike novel on his nightstand. Piece by piece, he put them in chronological order.

Sixteen years. That's how long it had been going on, the letters. The affair. But how was that possible? How did people keep a secret like that quiet for so long in a place like Fallen

Mountains? How had they kept it from *him*? Nosy as he was, he hadn't known, hadn't even suspected. Possum swallowed, a sick feeling lurching its way up his throat. He read the first letter, worn thin from folding and refolding, the ink smudged in places, then the second, then all of them, in order. Some of them were lewd, and he could feel the heat rising in his cheeks as he read the words that JT had written to his mother—at fifteen, there was nothing more nauseating than the idea of his mother caught up in a feverish affair. But some of the letters were tender, apologetic, sweet. *I wish things were different. I wish I could leave Marjane, but you know how it would look—not just for me, but for you and Tommy, too.*

Then, there was one line, from one letter, four years earlier: Possum counted the years backwards. *I was so proud when our boy won the spelling bee.* That line, Possum knew with a terrible certainty—that line was about him. Sixth grade. He'd won the school spelling bee. *Our boy.* Possum had been told that his father was killed in a car accident before he was born, and he'd never had any reason to doubt the thing his mother had told him.

But now the memories began to swim hard at him, a frightful torrent, and all at once he saw his life for what it was, an eddy of lies, all swirling around this one secret. Lavish gifts beneath the tree, birthdays, too: things his mother never could've afforded. An all-terrain Red Flyer wagon, a remote-control helicopter, binoculars, a microscope, a ten-speed red bicycle. He remembered Christmas concerts and baseball games: JT coming up after, looking him in the eye, squeezing his shoulder with a strange affection that would make Possum swoon and cringe.

A bewildering sense of longing swept through him. All those times, JT had used the word *son*. He'd claimed it a hundred times, in the school parking lot, at the baseball field. So why the letters? Why all the secrecy, on both sides? If JT had really loved his mother—and based on the letters, Possum felt sure that he did—why the sneaking around and lying? The longing fell away as Possum saw the truth: JT had made a choice. And he hadn't chosen Possum and his mother.

With an equivalent amount of dismay, it dawned on Possum that Transom must've figured it all out. Transom lurking behind his father at those concerts and ball games, that scowl. Also that appalling fury that Transom had been directing at Possum for almost a year. Although the two of them were the same age— only a few months separated them—Possum had inherited his mother's small bone structure and delicate shape, so that as a fifteen-year old he only weighed ninety-eight pounds. Transom, on the other hand, had already hit puberty and stood thick and menacing, a formidable force, all muscle and rage. Possum didn't stand a chance. When Transom held him under water during gym class when no one was looking, when he pissed on his shoes in the bathroom, when he murmured the ugly words, Possum didn't disagree; he didn't fight back. *Your mother's a trailer trash whore. And you're a trailer trash son of a whore.*

As he leafed through his mother's collection, he wondered: Were there letters at the Shultz house, sweet, incriminating words from Lissette tucked somewhere private, a desk drawer, a hidden spot in the garage? Had Transom, like him, come across them one quiet afternoon when no one was around? How much did Transom know? And then, a more horrifying thought: that mean blood pulsing through his worst enemy's body—it was flowing through his, too.

Outside the trailer, the spring night was closing in. Dave Matthews Band was playing a concert on MTV now, the flute and the alto sax flitting through notes, the crowd high and mesmerized. Possum wandered to the kitchen, where his mother had left a note: *Leftovers in the fridge. Love you.* He heated up his chicken casserole and ate it on the floor of his mother's room, pouring over the letters again. Anger knit its way from his gut to his throat. It was too much, all of it at once. This mess—Transom shoving him into the janitor's closet; the cruel, haunting words like knives in his chest—it was their fault. JT's. His mother's. If it weren't for their secrets and lies, none of it would've happened. Every day of his life, he was paying the price for their selfishness, and he'd had enough.

And then Possum made a decision. He stacked the letters, ordered by date now, and tied them together with brown twine from a kitchen drawer. He gathered the gifts—microscope, remote control helicopter, the binoculars, the ten-speed, too—and then slipped into his hat and light coat. In the front yard, he loaded the letters and gifts in his red wagon, the one he'd been given for Christmas when he was five, and he walked west, toward the sprawling ranch on the outskirts of town, the biggest house for miles. The wagon rumbled behind him, the stack of letters pitching and swaying. He looked over his shoulder at the sun dipping behind the ridge, the sky orange and pink and blue, and walked on. It was time to put an end to this, he thought.

At the Shultz house, the lights in the kitchen were on, and Possum could see Transom and his mother inside. Marjane Shultz wore an apron and stood at the counter, mixing something in a giant, stainless steel bowl. Transom sat at the table, watching her, smiling, papers and a textbook spread in front of him, doing homework while his mother baked. It was so perfect, so All-American. So false. It also represented everything Possum wanted in his own life but would never have. He leaned over and picked up the wagon and carried it to the front door so that no one inside would hear the roar of its heavy tires. He rang the doorbell, and ran as hard as he could into the night.

———

Now, seventeen years after that lamentable evening, as Possum walked across town in the February dark to Laney's house, he thought again of how things might have gone differently if he'd handled it another way, if he hadn't been bored and snooping in his mother's room, if he hadn't ever opened that box, even if he'd opened it and read the letters and kept the secret to himself. What had he been hoping to accomplish, anyway? In all the years since, he'd never quite been able to put a finger on it. Did he want his mother and JT to pay for the pain they'd caused him? Was he hoping maybe JT would change the path he'd selected, that Transom and Marjane would leave, that Possum and his mother would live a different, shiny life with JT in that big white house outside of town?

Instead, a week after Possum delivered the letters, Marjane Shultz, beautiful and perfect Marjane Shultz, tried to kill herself with a kitchen knife. People said she'd been shipped out to a psychiatric ward somewhere, but they were speculating, Possum knew. All anyone really knew for sure was that she never came back to Fallen Mountains. JT and Lissette stopped seeing each other. There were no more letters, no more secrets. More devastating was the fact that his mother sprouted a sadness he'd never before witnessed in her. A sadness he knew he was responsible for. Shortly after Possum dropped off the letters, his mother began dating that loser, Vance, who drank too much and beat the both of them. And Transom—well, Transom had tried to kill him.

As he climbed the steps to Laney's house, he pushed those ugly thoughts from his mind, shuffled the regret back into the stack of things he thought of only sometimes, and rang the doorbell. It was Tuesday night and Possum and Laney had a weekly tradition they'd been following for years, since the week Possum got out of prison. They took turns picking up Wheeler's fried chicken and mashed potatoes, then ate it at Laney's house, sometimes at the tiny kitchen table, sometimes in front of the television watching *Inside Edition*, sometimes, if the weather cooperated, on the covered porch. Their mothers were sisters— two half-stable women with appallingly bad taste in men—and, through all the ups and downs of their rocky childhood and adolescence, Possum and Laney had stayed close.

Kip bounded from the kitchen toward him and jumped up at the door, his claws scraping the glass. Possum let himself in, and Kip jumped up, paws sinking into Possum's bony chest, nearly knocking him over. Kip sniffed at the containers of fried chicken.

"Kip! Get down," Laney said, grabbing the dog by the collar. "Sorry. You know how much he likes you."

He handed Laney the food and kneeled to rub the dog's ears and scratch his back. "Feeling's mutual." He lifted his chin and let Kip lick his face. "Do you think I should get a dog?"

Laney walked into the kitchen and grabbed two sodas from the fridge. "Kip would not approve," she said with a laugh.

"True." He tussled the dog's ears again and stood. "How've you been?"

She shrugged. "Same old. You?"

He slid into the chair at the kitchen table and opened his box of food. "All right. Good, actually. I been talking to a girl, online." He felt a little embarrassed, saying it out loud.

Laney's face lit up. "Really? Tell me." She grabbed her first piece of fried chicken and dabbed it with her napkin, soaking up some of the grease.

"Her name's Alla. She's from Russia."

"Oh, like a mail-order bride? I've heard of those."

Possum snorted and rolled his eyes. "No, not like a mail-order bride. We met in a forum for antiques dealers." The truth was, he'd looked into it once, mail-order brides, one winter when he was feeling especially sorry for himself. Sometimes they worked out, those relationships. Sometimes not. He read a horror story about a woman who poisoned her husband and then took over his estate, a rich widow, and that was enough to make him give up on the idea altogether. He sunk his fork into the mashed potatoes. "We sort of hit it off. I mean, I think we did."

Laney paused and stared at her cousin. "Wow."

"I can't stop thinking about her."

She took a drink of soda and grabbed his hand. "Don't get mad when I say this, but—do you think she's real?"

Possum shrugged. "I don't know. It's like, I never thought of myself as falling for someone. I know I ain't handsome; I live in a trailer in a dumpy little town. And here in Fallen Mountains, you don't really get to unhitch yourself from your past. But I guess this has made me realize the world's bigger than I used to think it was."

Laney leaned forward, fingers greasy from the chicken. "Possum," she said grinning, "I've never seen you look like this. Your eyes, your face: you seem happy."

"I know." He took a swig of soda and smiled, unable to contain his delight. "It's scary." He thought for a moment. "It's like I'm so close to something I really want, and then there's this thing where if it don't happen, if things don't work out, the whole world will buckle. Sorry, I'm talking nonsense."

"No, I completely understand." She sighed, leaning back in her chair. "Believe me."

"Yeah? Any progress with Chase?" Possum was well aware of Laney's feelings toward Chase, and he approved, wholeheartedly. He liked Chase, and he loved Laney, and if the two of them could be happy together, he was happy for them.

"Well, with Transom back, things have gotten a little tricky."

Possum's face darkened and he began stabbing the mashed potatoes with his fork. So far, he'd managed to avoid any interactions with Transom because if there was one thing he was sure of, it was that he did not want to have to see that monster, face-to-face. Nor did he want to talk about him over fried chicken. "What does that loser have to do with anything?"

Laney traced the edge of a Styrofoam box. "We had a thing," she said. "Me and Transom."

Possum began to chew slowly. "I know. A long time ago." He remembered when he'd heard about Laney, from Jill Rispoli in his homeroom: *Your cousin and Transom, did you hear?* Possum had tried to warn her, back then. He'd tried to explain that Transom was dangerous and unpredictable, that he wasn't who he seemed to be, that she should stay away from him. But, without the truth of what had happened at the shale pit—Possum had never told her about it—his warnings held no weight.

Laney swallowed. "Well, it's a little more complicated than that."

"How so?"

"It wasn't just in high school."

He squinted. "What do you mean?"

"I mean we hooked up, every time he came home."

Possum slammed the table with his fist, the silverware clanging, the Pepsi in the glass fizzing.

Laney pulled back from the table, mouth open.

It was one of the things he hated most about himself, his tendency to veer so quickly into darkness. Judgment, rage. Try as he might, he couldn't seem to get a handle on it, that anger that could bubble up with just the slightest provocation. He opened his fist, took a breath. "Sorry."

Laney sat there for a moment, biting her lip. She slid her chair back to the table and dabbed her chicken with another napkin. "I know you've always hated him. I know he was mean to you sometimes, back in high school. He was mean to everyone."

He tried to kill me, Possum thought about saying: the words sailing out of him like a confession. Why was it, he wondered, that he hadn't done anything wrong, nothing except be himself—ugly and scrawny and awkward and poor, the son of two people who shouldn't have loved each other—and yet he felt like that's what it would be, a confession? A weight from which he could release himself, a freeing up, as though he were the one who needed absolution. He looked at Laney and took a bite of chicken. "Chase?"

She shook her head. "He doesn't know. I want things to work out with him," Laney said, balling the napkin in her hand. "I see that now. I care about him. I see a future with him. At least I want a future with him. I think now, he wants it, too. But at the time, I didn't know that. I mean, he hadn't even told Transom about us."

Possum tugged at his chicken. "Maybe that was out of respect," he said. "Chase is sort of old-fashioned. He isn't like some men, who go around announcing to the whole world every time they score." He remembered Transom's exploits in high school, the names of various girls rippling through gymnasium pep rallies and auditorium assemblies. Possum felt sick. Transom showing up and wreaking havoc, taking advantage, just like he used to. Would Possum ever escape that circle of damage that seemed to ripple from the man?

Laney's hands shook as she reached for her soda. "I was in love with him, a long time ago. Transom. He was my first. And I think a little part of me will always love him, like maybe every person you ever love takes up a little corner of your heart, and you don't ever really get it back."

"I wouldn't know," Possum said, unable to mask the bitterness in his voice. Lucky Wheeler's chicken and mashed potatoes were churning in his stomach now, food mixed with fury: a bad combination. He could forgive Laney for getting mixed up with Transom once, back when they were kids and stupid and Transom was a baseball star, rich and popular and Laney was a silly teenage girl, but all these years? She was older now, a grown woman with some sense, he'd thought. And with a good thing going with Chase, who, poor guy, was in the middle of this.

Laney frowned and looked at him hard. "I messed up. I get it. But don't look at me like that, Possum. Don't, please."

He didn't want to judge, he really didn't. When he'd gotten out of jail and everyone in Fallen Mountains had looked at him like some kind of violent freak, mothers tucking their children to their sides, old ladies crossing the street to avoid him, Laney had invited him over for fried chicken. He didn't want to judge, but this? This was sickening. "I should get going," he said.

"Possum, whatever happened between the two of you—it was a long time ago."

He wished it were that simple. "Listen," Possum said, his voice thin and unsteady, "I want you to be careful, that's all. Transom, he's not who you think he is." He wanted to say, remember back in high school, that night you called the sheriff because I didn't show up for work at the Dairy-Freeze? The next day I told you I had the flu, but that was a lie. What really happened was this: I was walking to work and Transom ran me off the road. He threw me in the trunk, drove around. When he finally stopped, he opened the hatch, dumped kerosene in, told me I would burn. Possum wanted to tell her. He wanted her to know. But the words lodged in his throat, the horror of that night, the shame of everything that had led up to that point, paralyzing him.

"You've said that before, about Transom not being who I think he is." She shook her head. "I don't know what that's supposed to mean."

"He's capable—he's done bad things. Very bad things."

Laney reached across the table and placed her hand over his. In that way that only his dearest friend could say and get away with, she whispered, "So have you."

Possum tore off a piece of chicken and whistled for the dog. He let Kip eat it from his hand, the dog's soft tongue licking his palm. He folded his Styrofoam box closed, tossed it in the trash, and washed the chicken grease from his hands at the kitchen sink.

Laney wrinkled her nose. "Don't leave," she said. "Don't be mad. What about *Inside Edition*?"

Possum forced a smile. "I'm not mad. I just forgot I have to post some new items tonight," he lied. He slid into his red vest and tugged his cigarettes from his pocket. One of these days, he kept on telling himself, he was going to quit. "See you next Tuesday," he said. On Laney's front porch, he pulled one out of the box and lit it and walked into the bitter winter night.

AFTER

RED SAT IN THE PASSENGER SEAT AS MICK DASHEL pulled his silver Buick in front of the Hardy farmhouse, and watched, dismayed, as the man grabbed his backpack from the back seat, sailed out of the car, and crossed the old porch. Mick knocked on the door, waited a minute, and when nobody came to answer, he tried the handle. For a moment he seemed surprised: it wasn't locked. He leaned in and hollered something into the house, then turned and looked over his shoulder at Red, who still hadn't unbuckled his seat belt. He held up his hands. "You coming?"

Red struggled out of the car, knees protesting as he stood, the heat assaulting him as he lumbered across the yard, brown grass crinkling beneath his feet. "You just going in?" he asked Mick.

"We have a warrant. We can do whatever we want." He walked into the living room and swung his backpack onto the sofa table behind the couch.

"It's just—it just seems—sort of rude." Red looked around the living room he'd seen many times over the years, by invitation, as a hunting partner of Jack Hardy's, as a guest. Despite the difference in age, they'd been close friends, the four of them. He and Sue would sit at the fireplace and drink coffee or come to dinner, Jack and Maggie and often Chase and his parents at the dining room table. Transom, too, sometimes. Laney Moore, once. Maggie and her Home for Semi-Orphans, Sue used to say of her friend, because, over the years, Maggie had seen each one of those kids in need, and she'd taken them under her wing. They were just children who needed a place to be kids, was the way Maggie put it. That's the type of home this had been, the type of people they'd been, Jack and Maggie both. They saw a need, and they did whatever it took to meet it. Red missed all of them at once—Jack, Maggie, Sue—and his loneliness gripped him hard there in the living room. How had he been so lucky as to clamber out of that blank and lonely chapter where he watched the city lights from The Rocks and stumble into such sweet and generous company? How had he been so unlucky to be the last one left?

"Rude?" Mick Dashel grabbed latex gloves from his backpack and handed Red a pair. "You're getting your stories crossed, man. What's rude is someone buys your land, gets you out of debt, free and clear, and you don't like what they do with it, so you shoot them dead, or worse, something uglier, and then you pretend like the person just left town. *That's* rude."

Red could barely fit his fat hands into the gloves, and the sweat didn't make things any easier, latex rolling up, his pinky about to burst through. He hated the idea of Chase Hardy getting dragged into this mess. "Don't get ahead of yourself," Red said to Mick. "We ain't found nothing yet."

Mick rifled through his backpack and pulled out a hard plastic case, inside of which was a small fingerprinting kit. He opened it and said, "Don't take this the wrong way, but maybe you haven't found anything because you don't know how to look." He grabbed a blacklight. "I don't mean any disrespect by that, please understand. JT tells me you've got an old-fashioned town here, no major crimes, just you taking care of things. And that's all well and good, and I envy you folks. But I double-majored in forensics and psychology, and I've been doing this for eight years now. This—" He waved his hands over his equipment, a magician with his bag of tricks. "This is what I do."

Red thought of JT Shultz, who knew of what happened at the shale pit half a lifetime ago now, for those boys. If Red had considered the possibility that Possum could be behind this, wouldn't JT have considered it, too? Would he have mentioned anything of that night to Mick Dashel? Or maybe JT had been keeping secrets all his life; maybe this was just one of so many skeletons that he'd already forgotten it.

Mick was in the kitchen, yanking open drawer after drawer, the silverware clanging, Pyrex dishes ringing. He opened the fridge, the freezer. He checked the pantry, his eyes scanning canned beans and Bisquick and fruit cocktail. "Nothing here," Mick said, and then moved into the room off the kitchen, the one that used to be Jack Hardy's den, the place where he had stored his hunting gear and written checks and ordered seeds. Red closed the kitchen drawers Mick had left open, and followed.

The room had been completely transformed since Red had last seen it, the fall before. When Jack was using it as a den, there were boxes of old knickknacks, heaps of hunting clothes, stacks of paper piled high on the desk. Now, all of that was gone, and the room had a tedious order to it. On the desk, a signed baseball in a glass case. Two framed photographs of Transom and Teresa. In a third frame, an old photograph: a woman and small boy, the boy leaning against the woman's side, the ocean behind them, a bucket hanging from his hand.

"His mother, I presume?" Mick asked.

Red leaned in for a closer look. It was her, Marjane Shultz, tall and lean and lovely. Sue had told him once that every woman in Fallen Mountains envied her, with her beautiful dresses, her style and sophistication they could barely grasp, her charm. They'd all been shocked when, out of the blue, she'd slit her wrists with a paring knife—she'd seemed so happy, so flawless. Red nodded. "Yes," he said. "That's Transom's mother."

There was a map of the Hardy property on the desk, too, with notes and sticky tabs. Mick leaned over and studied the map. "Looks like Transom had settled in here, maybe used this room as a sort of work space."

He began sifting through the desk drawers. One two three, lifting papers, then on to the next side. In one drawer, he found a small stack of photographs. He handed them to Red. "You know any of these folks?"

Red took the photos in his hand and flipped through. Jack, Maggie, Chase, and Transom, huddled together on the step of the front porch, the boys young, maybe twelve or thirteen, Transom already tall and thick, bigger than the rest of them, even Jack. Then another: Chase and Transom grinning and holding up fish by the mouth, bass. They were older in this one, larger. One with Transom with his arm slung over Maggie's shoulder, Maggie small and white-haired, laughing and looking up at him. A picture of the Hardy farmhouse, the barn. And two black-and-white photographs of Laney Moore, taken five or ten years ago, probably, but Red wasn't sure. Laney looking right at the camera, right at the person taking the picture, a smile playing at her lips, her shoulders bare, a blanket tucked beneath her armpits. In the next one—Red guessed the two were taken in succession—Laney was laughing, looking to the side, but again, under that blanket, naked.

"What is it?" Mick asked, sliding a drawer closed.

Red frowned. "Probably nothing." He studied the photo. Laney was one of those lucky people who hadn't changed a whole lot over the years—she could've passed for a twenty-two-year-old in high school, and she probably still could, even though she had to be in her thirties now—plus the photo was black and white, which made it harder to tell its age. "There's a picture here of a woman. She and Chase Hardy are a thing, a couple." He turned the photographs around and held them up for Mick. "Which is a little strange, don't you think? Transom having a picture like this in his drawer, even if it's old. It's his friend's girlfriend, plus he's engaged to someone else."

Mick shrugged. "People hold onto things. My wife held onto pictures from her junior prom, senior prom, middle school, tucked in a box in the attic. Friends, boyfriends." He paused and looked out the window for a minute. "Not that we have a model relationship or anything. When I came out here, she told me not to come back."

Red swallowed. "Ever?"

Mick studied a ticket stub in his hand. "Think so."

"Sorry to hear that."

"I wasn't home much. Work and all." Mick cleared his throat. "What's her name, the woman in the photograph?"

"Laney," he said. "Laney Moore." The thought flickered through his mind: Possum's cousin, his closest friend. Red saw them together all the time. This, combined with the discovery of the photographs, made him wince—had Laney managed to get wrapped up in something ugly? Had Possum dragged her into it?

"We'll bring her in, ask her a few questions," Mick said.

"Sure. Wouldn't hurt."

Mick stood and walked to the corner, where Jack Hardy's guns were lined up in an old glass-front cabinet. He reached up to the top, felt around, and grabbed a key. He took out his black-light and shined it carefully over each gun. Nothing. Then he took out the fingerprinting kit.

"Help me label these?" he said, handing Red a Sharpie.

"Don't see what the point is," Red said. "These guns were Jack Hardy's. Chase's now. Prints will be all over them."

Mick took out the first gun and began dusting for prints. He glanced at Red. "Remember, this is what I do. There's a process to all this. Trust it."

Red watched with interest as Mick worked through weapon after weapon, quick and precise, his hands skilled and confident. They were there for over an hour, working in Jack's den, until Mick was satisfied and said they could take a lunch break. The whole time, Red kept wondering if Chase would show up and find them searching his house, opening drawers and dusting his guns and leafing through pictures, and even though they had a warrant and weren't breaking any law, Red couldn't help but feel that they were the ones doing something wrong.

BEFORE

THE FEBRUARY WIND WHISKED THE SNOW FROM THE roof of the Lincoln as Chase loaded the last few items—a tackle box, a waterproof bag, beef jerky for the ride, and a Pennsylvania *Gazeteer*—into the trunk. He shut the hatch gingerly, careful to avoid breaking anything. One last time, he thought through his list of chores. He'd arranged for Cliff Miller, one of their old farmhands, to tend the cows for two days. He'd heaped the cats' bowl high with food. He'd banked the woodstove. It had been years since he'd left the farm overnight, and he was nervous about it, sure he was forgetting something important, sure something would go wrong without him there to handle it.

Somehow or other, he had gotten stuck with almost all the packing for their camping trip, both the food and the gear, while Transom made phone call after phone call from Jack's den, which he had sort of transformed into his own office over the past several weeks. Even though Transom had described his work various times to Chase, in vague, uninteresting ways, Chase still wasn't exactly sure what it was his friend did for a living.

Every time Chase asked about it, Transom usually came up with some line about how it was complicated and boring, and

Chase took that to mean that, whatever it was, it might not be entirely legal. He decided not to push it— if his friend was into something shady, he'd rather not know. That way, he wouldn't have to lie for him, the way he'd lied for him all those times to Jack and Maggie. He'd always hated that, being put in a position of having to choose between lying to his grandparents or getting Transom in trouble. Besides, if he and Transom were going to live together as adults, they needed to respect each other's privacy. No prying, no pushing for answers. Even though Chase had been nervous that Transom might make things awkward when Laney had stayed over after coming to dinner—say a snide remark or rap on the door or make crude gestures behind her back—he had done no such thing, and for that, Chase was grateful.

He headed back to the house and walked to the kitchen, the old, dark floorboards whining beneath him. Plates were stacked to the right of the sink. A frying pan with dry scrambled eggs caked along the sides sat on the counter. He plopped himself into a chair and contemplated where to begin, and then realized, with a strange sense of alarm, that the tablecloth hadn't been changed since Jack died. Because it was a pattern, yellow and blue and red checkered, the wide assortment of spills and stains weren't noticeable right away, but with a closer look, he saw it was disgusting. He cleared the table and removed the tablecloth, balled it up and walked it to the laundry room.

He began removing the dishes from the sink so that he could fill it with fresh water. When Chase was in high school, Jack had tried to convince Maggie to get a dishwasher, but she had always brushed him off, joking that she already had two, Chase and Transom. It had been their job to help with the dishes three nights a week. Although both boys hated that chore, when

Chase thought back to it now—Transom soaked to his elbows in suds, Chase laughing—he found himself remembering doing the dishes with an odd fondness. Life was simple, back then, and good.

Transom came into the kitchen then, grabbing a beer from the fridge. He reached into his pocket, grabbed one of his pills, and tossed it into his throat.

Chase twitched slightly. "You know it's not even ten o'clock in the morning," he said.

Transom cracked open the beer and took a swig.

"You can dry," Chase said, pointing to the drawer where the towels were. He scrubbed at the eggs on the frying pan. "Who were you on the phone with?" Chase asked. The question was harmless enough.

Transom shrugged. "An associate," he said, wiping out a glass with a towel and reaching to put it in the cupboard. "Business stuff. We used to be friends."

"Everything all right?"

"Yeah, just figuring out some details," Transom said.

Chase could tell he was lying then. Transom had this habit of pulling his head ever so slightly to the left whenever he lied. He had always done this, ever since he was a small boy. Sometimes, he would be telling a story that was completely true, but then, as soon as he began embellishing or exaggerating, he'd tug his head toward the left. He was angry, too, Chase knew, from the way he clenched his jaw. Remembering his intention to respect each other's privacy, Chase decided not to press for information, at least not right then. They finished up the dishes. Transom grabbed a six-pack from the refrigerator, and the two of them headed for the Lincoln.

—

It wasn't until late that evening that Transom brought up his plans for the farm.

They'd spent a half day hiking to their campsite. Dark swept in early and quickly in February, but Chase had set up his tent so many times that he could do it swiftly, even in the waning daylight. He unrolled the nylon and stretched it into its square shape, then he pounded the metal stakes into the hard, cold earth. Transom stomped around nearby, clearing a spot for a fire and gathering pieces of dry wood.

When he was satisfied that he could safely burn the fire, Chase arranged the larger pieces of wood, building a tepee of sorts over the dry leaves and kindling. He lit a match, leaned over, and blew softly so that the flames kicked up and caught the leaves. In a few minutes, the kindling was burning nicely, and the dry, outer edges of the firewood had caught, too. Chase grabbed his backpack, turned it sideways, and leaned up against it as Transom finished seasoning the venison steaks they'd brought along. He breathed in the cold night air, felt it dry and sharp in his throat. He loved that feeling, that coldness that burned just a little. He looked up at the sky, dark and clear and full of stars.

"This was a good idea," Chase said, "coming up here."

Transom squatted and carefully placed the steaks in the cast-iron skillet on the grate over the fire. He smiled, reaching for two beers and handing one to Chase. They sat in silence for a few minutes, the fire's cracking and hissing the only sounds in the night.

Transom grabbed a skinny branch and held it over the fire, letting the end catch and burn up orange. "Listen," he said. "I don't know how to say this, exactly, and I know you aren't going to like it, but here goes: we've got to get some timber off the farm."

Chase frowned. "What do you mean?"

Anxiety flickered across Transom's face. "I mean I signed with a logging company to come in. Forester came this afternoon to mark trees. Loggers will be there soon." He took a drink. "Maybe Monday."

"Monday? This Monday? Where?"

Transom shrugged helplessly, defensively, his face illuminated by the light of the campfire. "Hard to say."

A strange sensation welled up in Chase's chest, an anger and resentment and feeling of betrayal he hadn't felt in a long time. If those loggers were arriving Monday, this plan had been in motion for some time. Why hadn't Transom mentioned it before? Is this why he'd wanted to come on the camping trip, so he could drop this news on Chase in the woods, far from the farm, where nothing could be done? Chase rubbed his thumb over his knuckles and sat still, focusing his eyes on the fire, which spat and grew as the wind picked up. "How much are they gonna cut?"

"Just a few acres, probably. Enough to get some cash flow. The thing is," Transom continued, "there's a process to this sort of thing. It takes time. You got to trust me." He looked at Chase across the fire, his face bright from the glow.

"What do you mean, 'this sort of thing'?"

"Revitalization. You want to stay there, you want to farm. I get it. But things are changing. I've been looking at the numbers in Jack's books, and it wasn't just Maggie's illness that set you back. Things were going south long before that. Something had to be done."

"You should've run this by me. You should've asked."

"Don't take this the wrong way, Brother—but it's not your call."

Chase glared at him, his anger simmering. He thought of the farm, Church Hollow, the towering oaks that sighed and swooned. He loved the fields, the hills and folds of the land, the stream where the cows drank and cooled themselves. But that was all part of farming; that was work. The woods—they were sacred. Surely there was some other way.

Transom ran his hand over his stubble. "That came out wrong, man. What I'm trying to say here is that there's value in that land, plenty of value. And we can do a better job of managing it. We can make it sustainable."

"It's been sustainable for two hundred years," Chase snapped, pitching a twig into the fire. The Hardy farm had been in the family since 1802.

Transom shook his head. "That's what I'm trying to tell you. It's not sustainable. It hasn't been for years. The place has been going under for close to a decade."

Was it true? Jack in his office, pacing back and forth. Jack up at night, bent over his calculator, brow furrowed. Jack late on Chase's paycheck, saying he'd lost track of time. Had Chase been too blind to see it? Too naïve?

"Everything's different now," Transom said. "It doesn't have to be such a struggle, having a piece of ground. It doesn't have to be so hard." He paused and took a drink. "Here's the way I see it. The cows, the crops—that's what you know. That's your part and you'll keep doing that. Leave the management to me. I know what I'm doing. I've done this before. Things may look different for a while. They might change. But let me do my part. Can you do that? Can you trust me?"

Chase rubbed his hands together and held them closer to the fire. Change. He'd never been good at it, and he knew it. He thought again of Church Hollow, the towering oaks, the cherry trees with their wide, ambling limbs. He hated that his instinct was to feel angry: angry once more at Jack, for leaving him in the dark, for handing him such impossible odds. "Can you take another look at things?" he asked. "See if there's any way to keep the trees?"

Transom reached into his pocket and took out a pill. "Sure," he said, tilting his head back. "I'll see what I can do." He leaned over and nudged the steaks with a fork. "You ready to eat?"

—

The next morning, Chase lay cocooned in his sleeping bag, listening as the woods awoke. Crows hollered as they passed overhead, irritated, perhaps, by the unusual sight of the bright yellow tent. Something, a squirrel, he imagined—they always sounded so much larger than they were—lumbered loudly through the thick quilt of half-frozen leaves covering the ground. Chase hadn't slept well. He kept replaying the conversation from the night before through his mind, toiling over whether he should've asked all of his questions. He decided that he must be firmer with his friend. Transom had always been the more willful, more powerful one, and Chase had, for the most part, always gone along with what Transom wanted. That's how it had been when they were kids: Transom came up with the plan, and Chase went along with it. And Chase had never minded much, but now, things needed to change. They were adults. There was too much at stake.

Just before six, Chase forced himself from the warmth of his sleeping bag. He'd tucked his jacket down by his feet to keep it warm overnight, and he quickly slid it on. Transom snored softly, turning on his side as Chase unzipped the tent and climbed out. A white pine nearby swayed and creaked. He picked up a stick and poked at the coals from the night before. There were still some left, enough to get a good fire going, and he arranged some pieces of kindling and leaned over to blow on the coals. A few small embers swirled, and a thin curl of smoke snaked its way upward.

Chase settled his back against a fallen tree and watched as the fire grew in intensity, kicking a log that had rolled off. He thought of calling Laney to talk things over with her, ask for advice, but when he checked his phone, he had no service. He poured water from his canteen into the kettle and placed it over the fire and began thinking about all the strange events that had unfolded in the past several weeks. So much had happened, so quickly, that he'd hardly had a chance to take it all in. Losing Jack. Sitting at the attorney's office and learning of the dire financial situation he had left behind. Transom returning unexpectedly. Transom offering to help. Chase had heard people refer to such times as a roller-coaster ride, and now he understood why, so many ups and downs, no chance to get your bearings.

But now there was confusion, too. Doubt. He thought back to that December morning in the field, Transom gutting the rabbit. What was it Transom had said? Buying the farm was an investment, a business transaction. He'd come back to settle in, be home. Transom wouldn't have returned only to take over the farm and turn a profit. Chase shook his head and pulled his hat down over his ears. He kept telling himself that his best friend would never intentionally destroy the thing in this world that meant the most to him. Transom would never do something so deceitful, so treacherous. Chase should be ashamed for even entertaining such a thought.

But, as much as he tried to shake it, the thought wouldn't go away. As he sat warming himself by the fire, Chase began remembering events from many years before, things he hadn't even realized he remembered. Transom cheating on Mr. Coleridge's history test at the end of the year, befriending the nerdy merit scholar so that he could copy his answers in the back of the room. Transom taking money from his father's wallet, insisting, when Chase tried to stop him, that his father didn't need it. Transom lying to Jack and Maggie about spending a weekend visiting his mother when he really spent it camping with a girl. All the lies Chase himself had told, on Transom's behalf. Not real lies, not dangerous lies, but lies nonetheless. The more he thought about it, the more uncomfortable he became. Lies: lies stacked and placed like the stone wall at the farm, so many lies that one fit right into the next.

He reminded himself, though, that there was more to Transom than pretense and abuse, much more. He could be generous, warm, even kind. Until his parents split, Transom invited Chase on every family trip: crabbing in Delaware, whitewater rafting on the Youghiogheny, hiking in Yosemite. The Shultzes had taken him to Puerto Rico for a ten-day stay at an all-inclusive. They'd gone swimming in the rainforest. In eighth grade, Transom helped Chase learn algebra: they sat at the kitchen table at the farmhouse and did their homework, and Transom explained things that Chase was too shy to ask about in class. Transom had also saved him, once, a long time ago, from something dark and terrible that neither one of them had ever spoken of, at least not directly.

—

Chase's parents had gone out to celebrate their anniversary. He'd spent the night at the farm like he often did, but something woke him before dawn. He heard voices and went downstairs and found Jack and Maggie at the table, crying, while Sheriff Redifer stood in the corner with his handkerchief in his hand. Red told him what had happened: drunk driver, head-on collision, both his mother and father killed on impact.

Chase stood there, frozen, the words striking him but the news failing to register. Jack reached for him but he pulled away and instead walked to his grandfather's office, opened the gun cabinet, removed his Winchester 1873, and shoved a bunch of .44 bullets in the deep pocket of his work pants. Maggie called his name but he stormed out the kitchen door and headed for the woods, a natural choice for him since it was the place he'd always gone to clear his head. This time, though, it was different. There was no clearing of his mind; there was no making sense of what had happened.

For three days, he roamed the Hardy woods in a grief-stricken trance, lost, drinking from streams, sleeping against trees. Jack and Maggie were out looking for him, the farmhands, too. He heard his name echoing through the woods, but he ignored their calls, ducking down between rocks, the hundred hiding spots he'd discovered as a kid. The fact that he was adding anxiety to his grandparents' loss didn't occur to him until much later, once he'd snapped out of his stupor. What he knew was that he couldn't face them; he couldn't face anyone.

Until that point in his life, Chase had never lost a thing, not even a pet, and in the woods, the weight of his grief pressed so heavily on him that he was certain his heart, or brain, or something, would burst from the strain. He couldn't bear it, that untenable pain. He wanted his mom and dad back; he wanted to rewind the hands of time and make it so he'd gone along with them to celebrate; he wanted to die.

Instead, he killed.

Two magnificent bucks that had been roaming together for weeks, their antlers heavy in velvet, their summer coats golden brown and beautiful. He and his dad had been watching them each evening from their porch; they'd been looking forward to hunting them legally, come hunting season. But now that wouldn't happen. There would be no hunting together, no sketching plans about where they would sit, no debating about which buck had the better rack. The senselessness of his parents' death—it made waiting feel unbearable and also senseless. Why wait for anything? Why adhere to any rules? Why plan?

His mind spun. His parents, who never went out: the impossible odds that both of them would be killed at the same time. Had they suffered, even for just a few minutes? Had one died before the other? He was an orphan now. *Orphan.* Had he ever uttered that word in his life? His grief tilled deeper, tearing at him like the heavy metal parts of a plow, tunneling through earth. He shot one buck quickly and left it where it fell. The other, he intentionally shot in the spine. He let it kick and flail and suffer a long, slow death, and as he watched, he could feel a certain force taking over him. He surrendered to a brawny, animal side of himself he'd never felt before, and with that surrender came a swell of power. He gutted both animals with a primitive violence, plunging his pocket knife into the abdomen, up to his elbows in blood. Then he dragged the bodies to Church Hollow, kicked them into a heap, and set them on fire.

It was Transom who found him in a heap in the woods, slumped beside the embers of his animal bonfire. He pulled up on his four-wheeler, hopped off, and rushed over. Chase raised his head.

"You hurt?" Transom asked.

Chase shook his head.

"You sure? There's blood everywhere." Transom looked him over.

"I'm all right."

Transom pulled a pistol from his holster, a fancy gun from his father's Smith and Wesson collection, and set it on the ground. He squatted and handed Chase a canteen. "Drink."

After a while, Transom pulled him up gently to sit.

"What happened here, Boss?"

Chase shook his head, the woods muddled and bright. "I done something, T. Something bad."

Transom took his hat off, studied the remnants of charred bone, and then nudged the ashes with his boot.

"Don't tell no one," Chase said.

"'Course not."

Chase buried his hands in his palms and began to cry.

Transom picked up the handgun and turned it over in his hand. "Feels good, don't it? Kicking back at the world for what it done to you."

He was right about that, Chase remembered—Transom had put to words exactly what he'd been feeling. As much as he hated it, it was true: killing those deer, it somehow made his own pain more endurable, at least in the moment. Now that it was over, though, the pain was coming back, more visceral, more complex, because now there was guilt, too. A burning remorse for the violent things he'd done, and no way to take them back. He shuddered and shook his head.

"Yeah, you go ahead and tell yourself it don't. But I know better." Transom held the pistol up, cocked the weapon, and aimed at a squirrel that clucked in a nearby tree.

"No more," Chase said. "Please."

Transom fired, Chase flinching hard at the sound. The squirrel dropped to the ground, thudding in the leaves. Transom hollered in victory but then looked at Chase and scowled. He stood. "I lost them, too, you know. Your parents." He tucked the handgun back in his holster and looked up at the sky. "Come on, let's get you home."

He reached down and scooped Chase from the ground where he lay, spent and dehydrated, reeking and covered in blood. They hobbled to a stream close by, and Transom took off Chase's shirt and dipped it into the water. He wiped the blood and dirt from Chase's face, washed off his arms, rubbing gently at the dirt. Transom took off his own shirt and put it on Chase and left the stained t-shirt in the stream. When they got back to the farmhouse, Maggie and Jack sat at the table, waiting, dressed in black.

"Got into some liquor," Transom lied, hauling Chase up the steps and straight to the shower before either one of them could say a word.

"Get yourself cleaned up," he told Chase, yanking the curtain closed. "Funeral's this afternoon."

Days later, Chase tried to convince himself it hadn't really happened—it had been a bad dream, some ugly hallucination caused by extreme stress, because surely he wouldn't have done those terrible things. He went out to Church Hollow where Transom had found him, and it was there. Evidence. Charred leaves, a black circle on the forest floor. The shirt in the stream, too.

He got a shovel and dug a hole, buried what remained of both deer and the squirrel. He kneeled and prayed for forgiveness—from God, from his parents, from the land. He swore he'd never harm an animal again: a sort of penance, an oath. That land—his parents had loved it as much as he did, and he would honor them and do whatever it took to care for it, protect it. That day, he also vowed he'd keep his emotions at bay: he wouldn't let himself feel that much ever again because that was the only way to manage. He had to numb himself, hold back. He never thought about his parents. When he drove past their house, he looked the other way, every time. Through the years—Maggie's death and now Jack's, too—he'd kept that promise.

—

At the campsite, the water in the kettle was boiling now, spewing drops that capered into the fire. Chase grabbed the metal coffee cup and emptied a packet of instant coffee into it. He wrapped his hand in a towel, grabbed the kettle, and poured the steaming water into the cup. Transom emerged from his tent, shielding his eyes from the light of the fire. He crawled back in the tent and reemerged, wearing a thick wool trapper's hat. His eyes were bloodshot. Chase wasn't sure how many beers his friend had the night before. He wondered, too, about those pills Transom kept taking. Chase had asked once, and Transom had handed him the bottle. "Shoulder," he'd said. "Don't worry. They're legal." He pointed to his name on the label.

Transom ripped open a packet of coffee and dumped it into his own coffee cup, then motioned for Chase to pour water in his cup.

"Feels like rain," Chase said.

"You always say that."

Chase looked up at the sky. "Maybe it'll be snow. Depends on the temperature. But that sky, white and gray, that's precipitation, one form or another." Chase drank his coffee quickly, the warmth traveling through his chest. He dumped the last sip, then stood. He started dismantling the tent and stuffing it into its carrying case while Transom watched from his perch on a log.

Shortly after they packed up their gear and headed on their way, a few flakes of snow began to flutter downward. Chase, convinced it would rain at some point, suggested they scrap their original idea to take a longer, more rigorous route back to the vehicle, but Transom insisted they stick to the plan. They still had about five miles to go when the sleet began pelting them, cold blades against their necks. As they slogged through the steep, rocky terrain, Chase grew more and more morose. All he could think about were the trees back at the farm: the patch of towering white pines so big that Chase couldn't reach around them. The swath of walnuts in the low, swampy area beyond Church Hollow. The rambling red oak at the top of Maggie's field.

They skipped lunch. By the time they arrived at the truck, both of them were soaked and cold and miserable. Chase had slipped twice, so not only were his gear and upper body drenched, but his heavy pants and long johns clung to his legs as well.

Transom awkwardly attempted to lighten the mood. "There's a motel right down the road. We passed it on our way in. We can't camp like we'd planned. What do you say we crash there instead?"

"I was thinking we should head home," Chase said, heaving his backpack into the Lincoln with disgust.

"Come on, I'll buy you a drink, and dinner, too. You've got to be hungry. I'm starving."

Chase shrugged his shoulders. What he really wanted was to be alone.

"We come all the way up here. Let's not let a little sleet ruin it," Transom said with a grin.

Chase yanked his raincoat off his shoulders and shoved it in the back seat. "It's not the sleet," he muttered under his breath. "It's you."

From the other side of the Lincoln, Transom looked at him, waiting for an answer. Oblivious, as usual. Because Chase was soaked and hungry, he nodded in agreement.

At the pub where they stopped for supper, Transom gathered a crowd around the pool table. One by one, he pulled them in, a joke, a challenge—that smile of his, that laugh that rang up and up—he could read a person and know how to draw them, make them feel a part of something. Chase slumped in a stool nearby. He wished Laney were there. He'd had too many drinks, and he knew it, but he kept on drinking. He couldn't help it, sagging in misery as he watched Transom with all those people, laughing, throwing his money away, game after game. An attractive young woman had taken a liking to him, too. She was young, too young, and petite, and Transom's hulking figure made her look all the more so. She wore tight jeans and tall boots, and her red sweater kept slipping off her shoulder to reveal a black bra strap. Teresa, her name was.

Transom came over eventually. "Listen," he said, leaning in so close that Chase could smell whiskey on his breath. "You need to call it a night, buddy. I'm gonna drive you down the road to the motel."

Transom walked over to the woman in the red sweater and whispered something in her ear. She tossed her long brown hair over her shoulder and laughed, then walked over to the coat rack by the door and came back with a gray jacket and red purse. Transom slung Chase's arm over his shoulder and helped him stand up and head out the door, and the three of them walked to the Lincoln. The sleet had turned to a light, downy snow that was just beginning to accumulate on the roads. Inside the vehicle, all Chase could think about was how he could smell the woman's perfume, even though she had just been in the bar with all its smoke.

Transom told her to wait while he helped Chase to the motel room. It would just take a minute. He fiddled with the keys and opened the door, ushering Chase inside. Transom flipped on the light and watched his friend stumble into bed. "Don't wait up," Transom said with a wink as he headed right back out the door.

—

The next morning, when Chase woke in the motel room, it took him a few minutes to realize where he was, what he was doing in that strange, dingy place. He'd been dreaming that he was in Church Hollow, watching a black bear lumber through the woods, and the realness of the dream still hung on him. His head thumped and ears roared. Transom wasn't there. Chase lay back in his bed, grabbing a pillow and placing it over his face to shield himself from the light. How long had it been since he had woken up after dawn? Years? He couldn't remember the last time he'd just turned over and let himself go back to sleep.

Before long Transom showed up, with two tall, steaming Styrofoam cups of coffee. "Rise and shine, big guy," he said, placing Chase's coffee on the nightstand and plopping himself on the bed.

Chase moaned and pulled another pillow over his head.

Transom sighed. "I think I'm in love."

"I've heard that before. Many times."

Transom looked at him with a seriousness Chase had rarely seen in his friend. "No, I mean it this time. I think she's the one."

"You just met her."

Transom shrugged. "I guess when you know, you know," he said. "You better get dressed. She'll be here in a few minutes."

AFTER

Mick Dashel had just finished questioning Chase Hardy, and Red, who'd felt oddly embarrassed about participating in the interrogation of his deceased friend's grandson—especially since he'd already sort of done it once, out at the farm—had come up with a perfectly legitimate excuse not to sit in on it. Miranda Wilson had hit a deer with her car, and Red had hopped in the Jimmy to drive out to make sure she was all right and drag the deer from the road. He'd loitered there with Miranda, asking about her husband and kids, about work, the farm, the tractor that'd been giving them trouble, all in an attempt to waste enough time to ensure that Chase Hardy would be gone by the time he got back to the station. After all, Mick would record the entire conversation, so if Red really needed to, he could listen to it later. Although he doubted he would.

"He knows something," Mick said, after Chase had gone and Red had come back to the station from the Wilson place.

Red's heart lurched. That tug in his gut, telling him Possum might be behind this—the possibility that his own silence could be putting someone else at risk, let alone Chase Hardy, quiet and sweet and harmless as a fly, made him dizzy. The room spun and his knees threatened to give. He eased himself into his chair. "What makes you say that?"

"He's hiding something, I can tell."

Red shook his head. "I don't think he was that upset about what happened out there at the farm. Certainly not upset enough to hurt someone."

"I've seen people hurt over much less."

Red reached into the bowl on his desk and pulled out an antacid. "I'm telling you: you don't know him like I do. We still can't be sure what happened to Transom, if someone did something to him, but if someone did, I don't think Chase has it in him to do a person harm. The man don't even hunt." Red remembered something he'd witnessed, out the window of the police station, just a few weeks back: "Chase Hardy's the kind of person who pulls his truck over to help an old lady struggling to steer her walker over bumpy sidewalk. He helps with Vacation Bible School at our church. Kids love him." Red shrugged. "He's a good person. Maybe in a city, you don't know people well, but here, we know each other." As he said the words out loud, he realized just how untrue the statement was. Surely the good people of Fallen Mountains would say they knew him.

Mick smiled. "You never really know people, not fully. People are strange. They hold onto things, they have secrets. And trust me: we do things we didn't think we were capable of, good and bad. All of us. People can commit all sorts of atrocities, even normal people, good people. Think of wars. How else could such barbarities occur, if the deep capacity to do evil didn't exist in every one of us? I've seen it all, Sheriff. I've seen a sweet-faced mother of three who found out her husband was cheating on her and stabbed him to death in his sleep. I've seen a beloved pastor of a church of three thousand shoot the man who molested his daughter. And yes, I've seen people killed over land. The thing is, each of us can only take so much. If we're pushed too far, if we're backed into a corner, we'll snap. We'll do things we wouldn't, under normal circumstances. It's a fact."

Red thought of Possum on the floor of his trailer. At the trial, the defense attorney had provided proof that Possum had been being abused by Vance for over a year. Pushed too far, snap. He reflected on his own life: JT threatening to pull the health insurance, weeks before his little boy was to have the surgery he desperately needed. Backed into a corner, snap.

Mick continued. "The advantage to stepping into a case where you don't know anyone involved is that you can see the facts for what they are. With Transom Shultz, all the evidence is suggesting that he didn't just disappear. He'd just gotten engaged. He'd made arrangements—paid for them—to go somewhere with someone he cared about. All of his personal effects were in his vehicle. Now, as an outsider who doesn't know anyone personally, I can see that Chase Hardy very likely had a falling-out with Transom over the farm—he would've felt betrayed, angry—and he probably decided to do something about it. Plus, like I said before, Chase Hardy is the beneficiary on Transom's will. Now, it could be that they went at it and there was an accident. I don't rule that out. But I bet there's a body out there at the farm. Trust me, I don't like the idea of it any more than you do, but I can feel it. Somewhere in that ground, there's a body."

BEFORE

March. Chase sat in his truck, watching the large yellow machine rumble its way through the field, dragging another load of four long, branchless logs, leaving deep, muddy ruts in its wake. Within a week of his camping trip with Transom, the loggers had arrived at the farm, and that's when Chase realized Transom had never taken a second look at things to determine whether the trees might somehow be saved.

For two weeks now, the crew had been working from dawn until dusk. Chase could hear them, the whine of a chainsaw, the great crash of a tree hitting the ground. There was a skidder, too, and two log trucks that came and went. The first half of the month had been cold and wet, with alternating snow, sleet, and rain, and the field was torn up and crisscrossed with deep, black channels. Progress had been slow. Now, though, with the weather warmer, the work was in full-swing. A large pile of logs, thirty feet high, sat in what was called the landing. The loggers and the skidder, the machine that dragged the felled trees from the woods and into the field, had returned the day before. All day, the log trucks, one with a red cab and the other with a dark green one, had been heaving their way up the newly shaled road to the landing, where the drivers loaded up the wood.

In a few weeks, it would be turkey season, spring gobbler. Typically, Chase would see turkeys throughout the winter. They foraged in the fields, gathering scraps of corn that hadn't been harvested; they scratched among the crumpled brown leaves in search of acorns. Chase would count them and keep track of their numbers, and usually, there were at least two flocks on the property. Last year, there had been a flock of twelve and a flock of seventeen. This winter, however, he hadn't seen the turkeys, not once. He wondered if the loggers had caught sight of them while they were in the woods. Every time he saw them dragging out more and more trees—robust oaks, tall and straight; hard maples; walnuts—his gut churned with disgust. He hadn't yet been able to bring himself to walk the part of the property where the men had been taking trees. He wasn't sure he wanted to see Church Hollow; he didn't know that he could handle it.

What had been the cruelest blow of all, the thing that had truly set Chase over the edge, had just transpired the day before: Transom had signed with an oil company. *Frackholes.* Worse yet, he hadn't had the guts to tell Chase face-to-face. Instead, he'd left the contract on the kitchen table, where he knew Chase would find it. Chase came home to see the stack of papers, a lot of jargon that he didn't understand but which stated, at the top of the first page, that it was a lease agreement. Transom's signature was at the end.

Aside from brief, forced interludes, Chase hadn't spoken to Transom since their camping trip. He worked to avoid him, making sure he was in town, or in the barn, or, more and more often, at Laney's, whenever Transom was home. When Chase found the contract on the table, though, he confronted Transom about everything: about Transom misleading him, about promising to try and keep the trees. Transom hadn't denied any of it. He'd started to formulate an answer, a lie, Chase could tell—that twitching to the left that he always did—but then he'd caught himself.

He insisted that Chase had to ride it out, that things looked ugly now, but that, with time, it wouldn't be so bad. Different, yes, but not bad. Once they got the well pad in place, once the logs were cleared out and all the equipment was gone, there'd just be three metal tanks, a few pumps, about an acre of the whole farm. And that was the beauty of it, Transom explained: once everything was set up, you had a source of income for years to come. No more fretting about what portion of the crop was getting destroyed by whitetail, no more worrying about the fickle Pennsylvania weather, no more struggling. What Transom didn't seem to understand, though, was that it wasn't so simple. It wasn't just about the income; it wasn't about forging an easier way. There was a sense of pride in tending the land, in knowing it and caring for it, that was gone, that Transom had taken from him. There was no getting that back.

There were risks, too, with fracking, hazards that could unfold, troubles Chase heard about on the local news from time to time. A truck carrying fracking fluid toppling on a sharp bend, spilling thousands of gallons. As the person whose yard had been flooded by it told the reporter, pointing to a well pump, that stuff went somewhere, and in his case, it was right into his drinking supply. Recently, one channel had been featuring a family who said their children had been perfectly healthy, until an oil company put a compressor station on their farm. Now, the father explained, his arms draped protectively over his girls' shoulders, they were sick. And just last week, a woman had held a match to the well pump by her garden, and the water—or whatever it was that came out—had caught fire. The chances of any of those things happening were probably slim, Chase understood, but still: in his mind, no amount of money was worth risking your home or health.

From his truck, Chase watched the man driving the skidder. He pulled past the enormous heap of felled logs and lined up his new load with them. The logs dropped from the back. The man climbed out of his seat and leaped to the ground. He moved with dexterity and grace, and though he was too far off for Chase to get a good look at, Chase knew that it must be a young man he was watching. The man clambered back onto the machine, at its rear, where he leaned over and tugged at the heavy metal chains that, in the woods, he'd wrapped around the logs. He cranked and wound the chain. The man hopped down, then climbed back into his skidder, and trundled off to the woods again for another load.

Chase glanced at his watch. He was tempted, as he always was, to drive up into the field, and then into the woods, to check it out, see it all with his own eyes. He was supposed to meet Laney soon for their evening walk, but he could go through the woods quickly, not even get out of the truck. He had time. He pushed in the clutch and shifted into first. He climbed the hill and pulled into the woods with caution, navigating the deep ruts and trying to avoid the high spots where he might bottom out. He realized that he was following a sort of road—a route that the loggers used consistently to pull out the logs. The truck swung back and forth as it crept into the woods.

And then he saw it, as he crested the plateau: Church Hollow stripped almost entirely of the tall, straight hardwoods that

Chase had loved since he was a boy. It was so much worse, so much uglier, than he'd imagined it would be. Large stumps jutted up from the ground, and small trees, trees without timber value, had toppled and lay strewn about like pieces of a shipwreck. Limbs that the loggers had sawed off the trees had been collected into tall, precarious stacks. The ground was completely torn up, like a battle had taken place there. If Chase were to try to get out of the truck and walk, he would only be able to do so by climbing over the debris slowly and carefully—there was no clear area where a person could walk in a straight line for more than a few yards. He scanned the area, trying hard to get his bearings, but without the landmarks he'd always relied on—the white oak with wide, ambling limbs; the enormous boulder he'd sat on when he decided to sell Transom the land; the patch of mountain laurel—he was lost. He began to sweat, his heart hammering. When he saw the skidder headed toward him with yet another load of logs, he turned off the truck and jumped out. In a blinding fury, he navigated the ruts and heaps, quickly hoisting himself over the fallen trees. The driver of the skidder raised a hand in a wave and halted to a stop. Chase tugged himself up onto the machine, just as he had seen the driver himself do earlier, and tapped at the door. The young man, seeing the anger in Chase's eyes, cautiously opened it. Chase reached in and grabbed the man by his jacket. He pulled him in so that their faces were close.

"What do you think you're doing?" he said, teeth clenched.

Clearly stunned, the young man swallowed. "Sir?"

And then suddenly Chase saw the man's fear and confusion, saw his own knuckles white as they clenched the guy's jacket, saw himself standing on the skidder, throbbing with rage. All at once he remembered the things he'd done, the days in the woods after his parents' death: his vow to keep his emotions at bay. He let go and stepped out of the skidder. Besides, he told himself as he drove away, that driver—he was just doing his job. Though he was the one dragging trees from Church Hollow, he wasn't to blame. It wasn't his fault, any more than it was the man loading the logs and hauling them off the property, or the guy running the chainsaw. It was Transom's. Transom was the one behind all this.

—

Laney was waiting for Chase on the front porch of her house. Kip sat at her feet, his ears perked, watching her with excitement. The dog understood that she was waiting, that they were both waiting, and that they were probably going somewhere. She reached down and patted his head. The weather had grown suddenly warm over the past few days, and the sunshine, the melted snow, and the first signs of buds on the trees had her giddy and energized. Anxious to get her garden started, she planted some seeds in large, black trays: zinnias, begonias, lobelia, impatiens. She planted a tray of vegetable seeds, too. Broccoli, cucumbers, and some heirloom tomatoes, seeds she'd saved from the garden the year before. She'd never started a garden from seeds, and she realized they might not take off, but still, it felt good to hold those seeds, press them into the dirt, feel productive in that way. There was a hopefulness in the act that she savored.

Laney's heart was heading into dangerous terrain with Chase, and she knew it. She thought of him constantly, at home, when she was hauling firewood in from outside, or heating herself some dinner, or watching *Jeopardy* on her couch. At work, it was worse. Her role on the assembly line at the telecommunications parts factory was to shove metal prongs into their plastic housing, three thousand or more times a day. It was tedious work, especially after you got good enough that you didn't really even have to focus on what you were doing. When she first started at the factory, four years earlier, she would be nervous on the line. At the end of the day, her back and shoulders would be sore from sitting stiffly and focusing all day long. Her eyes would sting; her wrists would ache. But the body could memorize that precise angle that the prongs needed to be inserted, that particular movement that allowed the excess to be snapped off just right, so that after a hundred thousand shove and snap movements, a person barely had to watch what she was doing. Laney's mind would wander. Her imagination would veer perilously through happy and enticing scenarios: ambling the fields of the farm with Chase, the cheat grass singing. Waking Christmas morning with Chase, having children with Chase.

She saw him approach in his truck, rounding the bend and pulling into her driveway. He looked at her and raised his fingers in a wave, gripping the steering wheel. He turned off the engine and climbed out slowly. When she pulled him in for a hug, he was soaked in sweat.

"What's wrong?" she said, searching his face. "What happened?" Her mind raced. Had Transom done something else to the farm? Had someone gotten hurt? She swallowed as a third thought came to her: Had Transom told Chase about the two of them? Now that Transom had a new girlfriend—that young, silly, painfully pretty thing, Teresa—surely he could keep his mouth shut. Laney hoped.

Chase leaned against his truck, resting his weight on the front bumper. "I just had a run-in with one of the loggers at the farm."

"A fight?" Laney paused, confused. "Are you hurt? Did you hurt someone?" She could hardly imagine it.

Chase shook his head. The wind picked up and the branches of the dogwood in the front yard lifted and swayed. "I think I just scared him," he said at last. He sat down beside her on the porch and told her what happened, burying his face in his hands and hunkering over. "How could I have let this happen?" he said. "How could I have been so stupid?"

Laney leaned over him, pulling his head to her chest. "You weren't stupid," she said. "There's no way you could've seen this coming. Nobody could. He was your friend; you trusted him. You didn't do nothing wrong."

Kip whined, prodding her thigh impatiently. He watched her, waiting for a sign that they were leaving.

"We better get going," Chase said, standing up. "Not much time before dark."

They climbed into Laney's truck and headed to the woods. Laney wanted to ask more about the confrontation, but Chase didn't seem to want to talk about it, shifting the conversation instead to her job. There had been talk of closing the electronics plant for over a year. Month after month, people discussed it, said they'd heard there was some kind of meeting scheduled with corporate, said they'd heard they might be sending the work overseas. Laney had given up on worrying about it. On occasion, she thought about what she might do, where she might find work, whether she would have to sell her house and move. But for the most part, her mindset was that there was nothing she could do, nothing at all, so there was no point in losing sleep over it.

"Trina Johnson's pregnant," Laney said. Trina had gone to Fallen Mountains High and had graduated a year after them. Although they hadn't been close in high school, Laney and Trina had become friends while working at the plant. They worked on the same team, on the same shift, so they were around each other a lot.

"Again?" Chase said, surprised. He smiled. "How many is that now? Five?"

"Three. That's not really that many," she said, her eyes on the road.

"Seems like she's been pregnant off and on for six or seven years."

"They had them close together. She and Denny waited too long, that's what she says. She's thirty-one, you know. A woman's only got so much time." Too accusatory, the way she said it. She reached her right hand over and squeezed his. "Sorry. It's just that I'm feeling sort of jealous about it. I know that sounds crazy."

"Jealous?"

She shrugged. "I always wanted a family. You know, be a mom, have kids. Go camping. Have dinners together. I never had that growing up." Laney's mother, Kristen, had been severely depressed for much of Laney's childhood, after her husband left her. Laney was three.

She flipped on the turn signal and pulled into the parking lot of the national forest. Kip began to whimper, his jaw trembling with anticipation. Chase let him hop out of the truck and then climbed out. Laney slid into a light jacket.

Kip dashed off on the trail ahead of them, and the two followed at a leisurely pace. Buds were just emerging on the trees;

the air was thick with the sweet smell of dirt. The wind picked up and an old maple tree creaked under the strain. Laney shielded her eyes from the buds that sailed down and showered her.

"You'll be a great mom," Chase said softly. He paused to look at her face and then pulled her close to him. "What you said earlier, about a family."

Laney pressed her face against his chest. He smelled like the woods, like earth and sawdust, and she breathed him in. She liked this tenderness from Chase, a tenderness she was seeing more often. She loved that the direction they were headed felt like a good direction to her, like progress, finally. They saw each other every day now. They were establishing rhythms, like their evening walks and their morning coffee, and she loved that. They even went out together sometimes, to Wheeler's for breakfast on Saturday, when it was packed full of nosy people who craned their necks to get a look; or to Johnnie's Place for drinks on Friday night. People, Laney knew, were starting to consider them a couple. Trina teased her about it at work, and when she said she was waiting for Laney to get knocked up so their kids could go to school together, Laney had blushed and walked away.

Laney and Chase came to the stream that marked their traditional turn-around point in their walk. At the height of summer, the stream would almost dry up: a slow, tired brown that ran intermittently. In an especially dry summer, only the channel would remain, with pools of stagnant water here and there. But this time of year, with all the March rain, the stream roared, and the edges brimmed white. In a few spots, small chunks of old snow gathered at the base of the rocks along the stream. It was cold there, sheltered by the tall, stately hemlocks that towered nearby, and Laney pulled her hat down over her ears. Kip was perched on a rock, his tail hitting a branch of mountain laurel with each wag. He seemed to be contemplating a swim. Laney thought of him, his long hair drenched with the stream water, tromping back and forth in the front seat of the truck, soaking Chase and her and making the truck stink like wet dog. She whistled, and Kip turned to her, then bounded over.

"Not today," she said, scratching his ears.

They walked back to the truck. Some nights, they walked briskly, their faces red from the strain, their bodies growing warm beneath their layers. Laney never minded that pace, the feel of the work her body was doing. But tonight—with spring heavy in the air, and the day still warm even though the sun had set and the sky was churning pink and turquoise—tonight they walked in a dawdling, deliberate way, as if the night would wait until they returned to the truck to arrive, as if they could postpone the day's ending. Chase reached out and hung his arm over Laney's shoulder, and she pressed into him, content.

Despite her own happiness, and the glimpses she saw in Chase, too, Laney sensed that it wouldn't last, that it couldn't possibly last, so her pleasure continued to be fouled by a fear that always lurked in the backdrop of each good moment. What was happening at the farm would inevitably blow up, she knew that, and no matter how she imagined it panning out, it didn't end well. For now, Chase and Transom were avoiding each other at all costs, but Laney felt that eventually they would come to blows about all that had happened. It was only a matter of time. And then there was the issue of her secret—her history with Transom—which had remained a secret so far, but which continued to plague her, as much as she tried to shove it down and forget about it.

In fact, now that things were spoiled between Chase and Transom, now that there was no motivation to protect Chase from the hurt that the secret would bring, Laney worried that Transom had no reason to keep his mouth shut. One day, he might spill it, spew it out like a torch, just for spite. Transom could be mean like that, saying things, doing things, for no other reason than to inflict pain.

She'd spent a good deal of time contemplating a way to get rid of him: a lie. I'm carrying your child, she could say. If you leave Fallen Mountains and never come back, I won't tell Teresa. Would that work? The possibility of devastating Chase would no longer matter to him, she presumed, but he would, Laney suspected, care about how such information would affect his relationship with his new girlfriend. Maybe it would be enough. Maybe it would make him go away, his girlfriend, too. Laney considered asking Possum for advice—all the hints he dropped about being careful when it came to Transom, the way he'd pounded his fist on the table when she'd told him about her affair with him—maybe he would have some insights. Perhaps together, they could devise a plan. Because, of course, there was always more than one way to make a problem disappear.

AFTER

RED LEANED AGAINST A DESK INSIDE THE FALLEN Mountains Police Station, staring out the long, storefront window. The sun scalded the pavement. The Jimmy, parked in front of the entrance in a spot without shade, sent off a glare as blinding as a spaceship. The heat seeped into the building, and big drafts of warmth flowed inside every time someone opened the door.

"You ready?" Mick asked, tucking two bottles of water under his arm.

Red nodded. He grabbed his notepad and followed Mick back the hallway into the boardroom.

"I'm not a suspect, am I?" Laney asked Red, frowning. She looked up from where she had been sitting for fifteen minutes, waiting alone. She stood up. "That's not why I'm here, right?"

"Have a seat, Ms. Moore," Mick Dashel said, and then added, "Please." He placed a water bottle in front of her and eased into the chair across from her. Red followed suit, taking the seat beside him.

Laney slumped into the chair. "You didn't answer my question."

Mick shrugged. "Should you be a suspect?"

Laney turned and glared at Red. "What's going on here?"

Since Red had avoided the interview with Chase, he felt that, this time, he should stick around, although the truth was, he hated this whole situation, hauling one good, familiar face after another into the station, asking people to dig up their past. Looking at private photographs, too. It was different for Mick, who didn't know these people, who hadn't known them since they were kids and didn't see them at church or Wheeler's or the grocery store—to him, they were just pictures, just pieces of a puzzle. But Red didn't want to know who was fooling around with whom, he didn't want to be witness to any airing out of laundry.

Mick extended a hand to Laney. "Mick Dashel," he said. "I'm assisting Sheriff Redifer on the Shultz case."

Laney reluctantly shook Mick's hand. He clicked on a hand-held recorder and leaned back in his chair. "Ms. Moore, do you know why you're here?"

She shook her head ever so slightly, and stared at Red. "Sheriff Redifer called and said he needed some help with Transom's case. So here I am. He didn't say anything about me being a suspect."

Red shrugged and tilted his head in apology.

"Well, Ms. Moore, we haven't found a body yet, so no, you're not really a suspect, but evidence is suggesting that Transom did not disappear on his own volition this time." He paused, looking at her face. "So we're just trying to consider every angle here."

Mick opened a folder and took out the photographs Red had found. He slid them across the table. "We found these in Transom's desk," he said.

Laney took the photographs in her hand and studied them, her face burning red, her jaw clenching. "These pictures are from high school," she said, frowning at Mick Dashel. "Fifteen, maybe sixteen years ago." She skated the photographs back across the table to him and took a deep breath and Red felt sorry for her, for how embarrassed she was. "I hope you didn't bring me in here just to ask me about pictures from half a lifetime ago. I was a teenager when those were taken."

Mick tucked the pictures into the folder. "It's just odd, don't you think, that Transom would hold onto them? I mean, they were in a very small stack, with just a few other pictures, like they were something he'd intentionally set aside, like they were important." He looked at her face, searching for something there. "It's like those photographs meant something to him."

Laney shook her head and shrugged. "I don't know what you want me to say."

Outside, an eighteen-wheeler roared past, its brakes thundering, rattling the old windows. The air-conditioning units groaned, one on the front of the building and one on the western side, but they were not enough to cool down the building, not nearly enough.

"Tell me about your relationship with Transom Shultz," Mick said.

Laney folded her arms across her chest. "I've known Transom since I was a kid," she said. "We both spent a lot of time at the Hardy farm." She shrugged. "That's about it."

"But there's more to it than that," Mick said. "I mean, correct me if I'm wrong, but it looks as though you may have been naked in those photos? At least from the waist up." He took the photos out of the folder and studied them, as if to double-check.

Laney shot a glance at Red, who shifted uncomfortably. "We were involved, for a while."

Mick nodded. "But now, you don't like him. You don't approve of him."

Laney wrinkled her nose.

"Your mouth turns down a little bit when you talk about him," Mick explained. "It's a sign of contempt. Universally, actually."

She shrugged. "You're right, I didn't like him."

"And why's that?"

Laney paused. "He's selfish," she said. "He always has been. Look at what he's done to the farm. Jack and Maggie, they practically raised him. His parents, they were both crazy in their own ways. Trust me, I was at their house a few times when Transom and me were together. And I mean, even if Transom didn't have enough respect for Jack and Maggie, for what they stood for, at the very least he could've thought of Chase. Transom was supposed to be his best friend."

"Do you think Chase had something to do with this, then?" Mick asked.

Red shifted in his chair, took out his handkerchief, and began blotting his face.

Laney's eyes widened. "No. I didn't say that." She gripped the table. "I never said that. You can't go putting words in my mouth." She looked at Red. "Sheriff?"

"Mr. Dashel—" Red said.

Mick nodded. "Okay, tell me. What do you think happened to Transom?"

Laney twisted her mouth to the side. She reached out and pulled the cap off the bottle of water Mick had handed her earlier. She took a drink and looked out the window, and Red followed her gaze: old Widow Ross was shuffling past, struggling to navigate the uneven sidewalk in her walker. It was far too hot for a woman in her eighties to be out.

"I'm asking you what you think happened," Mick explained.

"You know he left before. Just disappeared, without telling anyone, without saying good-bye." She swirled the water in her plastic bottle and crossed her feet at the ankles.

"We know that," Mick said. "But we've got reason to believe that isn't what happened this time." He leaned back in his chair. "Tell me more about what kind of person Transom was. Who might want him to . . . disappear?"

For a moment, she was quiet, staring out the front window, watching Widow Ross. "I don't know," she said, finally. "I don't know what happened to him."

"Tell us why you hated him," he said. He folded his hands on the cream-colored formica tabletop.

"I didn't hate him," Laney said. She squirmed in the old chair and glared at Red again.

"All right. Tell us why you didn't like him. You seem like a nice person, a good person. Red has told me as much." Mick lifted his hands from the table. "Transom Shultz, on the other hand, well, he was probably not a nice person. At least that's the impression I get. I know his father, and like they say, the apple don't fall far from the tree. I hear JT came to Fallen Mountains, pushed people around, took charge of the town. And then Transom did the same thing, basically."

"I care about this town," Laney said. "I've lived here my whole life. I didn't like the way things were heading: Transom letting the oil company in at the farm, after all Jack and Maggie done for him. It just wasn't right." She paused, looking hard at Mick's face. "But that doesn't mean I did anything about it."

Mick scribbled a few things in his electronic tablet and leaned back in his chair, folding his hands across his chest. "One more thing. Where were you on Memorial Day weekend?"

Mick slid a calendar he'd borrowed from Leigh's desk across the table to her, and Laney looked at it, frowning.

"Well, Friday night I went to the shooting match. The rest of the weekend, I stayed home. I planted my garden. I didn't go anywhere."

"And can someone vouch for your whereabouts?"

"I was with Chase Hardy. He was with me, he was at my house."

"The entire weekend? You were together for the entire weekend?"

She swallowed hard, and Mick held her gaze before glancing over his shoulder at Red. "The entire weekend," she said.

The fan swung left, then right, pulling air into the room and lifting the edge of a stack of papers with each pass. Mick Dashel scribbled something in his electronic tablet and then clicked off the handheld recorder. "Thank you for your time, Ms. Moore. You're free to go," he said, rising, tucking his tablet under his arm. "But don't go far. We may need you again."

BEFORE

It was April and the timbering at the farm was finished: the skidder, pickups and log trucks, gone. In their place was a battlefield of stumps and treetops, deep ruts from machinery, mud and ruin—a haunting reminder of what Transom had taken away.

For weeks Chase had been avoiding him as much as possible, orchestrating his schedule based on whether Transom was in Empire with Teresa or there at the farm. But one night he came home to find the Lincoln in the driveway. He craned his neck from the truck, trying to look through the kitchen window to see if he could catch a glimpse of anyone walking around. He hoped Teresa wasn't there. Things were strained enough between Transom and him; the last thing he wanted to deal with was a run-in with her.

Teresa always put Chase on edge. She'd taken over the kitchen—Maggie's kitchen, his kitchen—and rearranged and gotten rid of items she didn't think were useful. Some of those items, like the Foley mill she pitched and the blue glass pitcher she took to Goodwill, had been sentimental, not just to Chase, but to Maggie. Maggie's mother had bought her that Foley mill as a wedding present. Jack had bought the pitcher for Christmas one year. Chase had warned Teresa, hissing, gritting his teeth, that she should never again throw any of their things away without asking. She'd rolled her big, brown eyes, laughed, and told him to lighten up.

In fact, Chase couldn't even find his way around the kitchen anymore. The spices, which he'd always arranged in such a way that allowed easy access to the most frequently used ones, were now ordered alphabetically. His favorite wooden spoon was gone. He suspected Teresa had tossed it because it was worn and stained purple from the time Maggie had used it to make raspberry jam. In the living room, Teresa added decorations: a candle, two framed photographs of Transom and her. Little by little, pieces of Chase's life were being whisked away and replaced; he no longer felt at home.

As he sat in the driveway, he contemplated what to do. He could go back to Laney's, which was where he'd just been, but she would understand. Still, he needed a change of clothes, so he turned off the ignition and headed toward the house. He opened the back door and walked into the kitchen, where Transom sat at the table, an array of papers spread in front of him. When Chase entered, Transom turned around to face him. He tried to make small talk—mentioned the weather, asked about Laney. He always did, acting like everything was okay between them when really, nothing was. Chase slipped his boots off and walked over to the sink. He grabbed himself a glass and filled it up at the tap, but then, when he tasted it and found that strange mud-metallic flavor he'd recently noticed, he dumped it out. He'd always loved the pure, sweet flavor of their well water.

"I got some folks coming over in the morning," Transom said. "Machines, too."

"Don't see what that has to do with me."

"Just didn't want you to be surprised is all."

He must've heard about the confrontation with the man in the skidder. "Surprised," Chase said. "That's an interesting word for all of this."

"Chase." Transom put down his pen and rubbed his eyes. "I told you there was a process to it, that you had to see it through, that you had to trust me."

"I did trust you," Chase hissed, the words burning on his lips. "I trusted you to take care of this place. I trusted you to be my friend."

"Come on, Brother."

Chase pointed a finger at him and grimaced. "Don't you call me that. Don't."

He took a step closer but then stopped, turned quickly, and walked away, and he told himself that the next time he came home and Transom was there, he would not engage in any conversation. He didn't like the feeling of rage and pain and regret that surged and boiled, the unsettling combination. It scared him, that sense that his emotions were taking over his body, swallowing his ability to control what his legs, arms, hands, would do, because he knew that feeling, from before: he remembered what it had led to.

Chase stormed to his room, gathered some belongings: a t-shirt, a clean pair of jeans, socks, underwear, from a laundry basket he had never unloaded. Maybe he would take Laney somewhere for dinner, maybe they'd drive to the next town, where they wouldn't have to talk to people they didn't want to talk to during their meal. And for a moment, he softened, reminded of Laney's warmth, her kindness to him. In a time of his life when he just kept losing things that were dear to him, when he felt he could no longer trust anyone, at least he still had Laney. At least he could trust her.

He grabbed a button-down shirt from his closet and placed it on top of his small stack of belongings. He closed his bedroom door and walked briskly down the hall, his feet heavy on the wooden planks. He walked back through the kitchen and slipped on his boots. Transom was no longer at the kitchen table, but Chase could hear him talking in the other room. The door was closed. He was always talking in there, with the door closed. Making plans, scheduling his meetings, negotiating with timber companies and oilmen. Didn't Transom feel just a little bit guilty about arranging the destruction of the farm, right there in the house where Jack and Maggie had lived, where they'd built a life together? In that same room, Jack had, for decades, sketched out his plan for the year, crunched numbers, bargained with seed companies and equipment vendors. With all his resources, couldn't Transom have figured out some other place to work? He could've shown some respect, if not for Chase, then at least for Jack and Maggie. In disgust, Chase thundered out of the house, slamming the door as he went.

—

The next day, Chase came back to the farm, took the .308 out of the gun cabinet, and drove the four-wheeler out to the middle of the property. Transom had finished the last of Jack's venison from the freezer, and Chase wanted the meat. At least that's what he told himself. But as he hunkered down in a small clump of trees, a spot he'd never hunted in his life, he shifted the scope back and forth between a doe standing at the edge of the cow pasture and a group of men as they worked their way across a field of corn he'd planted the week before.

When he'd first gotten back to the farm that morning, the field had been covered in a thick fog, but now it was lifting, like a stage curtain, floating upward, the sun flickering over the wet grass. He could now see that Transom was with the men as they mounted the hill and paused at the edge of the woods, what remained of them. Transom hadn't clear-cut everywhere, just some places. In that particular spot, a patch of evergreens and hardwoods remained at the top of the hill, creating a sort of border effect, but then, just out of sight, as Chase had discovered when he'd confronted the young man on the skidder, things had been cut hard. An hour earlier, bulldozers and an excavator had pulled up on flatbed trailers. The oil company had arrived, and they were to begin moving earth.

Chase continued watching Transom and his team of men through the scope. He felt mildly ashamed for spying like this, like some kind of creep, especially since it meant he was pointing a weapon in their direction. He thought of Pete Winslow, the peeping tom who'd been arrested after he was caught watching Kate Appleton through the bedroom window of her house on Main Street. But this was different, Chase reasoned. Pete Winslow was a voyeur, a weirdo. He hid in the bushes and fantasized. Chase was merely keeping track of what was happening to his family's farm.

He thought of leaving, sometimes. Packing up his truck, asking Laney to go with him. They could drive and drive until they found a place that seemed suitable, a new place to call home. They could land somewhere and start over, where nobody knew them or their histories. The idea of it was appealing, but it also terrified him, and saddened him, too. He couldn't really leave Fallen Mountains, could he? Everything he'd ever known and loved was here, on the farm, this tiny patch of the world.

In his more rational moments, Chase could remember that none of this was personal. This was just Transom being himself, being how he had always been. If he set his mind on something, it didn't matter what it took, who or what he had to plow through to get it; he would make it happen at any cost. He'd done it as a young boy, manipulating his mother, nagging and acting up until he had his way. He'd done it as a baseball player, insisting on a certain catcher until the coach had to refigure the whole lineup just so Transom had the guy he wanted. Chase was sure he'd been doing the same thing, all the years he'd been gone, and he was doing it again, now. Chase had always known that was how Transom worked; he'd just never been on the other side of things the way he was now.

As things at the farm became more devastating, the loss of Jack somehow grew worse and worse, the pain ebbing but then gathering weight and sweeping over Chase again. How was it that just six months ago he was driving Jack over the farm lanes in the pickup, mapping out the strategies for spring, calculating seed? Jack, giver of grace. Jack, patron of wisdom. Why hadn't he just told Chase everything? Why hadn't he let Chase try to help? Maybe something could've been done. Maybe the farm could've been saved. But instead, Jack had kept it all a secret, and Chase had been forced to decide with too little time, with too few options. Chase was angry about that, somewhere deep in his heart; he was angry at Jack for leaving a mess and for leaving him to face that mess alone. And now, as if losing Jack and the farm hadn't been bad enough, he'd lost Transom, too.

The men on the hill disappeared, one by one, into the woods.

Chase shifted the rifle to watch the doe through the scope, the way she lowered her head and nosed the grass, content and unsuspecting. He centered the crosshairs to the position just behind her front shoulder, where, behind the doe's summer coat, golden and glistening, were the heart and lungs. He waited, palms wet. It had been a long time since he'd hunted, a long time since he'd taken a life—was he ready? Could he do it? Of course he could. The steps felt familiar, second nature, right. He slid his thumb along the ridges of the safety and pressed it off with a sharp, hollow click. The wind picked up, and the doe raised her head, smelling the air, stomping a foot. He took a deep breath and exhaled, gathering courage, calming his nerves. His right pointer finger pressed in against the trigger, slowly, with precision and patience, so as not to cause any movement in the rifle itself. There was a terrible crack, a powerful kick into his right shoulder, and then the reverberations off the ridges. He palmed open the bolt, popped out the casing, and looked through the scope again. The doe jumped, one swift surge to her left, then took a few slow steps, stumbled, and fell.

AFTER

RED SAT ON THE BACK PORCH OF HIS HOUSE IN THE dark, crickets roaring, fireflies blinking across the yard, sweet melody of lights. A lifetime ago, he'd watched Sue and Junior as they'd run barefoot through the grass one summer night, palms stretched out into the dark, reaching and grabbing them. Sue had come up and hugged him and her hair was warm and soft against his cheek. They'd used a nail to punch holes into the metal lid of a Mason jar, and they'd let Junior keep them in his room for a night. A firefly night-light, he'd called it.

Tonight Red sipped whiskey alone, his third glass, and he never drank, so everything blurred and the noise was worse and the memories loomed with a greater tug than they would, minus the alcohol.

"I know what you're thinking," Red said aloud, to the crickets and fireflies, to Ghost Sue, to the heavy night. "I need to tell him about what happened with Possum. The investigator, Mick Dashel." He lifted his glass and swirled the liquid. "I need to come clean."

Ghost Sue leaning back in the rocker beside him, waiting for him to finish.

"You know, it seems so black and white now, but at the time, it wasn't. I need you to know that." He took a sip. "Junior hadn't had his surgeries yet. We were up most nights, you and me, and remember? He'd scream and scream and hold his ears and beg us to make it stop. Terrible thing, your own child pleading for you to take their pain away, and there's nothing you can do but hold him and pray and wait. Four years of that and I couldn't take it anymore." He finished off the glass and poured another. "And that's what it came down to. It was get Junior the help he needed, or let him go on suffering. Who knows how long it would've gone on, how bad things would've gotten. That's the choice I was left with, and yes, I chose my son, I chose to get him the help he needed. He was five years old and I'm his father and I did what any father would've done." The words slurring now. He leaned forward, elbows on his knees. "I don't regret it. I don't regret doing what I had to, to help him."

—

Seventeen years earlier, when Red drove out to the shale pit and found Possum in the trunk, he leaned in and squeezed the boy's bony shoulder. "Can we get you out of there?" he asked gently.

Possum sobbed, but in the light of the flashlight, Red could see him nod. He unfolded the boy, who'd wound his arms around his knees like a bat, and helped him out of the trunk. He was thin and short and too light for a high schooler. Wet, too: sweat and urine. How long had he been in there? Red handed him his own canteen of water and helped Possum ease down onto the shale.

"Take a drink, son." He went to the Jimmy and grabbed a blanket from the back, then hung it over Possum's shoulders.

For a long time, they sat there, night folding in on them, the roar of the crickets, the moths and mosquitoes quivering toward the yellow of the flashlight. Both of them jumped when a screech owl wailed, its awful sound too similar to a woman screaming in distress. Red flickered the flashlight over the lot and across the trees. Was someone there, watching them? The 30-30 lay beside him.

"Want to tell me what happened?" Red asked, after a long time.

"No," Possum said, voice shuddering.

Red pulled the blanket tighter around the boy's shoulders and sighed. "Do you remember anything?"

"I want to go home."

Red tilted his head and looked at the sky, the moon a white-gray crescent, the stars endless out there, no light from any city, different from the Pittsburgh sky he'd grown up watching. "Was it the Shultz kid?"

Possum began to shake uncontrollably, the air sputtering from his lips, his shoulders heaving. The words came out in convulsions: "Can you take me home, please?"

Red lifted Possum to his feet. Holding onto his elbow, he helped him limp over to the Jimmy, Possum so weak he couldn't stand. Red lay the blanket across the seat and lifted Possum in. He drove Possum home to his mother's trailer and helped him hobble inside, where they found Vance passed out drunk, slung across the couch, beer cans on the floor and coffee table, empty bottle of vodka on Vance's chest.

"Your mother home?" Red asked.

Possum shook his head. "She's at work."

"You need a hand getting cleaned up?" Red asked awkwardly, looking around at the mess inside the trailer. At the time, he couldn't have known that, a year later, he'd be there in that trailer yet again, under very different circumstances, Vance and Lissette on the floor, but Vance spilling blood from his head, Possum wide-eyed, figurine in hand.

"Naw," Possum said.

"I'll be by tomorrow," Red told him, stepping back onto the porch. He took Possum by the shoulder and looked him in the eye. "We'll take care of this, I promise."

But he hadn't kept that promise. After dropping Possum off, Red stopped by the house to tell Sue he'd be late—she would worry, he knew—and that stop had taken a little longer than he'd anticipated, Junior shrieking with ear pain, and Red giving Sue a break, holding Junior until he fell asleep. When, eventually, he made it back to the shale pit to check the vehicle for evidence, it was gone.

The next morning, first thing, he headed straight to JT Shultz's office, and that's when things really went awry. Red told him what had happened, the car in the shale pit, Possum balled up and soaked in the trunk, also what he'd seen in the woods, Transom standing there, watching him, then disappearing in the trees.

JT lit a cigar and sat in his wide leather chair, staring out the huge panel of glass that overlooked the factory floor. Below, half of Fallen Mountains worked in long lines, seated on hard rolling chairs, bent over their parts, sliding the next piece along the assembly.

"Been a tough stretch for him recently, Transom. What with his mother and all. He's the one who found her. Rushed her to the hospital. Saved her life, doctor said."

Red wanted to know what that had to do with anything, but he stood there in front of his boss, his wife's boss, everyone's boss, and kept quiet.

JT tilted his chin up and blew smoke across the room. He took a deep breath and looked at Red. "Life is complicated, isn't it? People are complicated. We think we know someone's story, but we never do, not the whole story."

"Your son's committed a crime," Red said quietly, shoving his hands into the pockets of his khakis. He thought of Junior, auburn hair like Sue, toothy smile and skinny legs. "You understand, I can't just sweep it under the rug."

JT tilted his head. "Well, you *could*." He leaned back in his chair, folded his arms across his chest. "Here's the trouble, Red. You had no witnesses, isn't that right? I mean, you think you saw Transom, but it was dark. You told me that yourself. You said there was a car, but—" he shrugged for emphasis—"there's no car." He took a deep drag from his cigar and blew the smoke toward Red.

Red clenched his teeth. "I'll talk to the victim."

JT took another drag. "Listen, I hate for it to come to this, but you should know that we're cutting back here at the factory." He paused, looking out at the little bodies at work. "How long has your wife been here?"

Red saw where it was going, the conversation, spinning and plummeting like an airplane going down. They relied on Sue's job for health insurance. Junior's surgery, just eight weeks away.

"Your wife, what's her name again?"

"Sue," Red said, through gritted teeth.

"And you've got a son, isn't that right?"

"Junior."

"Yes, Junior. He has some health problems, if I recall correctly. Costs the company a lot of money, to tell you the truth." JT smiled, his green eyes studying Red. He took another drag and then extinguished the cigar in a glass ashtray. "So what I'm saying here, Sheriff, is that we're all tangled up here, in Fallen

Mountains, the nine hundred fifty of us who live here. We're all connected. And we need to look out for each other, best we can. You understand my meaning?"

Red wanted to reach across the wide mahogany desk and take the man by the throat. He wanted to hold JT against the glass, still by the throat, so that every person working below could look up and see someone doing what each and every one of them had probably imagined doing, at one point or another. What kind of man used another man's child as leverage? Red's fury was burning on his face; he could see a reflection of himself in the glass behind JT. His pulse raced and he began to sweat. No, he wanted to say. I'm not going to be manipulated into covering this up for you. No.

And then he thought of Junior waking in the middle of the night, the sheets twisted around his small body, his hand over his ear, screaming and screaming, *Daddy, please make it stop, please!* Red thought of how long it could go on, how bad it could get for his son—hearing loss already, vertigo, too—and he swallowed hard and looked out the glass wall behind JT, and in that horrid room with the sweet-foul smell of cigar smoke, Red made a choice, a choice that would haunt him for the rest of his life.

He nodded slightly, spun on his heels, and walked out of the room.

———

On the back porch of his house on Crocus Street, Red sat alone in the dark with the glass of whiskey in his hand and the bottle on the table beside him. Two months after that conversation with JT, Junior had his big ear surgery. It marked the end of the night waking, the crying in pain, his little boy doubled over and pleading. Red had never gone back to Possum's trailer like he promised, not until a year later, when Possum himself called in his own different crime.

At the time, Red had been able to reason his way through his choices. When Red had asked him that night at the shale pit, Possum said he didn't remember anything. His mother wasn't home; her boyfriend, passed out on the couch. And the car, which may have provided some evidence, was gone. The only thing Red had to go on was his own memory, and as he played the events over and over in his mind, winding the moments back on themselves like an old videotape, he began to question himself, too. How sure was he that the person he'd seen in the woods was Transom Shultz? Sure enough to accuse him of a serious crime, potentially testify against him in court and send him to prison? Red didn't know Transom personally; he'd never really spoken to the kid. Sure, in a town as small as Fallen Mountains, they'd crossed paths: at the gas station, at the grocery store. But most of what he knew of Transom Shultz stemmed from what he read in the *Fallen Mountains Gazette*. Sports page stuff: no-hitters, district championships. Transom in a black-and-white photograph from a game, arm high in the air, releasing a baseball.

And it had been dark that night, mostly. Hadn't it?

He could almost convince himself, almost, but then the Faulkner quote would swim through his consciousness, the past not even past: times when Possum would look at him, those gigantic eyes of his, at Wheeler's Diner, when they both happened to be grabbing a meal, or at the dollar store, and Red could sometimes see little surfs of disappointment rippling across

Possum's face. Well, it had been disappointment, for a while. But maybe that wasn't what was there anymore. Maybe what he saw in Possum's face had shifted into something different. Eyes dark and shadowed, too many years of restless sleep. Mouth taut, a constant scowl. Maybe what Red saw there—and this was what really worried him—maybe it wasn't disappointment, but rage.

BEFORE

POSSUM WOKE IN A SWEAT: THE NIGHTMARE AGAIN, half-dream, half-memory, the two so knotted and twisted that they'd long ago fused together, so that by this point he was no longer all that sure which parts were true. Even back then, the night it happened, the day and the weeks right after, he couldn't quite remember everything. How his shirt became the thing that held his mouth and eyes closed, the thing that bound his hands and feet. How long he lay in that trunk, folded up and afraid. These were details he'd tried and tried to remember; he'd even tried to dream those parts, that's how bad he wanted to know, but still, nothing.

His eyes fluttered open, the light of day burning and sharp. He was in his bed, he was home, he was thirty-three. It was May. Each time, he walked himself through the same four steps back to reality: where he was at that moment, what building he was in, how old he was. Then, the month. He'd figured out that by using these steps, he could pull himself from the dream and get a grip on where he really was, both in time and space. Ground himself.

He sat up in his bed and reached for the glass of water he kept on his nightstand, the weight of the dream still heavy on his limbs, his neck stiff, his brain foggy. Seventeen years later and he still couldn't free himself from that night. A thousand times he'd wanted to tell Laney, because maybe that would be therapeutic, maybe it would do some good, but it might also make things worse. She'd have questions; he'd have to provide answers. He'd looked into therapies. Hypnotists, psychologists. He'd researched on the Internet and found plenty of ideas. Seven steps toward forgetting a bad dream. How to fall back asleep after a nightmare. Nothing helped. The one thing reading through all those posts and websites did for him was make him realize he wasn't the only person who suffered from recurring nightmares. Which was, he conceded, a small comfort.

Possum sat up. To the left of his bed, just above the nightstand, there was a picture: a stock photograph, in a thick frame with blue matte. He placed his hands carefully on the right side of the frame, and gave it a gentle tug. The front of the frame swung open, and inside, there was a handgun, the only weapon he'd ever owned, a gift he'd never told a single soul about, not even Laney. He reached inside, took it out, and slumped back into bed.

———

Years after Possum left the letters on the front porch of the Shultz residence, after Marjane Shultz attempted suicide, after Transom tried to kill him, after Possum bashed in Vance's skull and done time for it, Possum's mother gave him this gun.

"This was your father's," she said.

It was spring, a few months after he got out of prison. He'd already gone to his first auction and sold his first item online. He'd already found a good spot for morel mushrooms on Chase's farm, and he was tossing them in melted butter in a skillet in his mother's kitchen.

Possum turned to her, the mushrooms sizzling, water capering up and throwing steam. "My father?" He'd never told his mother about the letters he'd found, but of course she knew. Still, neither one of them had ever spoken of it.

She held out a wooden box. Possum wiped his hands on his jeans and set the box on the counter, then lifted the lid. Heavy. Inside, a pistol, shiny and new, the stock a tigered brown—antler, Possum figured. The barrel was black, etched with intricate designs and plated in gold. He'd never held a handgun before, and the weight of it surprised him. Smith and Wesson, .44 Magnum. He looked at his mother.

She leaned back against the counter and took a deep breath. "I know you figured it out. I also know what you done: the letters, the gifts. The wagon. We both knew it. From the start we didn't handle anything right, neither one of us did." She looked out the window and stared at the lilac bush in the small side yard, heavy with purple blossoms. "It was complicated. When I got pregnant, Marjane was already pregnant. JT was unhappy but couldn't leave her, not when she was pregnant, and he tried to convince me to—to consider other options. But I wouldn't. I knew it would be hard. I was twenty-one and I knew what I was getting myself into, and I wanted to keep you. I wanted you."

Possum turned the .44 over in his hand again, unsure of how to feel about it.

"A long time ago, he gave it to me," she said. "For protection. You were little. He worried about us, here in the trailer park."

Possum placed it back into the box and slid it toward her. "You should keep it."

Lissette shook her head. "He would want you to have it." She sighed. "Listen, I need you to know that we loved each other, in the way that we could," she said. "And we loved you, too. Both of us." She reached out and placed her warm fingers on his neck. "He wasn't a father to you; I know that. But he thought of you as a son. You were always his son."

—

Now, Possum sat on his bed, holding the .44. The gift still brought up an assembly of conflicting emotions for him. On one hand, it suggested JT really did care about him and his mother. He wanted to keep them safe. On the other hand, JT hadn't given the gun to Possum; he'd given it to Lissette. Possum placed the gun back into the frame and swung the front closed again. He grabbed his pocket calendar, on the nightstand. Wednesday. He was supposed to talk to Alla in twenty minutes. Then he planned to go out to the national forest to look for some king bolete mushrooms, which he'd seen growing there the week before. He'd also been working on mapping a way to access his good spot for morels on the Hardy farm from the national forest. Now that Transom owned the place, Possum wouldn't dream of going the way he'd always gone, up the farm road, right past the house and barn. But the morel cache was on the far end of the property, and he was fairly certain he could get there if he bushwhacked from the national forest.

Before he set out for the forest, though, he had to take care of a small chore for Lissette. She'd promised him a dinner of pork and sauerkraut in exchange for washing her queen-sized comforter set. Since it wouldn't fit in either of their small washing machines without causing some sort of problem, the comforter set had to be taken to the laundromat.

He stood up and stretched and peered out at the morning, the sun pulling through, the fog burning off the baseball field across the street, the trees greened up and swaying. He picked out a pair of jeans and a white t-shirt and went to the bathroom to wash his face. He stared at himself in the mirror for a minute, tried to press his cowlick down with a dot of pomade he'd picked up at the store. No luck—the hair shot right back up. He brushed his teeth.

He logged in and waited for Alla. He sat there for forty minutes, anxiously rubbing his pointer finger over the knuckle of his thumb. He checked the time again. Was he early? Had he gotten the time wrong? Miscalculated? At his desk, he kept a chart he'd printed from a website that listed all the time zones in the world. He counted the hours ahead to Moscow once more. Alla should've been there. With each minute, Possum's anxiety deepened—he always assumed the worst in people; he tried not to, but he couldn't help it—and he wondered: Was Alla standing him up?

It was in Possum's nature to fret, and he knew that. He'd always been a worrier, even as a boy, at least that's what his mother said. Whenever she brought it up, Possum had to resist the urge to point out that maybe if she hadn't been running around with JT during his childhood, that maybe if she hadn't married that good-for-nothing prick Vance, maybe he wouldn't be that way. Saying those things would only hurt her, though, so he never actually did. She meant well. Besides, he suspected she probably already knew all of that, somewhere in that head of hers. She apologized sometimes: vague, strange apologies. "I'm sorry,"

Lissette would say. And he would say, "For what?" And she would look at him, a deep, remorseful sadness in her eyes, and say, "For all of it." He would tell her it was all right, that she needed to let it go, that he had let it go, even though that wasn't true.

What concerned him today was that he'd scared Alla off. In their previous conversation, Possum had said something about how pretty she was, and as soon as he'd typed it, he regretted it, second-guessed himself, felt insecure. Why would a woman like her have any interest in a guy like him? Why had he gone and mentioned her appearance? He hoped he hadn't come across as creepy.

Almost an hour later, Alla logged in, apologizing. A client had come into the shop, asking lots of questions, poking around, delaying her trip home. So Possum hadn't scared her off, after all. He was ridiculously relieved about this. Giddy, even. And then he felt embarrassed for his relief. They talked for a while and promised to connect again the next day, same time.

He slid into his red vest, hoisted the mesh laundry bag over his shoulder, locked the trailer door behind him, and headed down the street, a skip in his step. Possum walked almost everywhere in Fallen Mountains. You could see a lot more when you walked. You noticed more. In the summer months, you could see the thistle, its prickly stalk and pinkish tufts, growing along the banks by the 4th Street Bridge where the train used to cross. You couldn't see them from a car. Nor did you notice the hornet's nest that hung from the locust tree behind the laundromat. Or the people in their vehicles. In fact, Possum was sure he knew more about relationships in Fallen Mountains than anyone else. He knew, for instance, many months before the man's wife ever found out about it, that Ted Martin had been running around with Melissa Dexter. Possum had seen them in his truck five or six times, always around lunchtime, and he had put two and two together.

He knew also that in the months since his reappearance in Fallen Mountains, Transom Shultz had been meeting up with a man in the parking lot just outside of town, close to Possum's trailer. The guy drove a white F-250 with a lift kit and a roaring diesel engine and always wore sunglasses, so Possum never really got a good look at his face. The most distinguishing characteristic of this fellow was that he was always squeezing a purple grip strengthener, pump pump pump. At first, it seemed like the two of them got along, Transom and the gripper, but more recently, they seemed to be arguing every time they met up. The gripper had stopped coming alone, as well. Someone else was sitting in the truck, though Possum never saw the person get out.

As he got closer to the laundromat, Possum noticed Chase's gray Chevy in the lot. Inside, the two exchanged hellos.

"Nice comforter," Chase said.

"My mother's," Possum said with a smirk. It was off-white, with a pattern of enormous pink roses and three layers of lace around the edges.

Chase smiled a little. "Sure it is."

He looked older, Possum thought. His eyes were bloodshot, and dark circles had appeared beneath his bright blue eyes. His hair, which he had always kept short, had grown longer, a thick and wavy mess, and even though it was spring, a time when Chase should've been spending a good bit of time outdoors, he looked pale.

"Your washer broke?" Possum asked.

Chase pointed to two garbage bags of laundry. "The water ain't been right out at the farm." He paused, folded his arms, and leaned against a dryer. "Ever since they started digging around out there, something's been wrong with the well. The pressure's unpredictable. And sometimes it tastes bad. Like dirt. At least, that's what I figure went wrong. I mean, all them years, things were fine."

"It's a shame," Possum said.

Chase stared out the window, his mind elsewhere. "You can't imagine."

A concrete truck roared by, its large beehive end spinning slowly.

Possum leaned against the washer. He *could* imagine, he wanted to say. Not so much on the matter of the land, but on the feeling that your whole world had been yanked out from beneath you. Feeling alone. Feeling helpless. The same monster who had betrayed Chase had hurt Possum in ways he wished he could forget.

"There's men out there, maybe twenty, hard to say. I think they're living on the property because I don't see them leaving at night, and where would they go, anyway? Not like there's a hotel in town."

Possum had seen a few of these people, picking up Styrofoam boxes at Wheeler's, drinking Yuengling beer at Johnnie's bar. Once, he'd seen a pair of men he didn't know buying hand sanitizer, toilet paper, and deodorant at the grocery store.

"I don't know where they sleep. There's a trailer, but it wouldn't fit all of them. Maybe in their vehicles. Twelve different trucks out there, I counted. Here's the thing that really gets me, though. No job johnny. And they sure ain't coming to the house to go. So where are they doing it?"

Possum shook his head.

"In my fields is where. In the woods. Which they aren't really much of woods anymore, after Transom had the loggers come in and cut. All them people and no job johnny. What kind of operation are they running out there that they can't get a portable outhouse? You mean to tell me the oil company can't afford to rent one?" He took a deep breath and adjusted his hat. "I'm sorry. I'm rambling, wasting your time."

"It's all right."

"It's just I love that farm," Chase said, voice hoarse, cheeks growing red. "Love it more than anything in this world, which maybe that's a sin, to love something so much you'd do anything to save it—Jack would've said so, he would say I've got my priorities out of whack—but he was never in my position, having to watch the place go to pot, and nothing I can do about it." He started grabbing clothes from the garbage bag and loading them into a washer.

Possum pulled the comforter from the mesh bag and shoved it into an open washing machine.

"Can I ask you something, man to man, friend to friend, and you won't say nothing to anybody?"

Possum pushed the last pillowcase in and closed the washer door. "Sure."

"Did you think about it ahead of time?"

"What?"

"With Vance."

Possum frowned. The day he came home and saw his mother on the floor of the trailer, he'd thought she was dead. Vance had finally gone too far; he'd done her in. In the moment, all that hurt and frustration, not just toward Vance, who'd been pushing him around and hissing meanness at him for months, but also at Transom, who'd shoved him in a trunk a year earlier, and at Sheriff Redifer, who'd driven him home and promised he'd take care of things. On the day Possum laid into Vance, it was like every mean thing that had ever been done to him, every punch from his stepfather's thick fist, every night in the janitor's closet, every broken promise, all of those things gathered up inside him like one massive wave, pulling strength as it moved. It was a powerful thing, that much anger, the sense that it was taking you over. An ugly thing, too. "No," he told Chase, shaking his head. He fed quarters into the machine and started the cycle.

As he watched Chase continue to push laundry into the machine, he wanted to offer something—some advice, or an indication that he could relate to what his friend was going through—but he wasn't sure what to say. He couldn't tell what it was—fear, hurt, wrath, maybe all three—he saw churning in his friend's face, but it was full of emotion, more emotion than he had ever seen from the man he had always considered laid back and composed.

Possum thought of warning Chase: Don't get swept up in it, your anger. Don't let it take you under. Because Possum, of all people, knew that you couldn't just pull free when you wanted to. No, just the opposite. He thought about cautioning his old friend to let it go, while he could. If he still could. But he didn't, because a tiny, foul part of him loved the idea that now someone else hated Transom Shultz as much as he did.

AFTER

AFTER HIS NIGHT ON THE PORCH WITH JACK DANIELS and Ghost Sue and the fireflies, Red woke up on the couch with a headache that blared and bloomed. The morning light a terrible affliction, the chanting cicadas outside the window, a greater travesty than usual. The family pictures on the wall, the television set, everything blurry, fringed in white. He lay on the couch, and the truth was he had no recollection of how he'd gotten there—had he walked? Crawled?—or when he'd come in. Middle of the night? First light? He squinted at the clock and realized it was midmorning already. Leigh. He fumbled for his phone but couldn't find it. Surely Leigh had called, worried, and if he didn't get moving soon, she might show up at his front door with the spare key she knew he kept in his desk.

He dragged himself up from the couch. The room spun. He sat back down. "I know," he said out loud, to Ghost Sue, to himself. "I shouldn't have drank so much. Trust me, I know."

He stumbled out onto the back porch and found his phone, right between his glass and an empty bottle. No wonder he felt horrible.

Three missed calls from Leigh.

He slipped his phone in his pocket, tucked the bottle under his arm, and headed back into the kitchen and sat there, looking at the stained glass trinkets suction-cupped to the window, items collected by Sue over the years. Anytime they'd gone somewhere new, she looked for some little piece of stained glass. A ruby-throated hummingbird, beak in a pink flower, from Canada. A cactus from a trip to Arizona one year. A waterfall from Watkins Glen. This is it, he thought. This is what you have after a quarter century of marriage. An empty kitchen and a bunch of stained glass knickknacks hanging in your kitchen window: shiny, colorful reminders of what you used to have.

Rapping. One two three. Knuckle to glass.

"Sheriff?" Mick Dashel at the front door, hollering through the glass. "Sheriff, you in there? If you don't answer, I'm gonna open the door. I got a key. Your secretary sent me over."

Red stood and ran water from the spigot into a glass and slumped into the captain's chair at his kitchen table and surrendered himself to the fact that there was no getting out of the predicament he'd fashioned.

Key sliding into the lock, door handle, blinds tapping the window from the movement. "Sheriff? You here?"

He heard Mick Dashel's footsteps on the floorboards, coming closer.

"In here," he called softly.

Mick Dashel appeared in the kitchen. "What's going on? Why didn't you answer? Leigh's about to have a coronary. We thought something was wrong."

Tell him, Ghost Sue whispered. Just tell him.

"I had too much to drink last night."

Mick eased into the chair across from him and looked at the empty bottle of whiskey. "Looks like it."

"There's something else."

Mick leaned in closer, his blue eyes bright. "All right."

"Long time ago, I think Transom Shultz may have kidnapped and tried to kill a person. Thomas Miller. Possum, he goes by. They were kids, both of them, fifteen, sixteen. I got a call, Possum hadn't shown up to work." He told Mick what happened at the shale pit and then afterward, all those years ago. His heart was racing now, the room gaining a new clarity, the stress subsuming the hangover.

Mick Dashel traced the outline of the placemat on the table and then looked hard at Red. "How long you been carrying that around?"

Red sighed, the secret that had haunted him, now out in the open. He closed his eyes, the room white and spinning again. "Seventeen years."

"And you're thinking maybe Possum has decided to seek his revenge."

"Yes."

Mick shrugged. "Statistically speaking, it's very unlikely. But you never know. We'll bring him in, ask him some questions if that'll make you feel better. I'll run him through the ringer."

"Nobody knows about it."

"I get it," Mick said. He looked at the window, his eyes scanning the pieces of stained glass. "Let me make you some coffee, Sheriff," he said, and walked to the kitchen to look for a mug.

—

A few hours later, they were in the boardroom of the police station again, with Possum across the table. Red wiped his hands, clammy with sweat, on his jeans. He took a deep breath and prayed he could hold it together. And then he prayed again that Possum wasn't involved with Transom's disappearance, because Red wasn't sure but maybe, maybe if Possum had indeed done something sinister, that meant Red was also somehow at fault.

"How'd you come across a name like Possum?" Mick asked.

Possum snorted and shrugged his shoulders.

"Would you prefer to be called Thomas?" Mick asked, leaning back in his chair.

Possum seemed to think about this, twisting his mouth to the side and tilting his head. "Possum's fine," he said after a moment.

"Okay, then," Mick said. "Possum, tell us about your relationship with Transom Shultz."

"Relationship? We didn't have a relationship."

"Fair enough. But you didn't like him, isn't that right? You two had a falling-out of sorts."

Possum grimaced. "A falling-out. Yeah, that's one way of putting it." He glared at Red.

"Care to elaborate?"

"Sheriff Redifer knows exactly what I'm talking about. He was there. Why don't you ask him about it?"

Red's face burned. He pulled out his handkerchief and blotted his forehead. It was so hot in that room, so unbearably hot. "Possum—"

Possum held his gaze. "At least you brought in backup this time, Sheriff," he said to Red. "So you don't forget to follow up."

Mick raised a finger to Red, a reminder of what he'd told him before Possum had arrived. *Don't say anything, not a word. You talk, I'm gonna ask you to step out.* "Sheriff Redifer's not the one being asked to answer questions right now," Mick said to Possum. "You keep that in mind."

Red reached for his water, his heart pounding loudly, chest, head, ears, roaring like a train racing closer. Right then, he was lamenting his decision to tell Mick Dashel about what had happened and have Possum come in for questioning. He was thinking, too, that Mick had probably been right—he should've waited outside, he should've gone to Wheeler's. He shouldn't be there.

Mick softened his tone. "Transom was a bully. Bullies never strike just once. Were there other times? Other things he did?"

Possum took a deep breath. "There were other times," he said. "But that was years ago. I'm over it."

"Wow," Mick said. "After what he did, the fear, the anxiety. I mean, the way the sheriff tells it, seems like he intended to kill you. And you've just moved on? Forgiven him?" There was no sarcasm in his voice or face. He folded his arms. "Good for you."

Possum leaned back in the swivel chair and looked at the ceiling. "That's right."

Mick slid a Coke across the table to Possum and opened a bottle of water for himself.

"What happened between you two?"

Possum shrugged.

"You don't know, or you don't feel like talking about it?"

"Both."

"I've always hated men who hurt women," Mick said. "Sounds like that guy, Vance, your stepfather, he got what he deserved."

Possum traced the rim of his Coke can.

"Did the same thing happen with Transom? He probably had it coming, too."

Red's heart thundered in his chest—please, please say no.

Possum cracked open the soda and took a sip, cringing at the sweetness. "You ain't gonna get me to confess nothing with Transom Shultz because I didn't do nothing."

Red breathed out heavily, relief sweeping over him.

Mick nodded. "But you can understand why you'd be a suspect in this investigation, man. Last time someone really pissed you off, you bashed in his skull. From where I'm sitting, it looks like you might have what we call an anger management issue, like you lash out at people you don't like. So when a person who tried to kill you—a person you have every right to hate—goes missing, well, we need to ask questions."

Possum had done nineteen months in the county jail for his violence toward Vance, who'd suffered minor permanent brain damage, not to mention an eye that strayed off to the left after that. Red had done what he could to make sure the judge and jury knew of the ongoing abuse—he'd gotten the high school guidance counselor to testify on Possum's behalf—and Possum had been treated with a good deal of leniency. It was, he felt, the least he could do.

"Yeah, I didn't like the guy," Possum said with a shrug. "Well, let's be honest: I hated him. But I avoided him at all costs. I did when we was in school, and I've been doing it since he come back."

"Were you afraid of him?"

Possum's mouth turned downward slightly. "Naw. I didn't want nothing to do with him is all."

"I'm sure you can prove your whereabouts for Memorial Day weekend."

Possum reached into the pocket of his red vest and took out a small blue calendar. He smiled, a wide boyish grin, his brown eyes big and round. "I was at an auction over in Empire on Saturday," he said. "On Sunday, I went to my mother's. I watched tennis on television. Monday, I went to another auction, over in Somerset."

"Tennis?"

"Okay, she watched tennis and I slept on the couch. But I was there. I spend every Sunday at her place. Everybody knows that."

"What about Friday night?"

"I was at the shooting match, then I went home and talked to my friend."

"You got any way of proving all of this?"

"I bought stuff at the auctions. I registered and wrote a check to pay for my things." He leafed through his wallet. "Here," he said, handing Mick two stubs from the auctions, both dated. "My mom can vouch for me for Sunday. And I talked to Alla— that's my friend—online, so there's record of that for Friday night. I'm sure you know how to track down a thread in a discussion board."

Mick tapped his tablet and photographed the dated stubs. He noted something else in his tablet, then stood. "You're free to go, Mr. Miller," he said. "Thanks for your time."

Possum tucked his calendar in his vest pocket, stood up, and walked out the front door.

Mick and Red remained at the table.

"He has an alibi, Sheriff," he said with a shrug. "Receipts, witnesses. I don't think he's our guy."

Red thought of that night at the shale pit. He thought of the scene he'd come to, a year later, at Possum's trailer: the blood, all that blood, pooled on the floor of the trailer, Vance's cheekbone protruding, the eyeball popped from its socket, and Possum sitting in the corner, eagle clenched in his fist, his jeans stained red, his shirt and face splattered, too. Red rubbed the handkerchief across his neck. "Appreciate you talking to him."

Mick slid his handheld recorder into his back pocket and tucked his tablet under his arm. "No problem."

Red headed back to his desk.

"Sheriff?" Mick said, leaning against the doorframe. "Hope you don't mind me saying so, but you might consider talking to him. Possum. Might make you feel a little better, getting things off your chest."

"What would I say?"

Mick shrugged. "Sorry, I guess. You could tell him you're sorry."

BEFORE

IT WAS FRIDAY, MEMORIAL DAY WEEKEND, AND LANEY had it off, one of six days each year that the factory closed. Chase told her he was taking her out. They picked up a pizza and drove to the woods, not where they usually walked with Kip, but up and up, over miles of dirt road. They hiked a trail to where there were thousands of boulders, high up on the mountain, where the trees had been cleared, so that you could look out and see the whole valley, all the farms and the town, too. Laney had always liked this spot, the way you were positioned above the world, the way some magnificent force of nature had left the boulders there like a giant's playground, although as they climbed out of the car, a memory from way back slunk its way to her. Transom and her, one chilly fall evening, a long time ago. She shook it off.

Chase spread out an old blanket on top of a rock that was big enough for the both of them and motioned for Laney to take a seat. He opened the pizza box, offered her a beer, and then sat down on the other side of the pizza. Today was warm, the first truly hot day they'd had in Fallen Mountains, a sudden shift in weather from a cool and rainy spring. The days were growing longer; summer was gaining ground.

Despite the ugliness unfolding at the farm, things were good. Transom was wrapped up in his new girlfriend; he'd bought her some preposterous engagement ring, and he seemed—well, he seemed happy, as far as Laney could tell. There were still times that her mind tiptoed toward him, when her body remembered. Over the past few months, she'd realized she had a lot of memories with Transom, some with Chase and some without, and it was possible she'd never be fully free of him, as a person can never fully be free of someone they loved. But he seemed to have moved on, and she was moving on, too.

She looked at Chase, studying his face the way she did sometimes. He used to blush and turn away, and she'd be embarrassed and look away, too. But this time he held her gaze and smiled. She gathered her courage. "Are we together?" she asked.

"What do you mean, are we together?"

She twisted her mouth to the side and narrowed her eyes. "You know what I mean."

"Do you want us to be together?"

"Chase."

He laughed then. "I'm just asking."

"Don't make me say it."

He slid the pizza box behind them and pulled her close. "I think we are. I think we're together," he said.

"I guess what I mean is, do you see this going anywhere?"

He shrugged. "I'm not ready to get married yet, if you're asking me," he said with a smile. He shoved a bite of pizza in his mouth.

She punched him on the arm. "I'm not asking you to *marry* me," she said. "That's the one thing I will not ask you, is to marry me, I'm warning you now." She took a sip of beer and put her arm around his waist. "I just need to know that this means something to you."

"Of course it means something."

That was enough, wasn't it? It had to be enough because, as much as she wanted more, this might be all she'd ever get. Chase would never be a person who tucked love letters under her pillow; he'd never be like Jack, who would regularly pronounce his love for Maggie, whose words and affection were so deeply a part of him that he couldn't have rid himself of them if he'd wanted to. And she could feel it, she kept on telling herself. In her heart, she knew: the way Chase looked at her, the way he touched her—something had changed for him.

—

Chase shifted his weight, the boulder growing uncomfortable beneath him. With Laney at his side, asking for some kind of affirmation, he wanted to say that he wouldn't have made it without her, that she had become everything to him because she was all that was left. He wanted to tell her that he loved the way the sun caught her blonde hair right then, the way her eyes would change each day and that he never knew exactly what color they'd be until he looked at them good and hard. He wanted to say, I think maybe I've fallen in love with you. But he didn't. The words just wouldn't come out.

Jack had always been so good at it, telling the people around him that he loved them. When Chase would come home from school as a boy, Jack would say, "Tell me one interesting thing you learned today," and when Chase would explain something he'd learned, Jack would nod his head in approval and pat Chase on the back. He'd tussle his hair or pull him in for a hug and say that he was so proud. Even when Chase hit the more awkward years of his youth, when he outgrew Jack and lumbered around the kitchen, Jack never stopped all of that, the hair tussling and hugging and saying he was proud. Jack also made it a point to tell Maggie how lovely she looked, how much he loved her, and he did it often.

Maggie was the same, her words flowing out of her like a spring. She was the type of person who noticed things. At church, or at the grocery store, when a woman got a new haircut, Maggie would compliment her on it. And she'd be sincere about it, so that even if it wasn't really a good haircut, Maggie would find a way to say something nice. Chase figured that was part of the reason why everybody loved Maggie, why they loved both of his grandparents. Both of them had a way of making you feel better about yourself, just from being around them for a while. It was like you became a better person from being in their presence.

Transom had soaked up some of that, one way or another. Not in the way that you'd feel better about yourself from being around him, but in that you felt important when you were with him, at least if he was in the right mood. Charisma.

But Chase wasn't like that. It was one of the things he hated about himself, his stoicism, his inability to express his emotions, but after his parents had died, after those three days in the woods, he'd walled himself off from all of it: highs and lows, happiness and sadness, anger and loss. It was the only way he knew how, the only way to protect himself. There was a steadiness in keeping everything and everyone at arm's length, a security. All these years, it had worked out well enough. But he was also missing out, and he knew it. He just didn't understand how a person did it—felt some things and felt them fully but not so fully that they swallowed you up. He wanted to let them out sometimes, like when Jack had died and he wished he could cry, or with Laney, when she looked at him with her ocean eyes, but he just couldn't. He hoped that his actions—the flowers he'd brought Laney earlier in the week, the picnic he'd planned—captured the way he felt about her, but he knew she still wanted to hear the words. And he wished, he hoped that one day, he'd figure out how to give her that.

The sun was beginning its descent. Down in the valley, it would be growing dark. People would turn on their porch lights and holler for their children to come inside. Neighbors would wrap up their conversations. Up on the ridge, though, it was still bright, and the sun was throwing wide, orange light at them.

"Your hair looks red in this light," he said, reaching out and touching her. "I never noticed it before."

She nodded and looked out across the valley, shielding her eyes. She finished her last bite of pizza and turned to him. "My mom used to say she liked my hair best in this light, in the last few minutes of the day. She liked that it looked red, when it never looked red any other time. I told her, your hair does the same thing, but she didn't believe me."

Chase didn't know Laney's mother, Kristen, very well, but he knew, like everyone else in town, that she hadn't been much of a mother for many years. Maggie told him once that Kristen had been severely depressed, and had even gone away for a while on account of the depression, but Laney never talked about that, and Chase never asked. He of all people could understand the desire for privacy—if she wanted to talk about it, she would. He wasn't going to press her to share things that were painful. He knew it was easier just to push down those memories, hide them deep in the caverns of your mind, where you could, at least most days, forget about them.

"Is it strange with your mom, not having her live in Fallen Mountains anymore?" Chase asked. Kristen had moved away to Maryland a few years earlier, after Laney bought her grandmother's house.

Laney shrugged. "I guess so. But she's happy, you know. She finally met a good guy. Larry. She always wanted to be married, have a normal family. She wanted to take better care of me, I get that. She just couldn't."

Chase smiled. "I like that about you. You see the best in people. You've got grace for them, I should say. You forgive."

She looked away, grabbing the two empty beer bottles and sliding them into the cooler. Chase stood up and reached his arms up into the air, stretching. Though it was growing dark, the air remained warm and heavy. "I've got plans for the rest of the evening," he said. "Hope you're free."

"More?" Laney said. "A girl could get used to this, you know."

"We're going to the shooting match. First one of the season." He grinned. "There's nothing like having your girl show you up, with the whole town there watching." Laney was an excellent shot, especially with targets.

She smiled. "Want me to miss a few on purpose?"

"I don't need your pity," he said. "Besides, if I beat you, I want it to be fair and square."

Chase held the cooler in his free hand, and Laney draped the blanket over her shoulder. The two of them looped arms as they scrambled over the boulders and walked back to the truck. "So that's why you brought the beer," Laney said as they climbed into the truck and closed the doors. "You're trying to get an edge. But I know I don't got to tell you that it would take more than two beers to throw off my aim."

—

At the shooting match, Chase was doing well until Transom showed up with Teresa. Everyone turned to look. Individually, the two of them would have gotten attention. Transom's thick, athletic build and handsome face had earned him notice for years. Teresa, as much as Chase hated to admit it, was beautiful. Stunning, really, and so young. She was the type of woman who, no matter how much you tried not to, you couldn't help but steal a look at. There was just something so perfect, so disconcerting and sweet, about her face. The two of them together, Transom and Teresa, they entered the room, and people gawked like they were royalty.

Chase tried to focus. He lined up the bead so that just the very top of it showed, centered his aim on the bull's-eye of the target, exhaled, and slowly squeezed the trigger. At least when he had his ear protection on, he could block out Teresa's irritating giggle and Transom's unmistakable, deep voice. But still, knowing they were there, knowing Transom was watching him, put him on edge. His shots grew worse by the minute. He began to feel hot, suddenly hot, but even downing his cold beer didn't help to cool him off. Sweat formed on his forehead; his safety glasses fogged up.

In between rounds, Laney found him. "Are you okay? We can go home," she said, her brows furrowed in concern. "Let's just go home." She squeezed his hand.

Transom approached. Teresa trailed behind him. "Laney," he said, nodding. "Chase."

He placed his gun case on the table beside Chase and began to set up. Teresa leaned over and whispered something in

Transom's ear, the thin line of her red underwear peeking from her jeans, then headed for the bathroom. Laney looked at Chase and smirked.

"I didn't know you had a shotgun," Chase said, eyeing up the leather case that Transom began to unzip. He thought, that was just like Transom to go and buy a brand-new gun, for a shooting match.

Transom said nothing in response. He slid the gun out of its case, and that's when Chase recognized it. The etching of the man and his hunting dog, ducks soaring overhead. Jack's prized possession. Transom's hand lay lightly, possessively, over the stock.

In that moment, something gave way inside of Chase: he could sense a shift, a thing turning, a sudden heave of dark. He pictured grabbing the gun, shoving the butt of it to his shoulder, swinging it up, the barrel pressed to Transom's cheek. He imagined it all, how fast his body could rattle through the movements. It could be over—all that destruction at the farm, all those lies—it could be over in an instant.

But then a hand, a calm and familiar hand, touched Chase's back softly. He twitched. Laney laced her fingers through his and pulled him toward her. "Come on, Chase," she said, and tugged gently. Chase turned and followed her. He could feel his feet moving beneath him; he could hear the guns firing at their targets and the people around him laughing and cheering. But as he moved, it was like he was outside of himself, like he was hovering above, watching, like he wasn't really there.

AFTER

RED CALLED TUCK PHILIPS, THE LEADER OF THE
Fallen Mountains Emergency Task Force, which had
been set up five years earlier and which had been called
upon exactly once, when a toddler had tumbled down an old well
at the Orvetto farm. The boy was scraped and bruised and petri-
fied, but thankfully, fine. The idea of the Task Force was that,
since Red had no deputy, no backup, he could make one phone
call and have help within half an hour, should the need arise.

One by one, the six members of the Task Force showed up at
the Hardy farm in their pickups, and Red gathered them around
Chase's garden, black and yellow bees scrambling up the orange
blossoms of squash plants, the cosmos happy and white and pink
and swaying in the breeze, the June air heavy and warm. The
men looked at him, all good Fallen Mountains men he knew
and trusted, three of them young and two of them older, and he
announced, his voice shaking, "We're looking for a body here,
boys. Or anything else out of the ordinary, really. If you find
something, radio it in. Don't mess with it, don't touch anything.
Just call."

The small crowd nodded.

"I want you all to avoid the construction site, up on the hill
there," Red said, pointing. "Nobody is to go anywhere near it,

understand?" He thought of his run-in with the foreman and his purple grip strengthener, the vague threat, the thick-chested guy hovering in the background. The last thing they needed here was another missing person. Another body.

"This here's Mick Dashel," Red said, nodding. "He's a private investigator and he's gonna give us some direction, because, well, as you know, boys, this isn't the type of thing that we're accustomed to dealing with here in Fallen Mountains."

Mick Dashel stepped forward. "We're gonna split up. Sheriff Redifer and I already went through the house a few days ago. But I want a pair of people looking through the barn, the silo, too, that outbuilding over there." He pointed to his left.

"There's a root cellar out back," Red added, remembering that Chase Hardy had been in there, the time he'd come out to check Transom's vehicle.

Mick nodded. "Check that as well. And then once those places are checked, I want three people combing that section, over there," he said, pointing. "The field that's grown over, and the pasture behind the barn. Red and I will take those woods behind the construction site."

Red's heart lurched.

"So, you guys divide yourselves up into pairs, and let's plan on meeting back here at five to regroup." He paused. "And, fellas, be careful, please."

BEFORE

A FEW HOURS AFTER HIS OUT-OF-BODY EXPERIENCE AT the shooting match, Chase was in his room getting dressed, about to head to the barn to milk the cows. It was early, not yet 5:00 a.m. and still pitch dark outside. All night, he'd tossed and turned, trying to convince himself that Transom was just being his usual ignorant self, that he hadn't meant any harm, that he hadn't known how important that gun was to Jack. Chase was still jumpy, though, still on edge: a peculiar, unnerving feeling that his own skin might be twisted right off him like a snake's, and he didn't like it. As he pulled on his socks, he told himself that tackling the chores in the barn would help. He'd keep busy, work it off, wear himself out. By evening, he'd have a handle on his emotions.

He'd almost convinced himself he'd be fine when headlights flickered across the ceiling. He heard gravel crunching beneath tires, heard the back door open, footsteps in the mudroom, then a pause: someone removing shoes. More footsteps, but lighter.

"Chase? You here?"

Transom.

Chase pulled on his shirt and walked out of the bedroom. He wasn't prepared to see Transom face-to-face, not yet: he needed time. The sound of Transom's voice fanned his anger, and his pulse thudded in his temples. The house was small. There was no avoiding Transom, but maybe Chase could make it quick, slide past him, dodge a lengthy exchange, get to the barn. He walked briskly down the steps.

Transom stood in the living room, staring out the front window, transfixed. Moths, tens of them, fluttered at the front door, drawn to the porch light, clumsy and graceless, yellow and white. Transom turned to him and smiled. "Thought you might be up."

Just as Chase had suspected, Transom seemed unaware of the turmoil he'd caused. But Chase couldn't help wondering: Was Transom really so oblivious, so out of touch? Or was he just so consumed with his own wants and needs that no one else's mattered at all? "What are you doing here?" Chase asked. He'd heard Teresa telling Laney they were heading back to Empire after the shooting match.

Transom reached for the sofa table and grabbed a glass. He took a drink of brown liquid and squinted. "I did so well at the shooting match last night, I decided to go out and sit in the Nest for a bit, see if I can call in a gobbler."

Jack's gun: Chase's skin prickled. *Move*, he told himself. *Go to the barn. Do the chores.* He tried to squeeze past Transom, who blocked his path to the kitchen. "I need—"

"Plus Teresa, she's on me about my pills," Transom continued, still watching the moths, still unaware. "Says she's gonna leave me. I'll ignore her for a day or two, make sure she misses me, and then go up to Empire with flowers or something on Monday. You know how it is with us." Transom sighed.

Chase didn't know, actually—their volatile relationship, the stress of being involved in something so unpredictable, bewildered him.

"Them pills, they cost you, one way or another. But you don't know that till you're too far gone." He stared at the moths as they danced about the light. "I probably should've quit baseball, long time ago, you know. My arm, it was so wore out." He paused, reaching for his chest pocket, but then seemed to change his mind, rolling his hand into a fist and holding it over his heart. "Doc gave me Vicodin, and I'm telling you—a few of them and that was it for me: no turning back. I never could get off of them." He shook his head. "They mess with you, though. Sometimes I would do things, bad things, just because I was mad. Mad at everyone. My father, my mother. Other people, too. I can't explain it, but especially back then, I had these times when all of a sudden I would need to hurt something."

Chase rubbed his palms against his thighs and pressed his lips tight. He wondered what Transom's angle was this time. Was he trying to explain himself? Was he looking for sympathy? Chase had no desire to sit through this soliloquy—this confession or whatever it was, a result of some cocktail of alcohol and painkillers and possibly something else, too—but he didn't trust himself to speak, either. He wasn't sure what might come out, what might be unleashed from the churning brine of emotions he was trying so hard to hold back. Maybe if he just remained quiet, let Transom say whatever he was trying to say, he could keep himself in check until he got some air. He cleared his throat and glanced at his watch, hoping Transom might get the hint.

"I haven't spoken to him for years," Transom said. "My father. Not since my mother attempted—not since she had her breakdown, and I came out here to the farm." He shifted his weight. "You know, I was always jealous of you, with Jack and Maggie. Your parents, too, when they were here. This whole place. It was always so peaceful, so full of love. Very different from the way things were with my family." An orange moth made its way through one of the screens in the front windows and began quivering toward the light of the kitchen. "I didn't mean for it to happen like this, Chase, for things to go the way they did here."

Chase could no longer keep quiet. He took a step forward. "You should've thought that over before you started signing papers," he hissed, the hostility in his own voice catching him off guard.

"I was trying to say sorry there, Boss."

"That wasn't an apology."

Transom ran his hands through his hair and took another drink. "Listen, Chase, I know you're not thrilled with how things look. I'm not either, but try to remember: it's just a piece of ground, just dirt and trees and rock, same as the next place. Fact is, I got a property over in Potter County that ain't that different from here, sort of reminds me of it. Big timber, nice fields."

"What are you talking about?"

Transom had never mentioned owning another property.

"I got land all over, Boss. Been at this for years now, buying farms, revitalizing. I told you I knew what I was doing."

In his mind Chase rewound the months to Transom's return, shuffling through the weeks like a deck of cards. The day after Jack was buried, Transom had come home. He'd said he wanted to pay his respects; he'd said he'd been missing this place, wanting to settle down. The memories fell into place: hunting rabbits in the snow-covered field, Transom asking about the farm, offering to buy it. "This was your plan all along, wasn't it? You come back here, act like we're friends, act like you're helping me out—"

"I never said that. I never said I was helping you out. I told you it was an investment. I made that clear from the start."

"I trusted you," Chase said, his throat so tight his voice was barely a whisper. "You were my friend."

"Come on, Boss. We *are* friends." Transom rolled his eyes and shook his head. "I don't see what you're so worked up about. It's just land. I use it, same as you. We just do it differently, that's all."

"No." Chase shook his head. He was trembling now, his hands juddering as he spoke. "What you and me do, it's not the same. You take every resource, everything good, and use it till there's nothing left. You turn it ugly because you don't care. I love this place; I take care of it."

"Don't start with your holier-than-thou bullshit," Transom said. "You with your poached bucks and bonfire, all Rambo in the woods. I'm the one who found you, cleaned you up, brought you home, remember? Never told a soul because you asked me not to." Transom held his gaze and took another sip of whiskey. "Don't get all high and mighty with me."

There it was: a sucker punch, a mean reference to the days in the woods, after so many years of silence. He should've known it would come eventually; he should've known Transom couldn't keep his mouth shut forever, not when there was some type of pain he could dole out. Chase wanted to say something, but what was there to say? He couldn't deny it or disagree. He'd done his best to put that time behind him; he'd been recompensing for it ever since. But of course Transom knew all of this; he mocked him for it. *You've become a regular pansy, you know that?*

A moth trembled in. It fell to the floor and began crawling around on the dark floorboards, making its way toward the table lamp. Transom stepped on it, a slight crunch, its guts and dust smeared in a yellow streak on the wooden floor.

"I got cows to milk," Chase said. He could feel the edges of his vision begin to blur, his anger about a hundred things knitting themselves together, making him dizzy. He pushed past Transom, heading for the back door.

"It's just land, Boss," Transom called.

Chase slipped into his boots and turned and looked back. "It was never just land to me."

AFTER

RED SAT IN THE SHADE, BACK AGAINST A PINE TREE, watching the parade of men in yellow hard hats shuffling across the construction site, maneuvering equipment. It was early, but already they were at it. One climbed into a forklift, another into a front loader. The machines roared to life, the forklift backing up and beeping loudly, the front loader heading over the hill and out of sight. He was far enough away that he could hear voices, men hollering back and forth, laughter rippling up, but he couldn't tell what anyone was saying.

The night before, just as Red was having a piece of butter toast and getting ready to turn in for bed, his phone had buzzed: a number he didn't recognize.

"This the sheriff?" the voice on the other line said.

"That's right." Red tried to place it—it was familiar but he couldn't put a face to it.

"This is Denny Morrison. We met about a week ago. I'm with Land Corp."

The trailer, the smug foreman squeezing the purple grip strengthener. Remembering, Red grimaced, his heart pounding faster. Paranoid, he pushed the curtain to the side and peered out the window. "Sure."

"Listen, one of my workers was out looking for a place to, uh, do his business this evening. Came across a body, he thinks."

"A body?" Red nearly choked on his toast. He reached for his glass of water. "Where?"

Deep sigh. "That's the thing. Scared him pretty good and he just took off running. Got lost out there in the dark, came through here in a panic. From what I could get out of him, straight back from the construction site, but pretty far off. I had someone drive him to the hospital, actually. He was so worked up I thought he might have a heart attack."

"That's it? He came across a body and he didn't think to take note of where he was?"

"It was dark and like I said, he panicked. He ain't the sharpest tool in the shed. I don't know why he had to go so far to take a crap, guess he just needs his privacy. Anyhow, couple guys saw him tearing out of the woods. At least I got him to calm down enough to get that out of him."

"I'll need his name. We'll probably have to talk to him."

"Yeah, I figured. You need anything else from me?"

"Naw, just keep your men out of the woods, would you? And, Denny," Red added. "For cripes' sake, get a portable outhouse."

He'd called Mick right away, and they'd agreed it was pointless to set out again in the dark: they'd meet up at first light. Red waited now, finishing the egg and cheese sandwich and coffee he'd picked up at the gas station on his way to the Hardy farm and stuffed the wrapper into his pocket. When all of this was over, he told himself, he was going to eat better. A long time ago, before he'd married Sue and he was living in the duplex back in The Rocks, he'd known how to cook, he'd at least been able to make a few staples. Bacon and eggs, stovetop macaroni and cheese, from scratch. But for the entirety of his married life, that had been Sue's thing, cooking. He wasn't sure how much he remembered, how good he'd be at it now, after so many years, but when he retired, he was going to start that up again. Enough with the gas station sandwiches wrapped in shiny silver paper. Enough with Wheeler's chicken in Styrofoam boxes, enough with the vending machine lunches of Cheese on Wheat and a candy bar. Once he retired, he would do better.

All night he'd been awake, his mind spinning through the details of the case, resenting yet again that he hadn't turned in that retirement letter just a few weeks earlier. He thought of Possum, too. Relieved as he was about Mick's assurance that Possum probably wasn't involved in Transom's disappearance, he still felt troubled about the whole thing. He still felt in the wrong, and he was fairly certain Ghost Sue was in agreement about that.

—

Mick pulled up to the edge of the woods and quieted the engine of his Buick. He reached out and offered Red a hand up. "Did you get any sleep?"

"No," Red said. "You?"

Mick shook his head. "Not after your phone call." He pointed. "You think here's where we should start?"

Red shrugged. "Guess so. Foreman said straight behind the construction site."

The two began climbing their way through the tangle of branches and stumps. Mick walked through a spider web. He grabbed it in disgust, shaking it from his hand and wiping his face, the thin white silk clinging to the stubble on his chin. Red couldn't help but feel just a little amused by seeing Mick Dashel, with his black polo shirt and khakis and aviator glasses, out of his element and struggling just a little in the woods, where Red was comfortable and competent. Mick had a look of intense focus on his face, a forced alertness that looked almost painful. The shiny black loafers he wore didn't make things any easier, the leather bottoms slippery on the forest ground.

They were heading downhill, almost into a valley of sorts. Red felt his knees growing sore from the pressure. He stepped in a small dip, and his ankle began to give beneath him, threatening to roll to the side and send him tumbling. He grabbed hold of a skinny tree and steadied himself. A long time ago, he'd hunted deer in this valley with Jack. Back then it was full of tall, towering oaks, their branches gray and wide like a church of worshippers. At least he thought this was the place. With most of the trees gone and the debris so thick you couldn't see more than twenty yards ahead, it was hard to say for sure.

And then, a scent. Foul, pungent. Something decaying, something dead. Could be an animal. A raccoon, a rabbit, a squirrel, maybe even something larger: a deer. Red didn't want to jump to conclusions, and besides that, just because he caught a whiff of something didn't mean he'd find it. He paused, looking around. So much land, so much mess. They kept walking, but a few minutes later, the wind shifted. Mick caught the scent, too.

"You smell that?" Mick asked.

Red nodded. He closed his eyes, concentrating. Sometimes, eliminating one sense could sharpen another. He wondered how far a smell could travel in the woods, with a breeze, with other scents—pine, dirt, that sweet and dizzying smell of autumn olive. Here, with so much space, he wasn't sure how to track it. A shadow crossed over him from above, a momentary break from the sun's force: a large bird circling. He looked up.

Red leaned back a little, watching the bird, trying to assess its path, determining where it was circling. He shielded his eyes and began walking west. Mick watched him for a moment and then wrapped the flagging around a tree to mark the spot where they left their course, and followed.

Red was focused now, like a predator honing in on its prey. He looked up, then down, up, then down. He stumbled awkwardly through the obstacle course of limbs and stumps. He tripped over a branch and fell to his knees, but climbed up quickly, keeping his eyes on the bird. Mick followed a few yards behind, slipping in his loafers, struggling just as much as Red with all the limbs and treetops tangling the forest floor.

"There," Red said, pointing to a spot forty yards ahead.

Three more birds, these on the ground, eyed them with contempt. With their horrid red heads and black bodies, their beady eyes, they were ugly and menacing. One of the birds leaned over, pecked at something, and then opened its wide, sobering wings—seven or eight feet across—and took flight. The others followed suit. They flapped awkwardly to a nearby tree, a tall, scrawny pine. And there, they waited, high above the men, hovering, keeping watch.

"What are they?" Mick asked.

"Turkey vultures." Red began walking to where the birds had been hulking along the ground, slowly, cautiously. Beside him, Mick reached for his piece, strapped to his belt. He rested his hand on it, following Red. Red pulled his handkerchief from his pocket and held it over his face. The smell was overpowering now, a dense, vertiginous smell of death. One summer, back when he was a kid living in The Rocks, a neighbor's cat had died under the porch, and for weeks it just rotted there, stinking.

They couldn't figure out what the stench was or where it was coming from. Morning after morning, he complained to his mother, until finally, he went on a search, circling their property, following his nose. At last, he found it. He grabbed a garbage bag, scooped it up, and took it out to the dumpster. He didn't have the heart to walk over to poor Mrs. Gorajczyk's house and tell her that her beloved white cat had somehow elected to kick the bucket under their porch.

In the clearing ahead, a throng of flies thicker than Red had ever witnessed hovered loudly over something they couldn't see just yet. Red stepped to the side and waved Mick ahead. He doubled over, vomiting in a felled treetop, the smell too much.

"You all right?" Mick called over his shoulder. Red raised his handkerchief in response, and Mick slowly approached the place where the flies buzzed. When he recovered, Red followed.

A body lay in the dirt: a tangle of muscle and bone, the face gashed up, the eyes gone. The abdomen and chest had been splayed open and ripped up and—removed. There was no heart, no stomach, and over the rib cage lay a black and yellow Pirates t-shirt that had been torn to shreds. Next to what was left of the right hand lay a pistol, and farther away, a shotgun Red recognized as Jack's.

"It's him," Red said, his voice hoarse. He wanted to run, far from that place, from the smell and sight of death, and he understood why the man had panicked and taken off the night before.

Mick kneeled at the bottom of the body. "Now that," he said, pointing to Transom's leg, caught in a rusty, bloody contraption of metal, "that is something I haven't seen before." He reached into his backpack, took out his tablet, and began circling the body, snapping photographs from various angles, kneeling, standing, leaning in close. He tapped some notes into his tablet and then began talking logistics—how they would get the body out of the woods, how they would preserve the evidence. If there was any evidence.

Red doubled over again, vomiting, hand wrapped around a tree for balance. It was all too much: the terrible sight of that body, the flies, the stench, the vultures flapping in the pine.

"I need you to call Tuck," Mick said. "Tell him to come right away." He wiped his brow with his shirtsleeve. "Do you think we can get a truck up here?"

Red shook his head. "Not with all these trees down. Could try a four-wheeler, rig something up to it, maybe. Or a UTV with a bed in the back." He thought for a moment, attempting to focus in the midst of the mess and smell, hoping to come up with a name of someone who might have a Cub Cadet or a Gator, someone who might be willing to loan their farm vehicle to haul a dead body out of the woods. How would he explain that, exactly? Who in the world would want to sign up for such a thing?

"Need you to call the coroner, too," Mick said. He frowned. "You do have a coroner, don't you?"

Red nodded. "Got someone we use over in South Tier. I'll give him a ring."

Mick opened his backpack and took out some fluorescent orange flagging. "Also, we need to mark this spot," he said, "make sure we know how to find our way back. We need to figure out a way to get this body out of here, preferably in one piece, and we need to bring in Chase Hardy."

BEFORE

CHASE HAD HOPED THAT THE DULL FAMILIARITY OF milking the cows would allow him to clear his mind, that the labor would help burn down his anger. He'd thought that the barn, the soothing melody of the machinery, the low moan of the cows, might ground him, ease the throbbing in his head. Instead, the monotony seemed to have the opposite effect. Slogging through the chores spurred his wrath: as he worked, he reconstructed the past six months, piecing together the details. Transom had come at the precise moment when he knew Chase needed him, when Chase was grieving and alone and had no one else to turn to. He'd planned that camping trip the same weekend the forester was coming to mark the trees. He'd lied about trying to save the trees. He'd gone against Chase's wishes—Jack's wishes—and signed away the mineral rights. The one remnant of his family's legacy, the one thing Chase had left—Transom had destroyed it. And it had been his plan all along, to take and take, no matter who got hurt along the way. It had been his plan all along to betray.

When Chase finished the chores, he walked briskly back to the house. It was still dark as he entered Jack's office, slid his lightweight camouflage coveralls over his jeans and t-shirt, grabbed his headlamp and his Winchester 1873, still dark as he hiked quickly up the farm lane, loaded the weapon, and slipped into the trees. There'd been a miscommunication, he would say, later. A hunting accident. He'd say they'd both gotten turned around in those woods.

A thousand times Chase had walked this land without light; he knew the slant of the hollow, the strain on his knees as he traversed it. He knew the dip where Jack had removed some soil and hauled it to a wet and failing field; he knew to avoid the huge rotting log that some creature or other used as a den, year after year. But now, with most of the trees gone and stumps and branches strewn about like wreckage, everything looked different. Felt different. Smelled different, too. He switched on the headlamp, struggled to get his bearings, then switched it off again. He came to a large tulip poplar, and in the dark ran his fingers along the smooth bark. With its wide, magnificent branches and tall, straight base, it had been a beautiful tree, and still was, especially compared to its new surroundings—he could just make out its shape in the coming light. Chase flashed his light again and saw a rusty metal burn barrel nearby; the loggers must've forgotten to remove it when they finished. Or maybe the *frackholes* were still using it. He flicked off the light.

He leaned against the tulip poplar and closed his eyes. Something rustled close by, dry leaves shifting on the forest floor: a living thing, moving. He squinted, trying to discern a shape stirring in the dark. Transom? His heart thumped, pulse hammering at his temples. He flashed his light and caught a glimpse of glowing yellow eyes: bright, glittering beads in the dark, then a tail, gray and bushy. Fox. He breathed out and wiped his brow. Though the sun had not yet risen, it was hot, and he was overdressed and hadn't thought to bring water. The woods spun.

Even in the dark he could see how ugly this sacred ground had become, how spent and abused and ugly. He fumbled along slowly, unsure of his footing, thinking about the afternoon, the winter before, that he'd lain back on the boulders and decided to sell Transom the farm, to trust him. He remembered all the Sundays he'd spent in that hollow as a teenager, sorting out his thoughts when the details of his life confused and overwhelmed him. Now, the boulders he used to climb were no longer reachable. A colossal pile of trees, either dead or of little timber value, had been pushed and stacked close by, blocking access. As he took it all in, a swell of grief rolled over him: his parents, Maggie, Jack. The land, too—trees, field. So much had been lost, so much taken. Chase felt that same sadness, same rage, that sensation of losing himself, seething deep inside his gut. Usually that feeling disturbed him, made him uneasy, but this time he felt a familiar thrill, one he hadn't felt in a long time: a dizzying rush like the quick burn of moonshine. What was it Transom had said, all those years ago in the woods? *Feels good, don't it. Kicking back at the world for what it done to you.*

Yes.

He began making his way east, up and over the steep ravine and down into the next hollow. He moved quickly at first, knowing that Transom wouldn't be able to hear him from far away. As he got closer to the Nest, he slowed his approach, moving carefully among the stumps and branches. He was feeling a little disoriented, with the trees and space he'd always used as landmarks gone, and so many new shapes and obstacles to negotiate along the way. There was plenty of cover for him, though, and he hunkered low, moving from one shadow to another. Around him, the gray light was growing lighter: soon, the sun would crest the ridge and the woods would become a labyrinth of beam and shadow. He had to hurry.

He could almost see the dying oak tree where Transom had told him he'd be: the Nest was still there, it hadn't been destroyed in the logging. He walked a few more steps and then knelt behind a stump, about three feet tall, and peered over the top: it was a good place to hide and take stock of his surroundings. The Nest looked no different than it had the fall before, when he'd dropped off Jack to hunt there. He saw the branches he and Transom had dragged and stacked at the base of the tree to create a little wall, many years before. A fort it was, back when they were boys, a place where they'd played and hunted and pretended.

And there was Transom, tucked in behind that wall, leaning against the tree, staring at a white pine the loggers had left behind. What was he doing? Chase raised the Winchester, nestled the stock into his shoulder, found Transom through the scope. His camo jacket was open, a bright yellow and black Pirates shirt taut across his belly. Chase panned left and right. No turkey decoy set up to speak of, either. Transom slowly raised his hand and placed something in his mouth, tilted his head back, and continued gazing at the white pine. Another one of those pills.

Through the scope, Chase shifted slowly to find what Transom was looking at, watching with such intensity, and he saw that it was a nuthatch, Jack's favorite bird, walking sideways, upside down as nuthatches do, its tiny white and black body hopping down the pine, its long black beak pecking at the bark, its small head turning to look at Transom from time to time, and Transom watching, mesmerized, at peace.

Then, just as quickly as his plan, his disturbing resolve, had come to him, it was gone, like a light switching on: Chase knew he couldn't go through with it—his hands and body began to quiver and all at once he was fully aware of himself. He stayed low and turned away, crouch-running in the opposite direction, back toward the barn, sobbing and shaking and sweating hard. He dodged stumps and leaped over fallen branches and when he knew he'd moved out of Transom's sight he dropped to his knees and buried his face into the bed of leaves on the forest floor and, for the first time in many years, wept.

AFTER

RED HAD ARRANGED FOR AN AUTOPSY THE DAY HE and Mick found Transom in the woods, and earlier that morning, the report had come in. It had been hard to determine what had happened, exactly, because the body had been carrion for over a week. Not only the vultures, but other animals, too, had been feasting on the corpse, and that fact, combined with the regular process of decay in such immoderately hot weather, had made quite a mess of what remained. But the coroner, whom they'd summoned from forty miles away, felt with a good degree of certainty that he knew what had happened.

Transom had stepped into an old bear trap. The force of the trap snapping shut would have severed tendons, *peroneus ongus muscle, extensor digitorum longum muscle*, although much of the body's flesh was gone by the time they found it. The trap had broken two bones, the *fibula* and *tibia*. Red carefully studied the coroner's report; he'd seen the white shards of bone thrusting through the ruins of Transom's battered body. He'd even looked up the bones on a sketch of the human body, trying to picture how it might have happened.

Eventually, Transom probably would've bled out, the coroner said, but the thing that had killed him, the actual cause of death, had been a gunshot wound to the head, a .44 bullet from the fancy pistol they'd found with the body. Suicide, Red concluded, ready to close the case. Transom's prints were on the grip; traces of gunpowder residue were found on what was left of his hand. It was clear he'd been the one to shoot the weapon.

But Mick wasn't ready to shut things down, not just yet.

Which is why they were at the back of the police station again, sitting across from Chase Hardy, contrite and grief-stricken. As much as Red missed Jack Hardy, he was glad his old friend didn't have to see all of this, because, sensitive soul he'd been, he may not have been able to handle it. Not just those beautiful woods, now pushed and cut to a wasteland, not just the compressor station being installed at the top of his field, but also this, now, too: the mangled, eaten-up body of someone he and his wife had raised as a second grandson, dead on Hardy property.

"Here we are again," Mick said, the oscillating fan whirring in the doorway, lifting the papers on the edge of the table every few seconds as it made its rotation.

Chase leaned over the table, his hands folded, a position of penitence, of prayer, maybe.

"I thought he'd up and left," Chase said, finally. He didn't look up, but he began to rub his thumb over the back of his hand. "I thought he felt bad about everything—the farm, me—and he just decided to leave." He paused again, then turned to face Red, his blue eyes startling and sad. "That'd be the way he'd do it," Chase said, "if he wanted to make things right. That's what I thought, at least."

Mick reached behind Red and grabbed a photograph of the .44 they'd found on Transom. "You recognize this?" he asked, sliding it across the table to Chase.

Chase frowned, eyeing the black grip and fancy gold filigree. "Transom's father collected them, fancy pistols like that. Had a thing for Smith and Wessons."

"It wasn't registered," Mick said.

Chase shrugged. "Probably bought it a long time ago, before they had all these rules about guns. Besides, Mr. Shultz was never really one for playing by the book."

"That's for sure," Red muttered. He leaned forward and started to stand. Chase had confirmed it: the weapon was Transom's. They were done here.

But Mick folded his hands. "What do you think Transom was doing out there in the woods?"

Gripping the table, Red eased back into his chair.

Chase swallowed.

"He didn't have a hunting license—we determined that right away with a call to the Game Commission—but it looks like he was hunting." Mick slid another photograph across the table: Transom dead, face swollen, flesh missing, the camo jacket rumpled and dark with blood.

Chase turned his head and shuddered.

"Come on, Mick," Red said. There was no need to put anyone through the pain of seeing the photographs. Red could barely look at them himself.

Mick took a swig of coffee, stood, and leaned against the filing cabinet. "Did you know about the trap?"

Chase shifted his weight around in his chair. "Yes and no."

"What do you mean, yes and no?"

"He said he was going to set it. I told him I thought it was a bad idea." He wiped his brow. "I thought he was just messing around, just talking. He did that sometimes, mouthed off. I didn't know he was really gonna do it."

"Are there more?"

Chase shrugged. "Jack only had the one bear trap. But I guess there might be other ones, smaller. Hard to tell."

Mick jotted something down in his tablet. "It could've been you," he said. "You could've stepped in it. Or those men who are out at the property working. Or Red, or me."

Chase nodded. He turned to gaze toward the front of the building, out the window. "I know." He traced a crack in the tabletop.

"If Transom's the one who set the trap, why didn't he know it was there?"

Chase shook his head. "I told him he needed to do a good job of marking where they were. I told him he needed to keep track of them." He wiped his eyes. "I don't know. Like I said, I didn't think he was really gonna go through with it."

Mick sighed. Earlier, Red had also pointed out that the woods would've looked much different than they had, the winter before. "How do I know you didn't set it?" Mick asked. "You had motive. You stand to inherit the whole farm."

"I haven't been trapping since I was a kid, sixteen. I used to run lines with my grandpa when I was a boy, but I gave that up, long time ago. You know that, Sheriff." He looked at Red. "But besides that, do you know what the odds would be of me being able to get another person to unknowingly step into one, to step their foot onto that small area, at just the right angle that he couldn't get out of it?" Chase held out his hands, forming a circle. He shook his head. "It'd be put near impossible."

Mick seemed to consider this. "Why do you think he was wearing camouflage?" Mick said, leaning close to Chase. "Why did he have two guns?"

Chase unfolded his hands and wiped them on his jeans. "Can I get a drink, please?" He breathed in deeply, placed his hands back on the table, and folded them again.

Red stood and grabbed a paper cup from the cupboard, then filled the cup with water from the sink and handed it to Chase.

Chase took a drink and placed the empty cup on the table. "It was turkey season," he said, at last, then wiped his hands on his pants again. "It would appear that he was hunting."

"Sure, the shotgun I understand. But that fancy pistol?" Mick said, studying Chase's moves, glancing at Red. "I don't know much about hunting, but I'm fairly certain most people don't hunt turkeys with a .44."

Note the anxiety, Red imagined him saying. *He's hiding something.* Red could see it, too.

Mick frowned. "I mean, he didn't have a license, but fine. Let's say he was hunting. We found four empty shells at the scene, three from the shotgun and one from the pistol, but no dead animals anywhere near, and the .44 bullet in his head."

Chase looked Mick in the eye. "My guess is that when the animals were pressing in on him, and he couldn't keep them away no more, he shot at them." He twisted his mouth to the side, swallowed hard and looked out the window again. "Saved the .44 for himself. I would've done the same thing."

Red pictured how Transom must have struggled, how he must have come to terms with the fact that they would devour him eventually, the coyotes and vultures, the beetles and mice, maybe a bear. They would descend on his body, dead or alive, as he lay there, weakening as the blood gathered at his feet. He imagined the fear and anxiety Transom must have felt in his final moments. It had been ten days since he'd disappeared, but how long had Transom lay there, in the woods that he had both loved and destroyed, before he died?

Mick steepled his fingers on the table. "Here's the thing I just can't get my head around. Why couldn't he have pried open that trap? He was a big guy, an athlete," he said. "He should've been able to open it, right?"

Chase kept his hands laced together, propped his elbows. He began shaking his head, squinting. "Transom had a bad arm. Weak. Besides, that trap hasn't been used for decades. Something could've broke, maybe a lever got rusty or something. A thousand things could've happened. How the heck would I know?"

The coroner had called in a trapping expert to have a look at the thing—there were two broken hinges and a faulty screw. Chase was right.

Mick noted something in his tablet.

Red looked at Chase, that posture of repentance, hands folded, head bowed. He seemed sorry, but maybe that was sadness he saw, not remorse. There was a fine line between the two, Red knew. A very fine line.

"You're free to go, Mr. Hardy," Mick said. He took out his phone, excused himself, and left the room.

Chase stood and nodded at Red. "Sheriff," he said.

"Sorry for your loss, Chase. I imagine there was some tension, lately, with what happened at the farm, but I know you two were close, deep down. Like brothers, you two. That's what Jack always said." He thought of his own brother, ripping through

McKee's Rocks in their father's Chevelle, punching Red in the face once for saying the Steelers sucked.

"It's been a bad year."

"What'll you do now?" Red asked him. "You gonna stick around?" He'd been wondering what would happen to his old friend's farm, whether Chase would stay or go. The oil company was finishing its compressor station in Maggie's field, an enormous patch of cleared earth with a huge metal-sided building, two stories tall. Outbuildings, too, and some convoluted tan structure of pumps and cylinders that Red assumed to be the workhorse of it all. Trucks would come and go, hauling the extracted gas to be processed and then sent out again.

Chase leaned against the filing cabinet. "I thought about leaving. Thought about it ever since Jack passed, to tell you the truth. Sell the place, cut ties, go somewhere new. Out West, maybe. One of those big states where there's more wildlife than people. But I don't think that's what Jack and Maggie would've wanted, do you? My parents, too." He looked at Red, his blue eyes searching.

Red shook his head. "That's not my call, son. You know that."

"I think they would say, if you love something, you love it no matter what. You find the good in it and you work at what's not good. They all used to say that." He took his hat off and ran his hands through his thick hair. "So that's what I intend to do. I'm gonna walk the place with garbage bags, and piece by piece, clean it up. I'm gonna take my front loader out and push the logs into piles, cut the stumps low. They'll come back, the trees, the woods. Not in my lifetime, not in my kids'. But someday." He nodded. "Someday, that place could be beautiful again."

Red knew Chase understood that the oil company would always have a presence there, that every time Chase looked out his front window, or worked in Maggie's old garden, the compressor station would loom in the distance, a constant reminder of what used to be, and he admired Chase's optimistic perspective. "You let me know if you need a hand. I might be getting old but I can still run a chainsaw and pick up trash," Red said with a smile. In a matter of weeks, he'd have a lot more time on his hands, and working to clean up Jack and Maggie's place would be the perfect way to spend it.

"Appreciate that, Sheriff. I'll give you a ring." Chase turned to go but then stopped. "Oh, I wanted you to be the first to know. I'm gonna ask Laney to be my wife."

Red smiled and extended a hand. "Congratulations," he said. "I'm happy for you." He paused. "Your family, they'd be happy, too."

Chase nodded. "I know."

—

Red had three things left to do. First, he had to arrange a time for Teresa to come into the station. He'd already called her to tell her what they'd found in the woods, what the coroner had said. He'd already explained, in the gentlest way he could, that, no, she didn't need to come in to see Transom's body—he'd been positively identified with the tattoo, the number 7 on his shoulder clearly visible once they'd cleaned him up, and there was no need for her to put herself through the agony of seeing him—and that, yes, she should go ahead and make arrangements for a funeral. But he felt that she should know about her fiancé's plans, too. He would give her the packet with the wedding plans and plane tickets from the Sea2Sea Travel Agency in Pittsburgh. As painful as it might be, Red felt she deserved to know that she'd been right, after all. Transom hadn't left her.

The second task was one Red handled with delight. He took out the envelope from his desk drawer and laid it on Leigh's desk, where she would find it the following morning. He would go out on patrol first thing, maybe nab a few frackers flying toward town on 28, bring in a couple tickets for her to process so that she had some things to do and didn't spend the day fussing over him and making a big deal about his retirement. It was a job for a younger man, this work, taking care of a town, watching over everyone, especially now that things were changing, moving faster, new people and new problems drifting in. He laid the envelope on Leigh's desk with a sense of intense relief, gathered his hat and his lunch bag, and locked the door of the police station behind him. Keys in his pocket, he walked over to the Jimmy and began pumping the pedal.

One thing left.

—

Red pulled into the small patch of gravel and parked between the trailer and storage unit. He wiped the back of his neck with his handkerchief, sweat trickling from him. He climbed out of the vehicle, smoothed his shirt. Knees creaking, he struggled up the stairs to Possum's stoop and knocked on the door. He saw Possum watching him through the curtain, then heard footsteps crossing the trailer. His heart thundered in his chest.

Possum cracked the door. "Sheriff?"

"Sorry to bother you, Tom," Red said, shoving his hands deep into his pockets. "You got a minute?"

Possum opened the door wider and stepped out onto the stoop. He looked beyond Red, squinting his big eyes, suspicious. "What's up?"

Red could feel the words catching in his throat, anxiety pulsing through him, making him light-headed. He wrapped his fingers around the metal railing, steadying himself. "I owe you an apology," he said, and he couldn't help it—his grief began to spill. He wiped his eyes with his sleeve. "What happened all those years ago out at the shale pit, it was wrong of me. There were things that went on, things you didn't know about, but still—I should've come back like I said I would, I should've gotten to the bottom of it and set things right, whatever it took, and I didn't." He paused, shuffling his feet. "I mishandled it, I let you down. And I know it's awfully late but I wanted to apologize."

Possum swallowed, looked past Red like he wasn't even there, watching a big truck with fracking fluid drive over the bridge, the tires roaring across the metal.

Red wiped his forehead with his handkerchief again. "I know that don't make up for the wrong I done. I just needed to say it. I need you to know: I'm sorry."

The wind picked up and the geraniums in a pot shivered. Red tucked his handkerchief back in his pocket and sighed, a great sense of relief sweeping over him. In the days since Transom had disappeared, he'd realized his father had been right. The past was never dead; it was never past. But it didn't have to own you, either. It didn't have to be all you were. He hobbled down the steps, and walked back to his truck.

"Sheriff?" Possum called out.

Red turned.

Possum gripped the railing of the stoop and looked at him, lip quivering. Red waited for him to say something, but Possum just stood there, face twitching hard. Red could see it: the boy who, long ago, had smashed his stepfather's face, who'd been folded in a trunk, who'd been dealt so many ugly things but who had, in the end, survived. After a long time, Possum dipped his head and nodded.

Red held his gaze. "You take care of yourself, son," he said.

BEFORE

IT WAS MEMORIAL DAY AND POSSUM WAS THRILLED because he'd just scored a pair of French porcelain compotes in perfect condition for twelve bucks at an auction. He was sure he'd turn a good profit on those, and he might even have enough to pay off the plane ticket to Moscow he'd bought for the end of August. Alla was going to show him some hand-painted lacquer boxes by a Fedoskino artist she'd been collecting, each worth thousands. They were going to discuss antiques. And other things, too, he hoped, though the truth was, he still wasn't convinced it would happen—the flights, the visit, meeting Alla. It seemed too good to be true.

On his way home from the auction, Possum stopped to hunt for mushrooms. He'd finally found a route to his best morel spot, the place on the Hardy farm where the elm trees grew, a course through the national forest that took him nowhere near the farmhouse or barns. The fancy restaurant eighteen miles west had just requested more, and Possum figured it was worth the risk. A lodge it was, technically, a place where rich city people came and paid a mint to fish or hunt, depending on the time of year, and then have whatever they harvested cooked for them by a professional chef that night. It was, Possum had often thought, one of the most laughable and ingenious ideas he'd ever heard of. Justin, the chef there, paid him twenty bucks a pound for morels, and Possum had promised him three pounds by Thursday—some big-time clients in from D.C., Justin said, and based on the poor performance at the shooting range and their complete lack of dexterity at the lake, the morels might end up being the main course.

Possum parked in the small national forest lot and tucked his keys in his pocket. He loaded his mesh bags into his Adirondack pack basket, walked past the metal trash cans, overflowing and reeking, and headed into the woods on the worn trail. He hunched over, ducking through the thick mountain laurel. About a half mile in, he veered off the trail to the right, where he knew the terrain changed a bit, dipping lower and opening up to more sweeping woods, larger trees, oak and elm. He crossed into Transom's property, marked by the No Trespassing signs, and his heart began to thump.

At last he came to the elm trees, their bases dotted with morels: large and yellow, miniature Christmas trees, they looked like, cut from a thick industrial sponge into cone shapes. The air warm and heavy with the sudden heat wave, the trees swaying, a nearby maple showering hundreds of double samaras around him, helicoptering their way from above. As a kid he used to love finding them, throwing them up and watching them spin round and round, back to the ground. Whirligigs, his mother called them.

He knelt and removed a mushroom, pinching carefully at the base and then placing it into the first mesh bag. Close by, there were more, and he gathered them, too, plucking them one by one and putting them into the heap. Later, Justin would soak these in water to clean off any dirt or bugs that were inside the folds, then he'd sauté them in butter. Possum had taught him the whole process.

He was gently pulling at a big one when he heard the sound: an animal noise, something suffering. In his pack basket, he had the .44 from JT, which he always kept with him in the woods for spring foraging, just in case he were to stumble upon a black bear, up from a winter's nap and hungry.

Again, the sound.

A fawn, maybe, newborn and helpless, a high-pitched scream of agony, something killing it. Perhaps a bear. Possum winced at the thought of a spindly-legged deer, spotted white and beautiful and pathetic, dragged from its mother through the woods in the jaws of some predator. At the same time, he knew better than to try and interfere.

Help.

Was he hearing things? He dropped one more morel in his bag and then stood, frowning, forcing his ears to work their hardest. Had someone called for help? A samara spun down and he reached out and caught it in his palm: delicate, feathery thing.

Help.

He began walking, up and up the ravine and then across its top and then down, faster and faster, the morels rolling about the mesh bag, the voice a coiling scream now, louder and more animal-like. He began to run, sliding his pack around to his front as he moved, pulling out the .44. Half the morels tumbled out but he didn't stop.

As he descended into another valley, he realized he was moving deeper and deeper into Transom's land, and he worried that he could lose track of where he was, but someone was hurting, someone needed help, and he'd figure that out later, how to get back to his truck in the parking lot. He'd find his way.

He heard a jangle of metal, heavy and dull, like the sound of a chain being dropped to the ground, and then ahead, in a tiny clearing, he saw movement, a person on the ground, stretched out and writhing and weeping and he moved quickly now, closer, stumbling through the stumps and debris but he froze because the person pointed to the sky then and shouted, "Don't! Don't you dare. I'm still alive, dammit. I'm still alive!"

The voice. He recognized it, the threats hissed through the door of the janitor's closet, the words just before the trunk of the car had closed. *You're gonna burn. You're gonna feel the heat coming at you but I don't want you to be afraid.* Possum looked up and saw two large birds, perched on the branch of a tree, way up. Vultures, sensing death, waiting. He eased down, tucking himself behind a thick stump, an ugly remnant from some magnificent tree, and watched.

Transom's leg was caught in something, the sound of the metal thrashing against the ground and ringing through the woods. A trap. He reached down and tried to pry it open, spilling a horrible sound that made the hair on Possum's arms rise when the trap didn't budge. Silence. Then Transom was struggling again, rolling and twisting and swearing and crying, and sometimes, he would call for help again. For one tiny spark of a moment, Possum pitied him, lying there, bleeding, unable to free himself, the scavengers looming overhead.

Possum watched and watched. He grabbed a morel and ate it raw but it was no good without the butter and garlic soaked in and, unwashed, the dirt from it crunched between his teeth.

All those years. He could still feel Transom's strong shoulder slamming him hard against the lockers like a hockey player checking an opponent; he could still hear the metal juddering through the halls of the school. He could still smell the dank gray of the trunk of the car. He turned away and rested his back against the stump, and although he knew they were toxic raw, he ate another mushroom, the sun high in the sky now and the air hot and still. Pondering what to do, he closed his eyes and listened as Transom lashed about.

Possum took a rag out of his pack basket, a piece of cloth he used to brush dirt off the mushrooms. He wrapped it around the pistol JT had given his mother a long time ago, and began rubbing it carefully. Over and over he went, starting at the muzzle, working his way back with an intense precision, swirling the rag in tiny buffing circles, covering every centimeter of the weapon, pressing the cloth into each nook. When he was finished, he did it again and then again. Next, he used the rag to remove the five bullets, then cleaned one carefully, and loaded it.

He wasn't sure how long he sat there, sweat sliding down his brow, his back drenched and his throat parched but finally, he slid out of his boots and stood and walked in his socks toward Transom, who lay bloody and limp on the ground, flies swirling at his leg. White pills lay scattered beside him in the dirt, a brown bottle with the cap removed, a shotgun, too—all out of Transom's reach. Transom looked up, his face drained of color, his lips cracked from sun. He blinked.

"I came to check on it," Transom said, pointing a weak finger at the trap, his bloody leg. "Damn thing was a lot closer to that tree than I remembered." He began to laugh, the same unforgettable laugh, only weaker, and then he coughed violently, blood spewing from his mouth.

Possum swallowed. "How long you been out here?"

Transom held up two fingers.

"Two days?"

He nodded.

"You're dying."

"Yes."

Transom was looking at him but Possum wasn't sure—did Transom recognize him? So much of his blood spilled on the forest floor now and the sun bright and blinding. Did Transom know him? And in that moment, did Transom remember all that he'd done, those years of torment, all that damage? Did he understand what this meant, Possum standing over him with all the power now, Possum with a gun in his hand, Transom's fate in his palm?

He bent down and kneeled next to Transom. "You ruined my life," he whispered, the words sour in his mouth. He pressed the barrel to Transom's temple, the stock still wrapped in the rag. He took a deep breath. That beautiful and terrible face, so close he could hear the breaths that came from Transom's lips. So very close.

Transom blinked. "You ruined mine first."

Possum had never seen it that way. Curled up in his own anger and hurt, he'd felt justified—he'd seen leaving that wagon on the porch as an act of integrity, a means of shedding light on a thing that had been wrongfully hidden. He was the one who'd been wronged, who'd been hurt beyond imagination. But now, he thought of the day he'd stood on the porch of the Shultz house, peering through the window and seeing Transom's perfect family, his perfect life, and for the first time, with Transom pale and pathetic and bleeding out, Possum understood that surely there was some truth in that statement, that he'd taken something from Transom, too.

Possum pulled back, sat on his haunches, set the pistol on the ground. Waited and waited until at last, he leaned forward. He placed the gun into Transom's hands, and as Transom's bloody fingers wrapped around the grip, Possum slowly tugged the cloth away. Their fingers touched. He reached over and picked up one of the white pills from the dirt and pressed it to Transom's dry lips. Transom opened his mouth and took it, and Possum picked up the rest of them, one by one, Transom holding his mouth open like a bird waiting to be fed. Transom stared up into the pine trees that breathed overhead, at the vultures watching from a branch, his eyes wide and blue. He put his hand on Possum's and squeezed lightly. "Thank you."

That small gesture. It wasn't an apology and yet somewhere deep in the cavern of Possum's belly, something rumpled then: the cache of anger and hatred—the thing he'd clasped tight all those years like a kid's stuffed animal—something began to fold a little. Give. Could it be that he'd been wrong? That holding onto that anger wasn't the way to get through your pain, after all? Maybe in the end, not letting yourself forgive someone— you were the one who paid the price for that, nobody else. He turned from Transom and stood.

Possum grabbed a pine branch and swung it back and forth across where he'd walked, just in case he'd left tracks, though the ground was so dry and hard that he knew there would be no sign he'd been there. He walked back to the tree stump, slipped his boots back on, and grabbed his things. He turned and went away, back up the hill, across the top of the ravine, and down into the next valley over, to the pair of elms. As he finished gathering the morels, he heard a gunshot. Another samara spun down and landed on his shoulder, and he closed his eyes and lifted his head to the sky, the grace of sun warm on his face. His pack full of mushrooms, Possum headed back to the truck, back through the dizzying white of the mountain laurel, home.

ACKNOWLEDGMENTS

ALTHOUGH IT'S THE AUTHOR'S NAME THAT APPEARS ON THE cover, the truth is there are so many people who help bring a book into being. There are so many people to thank.

I am deeply indebted to my incredible agent, Amy Cloughley, for seeing something worthwhile in my slush pile submission, and for offering me such keen editorial guidance, honesty, and support throughout this process. I'm eternally grateful.

To Cassandra Farrin and the rest of the team at Amberjack, thank you for reading my work with such enthusiasm and wisdom.

My deep gratitude to Bethany Spicher Schonberg, for reading and making a small suggestion that ended up changing the course of the novel for the better.

To Erica Young Reitz, for reading and giving guidance and encouragement, and for talking me through a different ending.

To friends and early readers Paula Closson Buck, K.A. Hays, Corrie Passavant, and Megan Bridgwater: thank you for your time and support.

To my father, for fielding questions about weapons, hunting accidents, and traps.

To my sons, who've woken to find me hunched over, pecking at the keyboard, most mornings, since they were out of cribs. May your brotherlove be a strong river, an unspoiled forest.

Thank you, most of all, to Chris, who has lived with me and this novel, at times with my mind half in it and half in our real life: you've nudged me from the edge of despair and believed in me when I didn't believe in myself or my work, and I couldn't have done this without you.

ABOUT THE AUTHOR

KIMI CUNNINGHAM GRANT is the author of a memoir, *Silver Like Dust*. She is a two-time winner of a Dorothy Sargent Rosenberg Memorial Prize in Poetry, as well as a Ruth Lilly Poetry Fellowship finalist. She's also a recipient of a Pennsylvania Council on the Arts fellowship in creative nonfiction. Kimi studied English at Bucknell University and Messiah College. She lives in Pennsylvania, where she enjoys writing, teaching, and exploring the woods with her family. *Fallen Mountains* is her first novel.